WHAT IF IT'S TRUE

D. M. BOURGEOIS

What If It's True/D. M. Bourgeois
Marrero, Louisiana
www.dmbourgeois.com

Book Cover Design by ebooklaunch.com

WHAT IF IT'S TRUE/ D. M. BOURGEOIS -- 1st ed.
ISBN 978-1-7357823-6-2

For my dearest friends – some old, some new.
Your friendships means the world to me. Thanks for
being the type of friends who would keep my secrets.

This is something my mother used to tell me when I was
growing up and I thought it was fitting for this book:
To your friends no secrets tell,
for when your friends become your foe,
your secrets everyone will know.

Friendship is the only cement that will ever hold the
world together."
—WOODROW WILSON

WHAT IF IT'S
TRUE

CHAPTER 1

Katie

Friendships are fragile. Friendships that last a lifetime are precious. Commitment and willpower to give and take in a relationship are gifts. Unfortunately, many miss out on a lifetime of friendships that are unforgettable. Katie reflected on those thoughts and smiled as she waited for her friends, some of them from childhood, some new.

Each of her friends brought something different to the group. Aside from Hannah, she was the most cheerful and optimistic one. Katie was blessed with big, beautiful eyes that changed colors depending on the day. Her lips were full and were naturally red, creating a perfect frame for her smile. As a child, people often asked if she was wearing lipstick. Being the queen of procrastination came easy to her, but she always followed through with the important things. Loyalty was one of her greatest attributes, with quirky humor coming in a close second. Laughing and having fun was what she lived for, and she made sure her friends did as well.

Katie smiled as Hannah's long brown hair and hazel eyes came to mind. When she smiled, her whole face lit up, drawing you in. She was a lot like Katie, equal in heart, but more reserved. Where Katie was often loud and boisterous, Hannah was soft-spoken and cheerful. Lizzy was a mixture of both of them. She loved to have fun too, but she wasn't as concerned with everyone's happiness. She was warm and welcoming, but she didn't go out of her way to converse with people. Even though her long dark hair and eyes commanded attention when she walked in a room, she'd preferred to keep to herself.

Cory Ann was tall and beautiful. Her dark green eyes and black hair were deceiving because she was a force to be reckoned with when things got complicated. And things often got complicated when Katie and her group went out to the bars in New Orleans. She wasn't always confident of her choices, but Cory Ann went with them, anyway.

Sara, Allie, and Marci leaned more toward the shy, quiet type. Sara and Katie had been best friends since preschool and couldn't be more opposite. Katie loved Sara like a sister and her big blue eyes had won her battles more often than not. Allie was a little more outgoing and had a great sense of self confidence. She was more like Katie, with her quirky sense of humor. Marci was quiet, but silently strong and independent. She was probably the most compassionate one of them all. Her beautiful brown eyes were soft and lured you in from the beginning. Hannah, Allie, and Marci had been best friends throughout school. Their unique personalities accented each other, and Katie loved that about them.

Millie was tall and beautiful, but there was something about her that screamed 'trust issues.' She was the most private person she'd ever met. Katie thought she'd make a perfect spy in a 007 movie. She laughed and drank with them but never volunteered too much information about herself.

Helping Millie cope with her recent breakup was the reason for their weekend getaway. Everyone loved Katie's idea of visiting The Myrtles and were all on board from the beginning. Stories of the plantation being haunted attracted people from all over, curious to see if they were true. She was skeptical, but secretly hoped to see a ghost or two.

The spectacular display of color, which covered the trees in autumn, swayed with the whistling wind. October was her favorite time of year because the crisp air made her feel alive. Katie stretched out her arms, took a deep breath and enjoyed the tickle in her nose when she let it go. She looked forward to another fun filled gathering with close friends. She twirled almost childlike, laughing as she made each turn. From the corner of her eye, she noticed a woman standing by the plantation and, for a moment, she felt foolish. She stopped abruptly and once the dizziness calmed, she realized she was all alone. A shiver ran through her body, but left just as quickly as it came. Had she just encountered a ghost?

Most of her friends had been with her since pre-k and shared an unbreakable bond. Not that the world around them hadn't tested their relationships because they had their moments, but in the end, friendship won the battles. She was glad they had made it through together stronger than ever. And now they all had an important role in her life.

Marci, though a more recent friendship, was as strong as the rest. When she talked about her coworker Millie's struggles with her current breakup, Katie suggested the trip to cheer her up. Millie had joined a few of their outings and quickly became part of the group. Katie felt blessed to have so many special people to share life with and was even more pleased that they were a fun bunch. Through the years, she'd experienced hardships and heartaches, but with her amazing support system, could heal and move on.

Katie loved Halloween. As a child, her parents hosted elaborate parties and invited all of her friends. When she was in eighth grade, she had her first trip to the Mortuary Haunted House in New Orleans. She screamed the entire way through, clinging to the man in front of her. By the end, her face print was plastered onto the back of his shirt. Since then, every year, she and the group continued to visit haunted houses.

Katie walked the ten acre grounds, admiring the natural beauty. She'd wondered how such a beautiful, serene place could be haunted. As she strolled by an old storm cellar, she noticed an entrance, but the padlocked door discouraged her from entering. A closer look revealed that the lock was open. Something was tugging at her, but she remained frozen. Finally, she reached for the handle, but someone called out, causing her to become distracted. A burst of cold air passed through her body when she turned away.

"Katie!" Hannah ran and threw her arms around her.

Another set of arms wrapped them both up, and their laughter filled the surrounding space.

"What were you doing? We said your name a few times." Allie glanced at her surroundings before she asked.

"Nothing. Come on, let's go get settled in." Katie walked forward, but not before stealing a peek back at the padlock. A strange feeling enveloped her as she walked away. You'll have to wait. The excitement of watching her friends arrive trumped her curiosity, so she tucked it away and focused on the weekend.

"How is it? Have you seen a ghost yet? You know I won't be able to sleep at all tonight, so be ready. I can't believe that no one backed out." Hannah was nervous, and it was showing through her rambling, shaky voice. "Noone backed out, right?"

Katie thought back to the vision she'd seen earlier and wondered if it was a ghost. As soon as she saw the woman clearly, she was gone. She stepped onto the veranda and hesitated. There were several doorways reaching from one end to the other. Could that be where the mysterious women disappeared to? She reached out to one and turned the handle, only to find it locked. The woman could've locked the door behind her. They were taking a ghost tour later that night, and she hoped to find out more about the house. Usually, she was on top of these things, googling everything about the place the minute the trip was planned. She remembered a woman named Chloe was murdered there, but that was the extent of her knowledge.

They entered the house to check in and she immediately noticed several mirrors around a room that was decorated with antique bust, old portraits, and dated wallpaper. Magnificent chandeliers hung from the more recently painted ceilings. The plantation was built in 1776, and the décor matched that era. It looked as if time stood still. Different from the little shudder she felt earlier, peace and tranquility filled the space and relaxed her mind. She wondered what her friends were thinking about seeing a ghost. Figuring it would be evenly split, she knew exactly who would be more scared than curious. She considered herself brave, but she wasn't sure how she would react if she saw a ghost. Only time would tell. Her mind was already playing tricks, and it was still daylight.

When they made the reservations, they booked the whole second floor so they would be together. There were two bedrooms on each side of a long, steep staircase. That was spooky in itself, not to mention the attic doors that hung partially open from the ceilings above the antique beds. There would be two of them in a room, eight in total. Hannah and Allie were sharing the room next to Katie's. Things were already heating up, starting with Hannah's fear of an old porcelain doll in the back of her closet. She claimed it opened the door. Her phone buzzed, and it was Lizzy announcing her arrival, so Katie yelled back as she headed down the stairs.

"Lizzy and Cory Ann are here, so I'm going down to meet them." She didn't wait for a response. Lizzy was her older cousin and was just as crazy about Halloween as she was. They were just alike because scary stuff made them nervous. They laughed uncontrollably, which meant they were going to spend a lot of time running to the bathroom. Katie giggled as she galloped down the stairs and, by the time she saw Lizzy, burst into full laughter. It didn't take long for Lizzy to lose control and join her cousin.

They grabbed their luggage and headed back up the stairs.

"This is creepy!" Lizzy mumbled as she followed Katie to their room.

"I know! Don't you just love it? We've always wanted to come and here we are." Katie walked into the room with Lizzy in tow. Cory Ann tagged behind. "You two will be in this room across the hall from me and Sara."

"No way!" Lizzy stopped in the doorway.. "I can't sleep in here with that attic door open like that." Before she knew what happened, Hannah and Allie pushed her into the room, and they all fell onto the bed.

"Y'all, this place is spooky! I don't know if I want to stay." Hannah looked at the others for encouragement.

"Oh, you're staying. We all agreed to do this. You're not backing out now." Katie watched as Lizzy shook her head in agreement.

"Yeah, we all agreed and besides, we just got here. It's still daylight. Let's go outside and wait for the others." Lizzy let her friends go first, then followed behind.

Katie hesitated because she thought she heard a creaking sound behind her, but hoped it was just an old house crying out. Whatever the source, she got a bad feeling and realized the night was far from over.

CHAPTER 2

Lizzy

When her cousin Katie suggested the weekend trip to the Myrtles Plantation, Lizzy prepared herself for a wild time. They always had so much fun when they were together. Thinking about Katie and her quirky humor brought a smile to Lizzy. She wondered how that was going to hold up in a spooky setting like the Myrtles. Both Katie and their friend Cory Ann were sure to bring plenty of laughter and definitely a lot of screaming. She and all of her friends loved going through haunted houses, but that experience usually lasted less than an hour, not continuously for an entire weekend. She was already waging odds in her head who would bail first. Sara. Katie's best friend Sara would definitely be the first to consider bailing. But they came as a group and would leave as a group. That was the deal.

Lizzy loved her job. Usually, she worked every Friday and Saturday nights at the bar because the money was good, so she welcomed the break. She was ready for a fun, relaxed weekend. She chuckled because she realized this trip was going to be anything but relaxing.

When she arrived, the first thing that struck her was the old, weathered dormers atop the main house. She sat in her car, staring at the windows, and would've sworn she saw a slight movement of one curtain but passed it off as weariness. Lizzy flipped her long, dark brown hair over her shoulder and tucked it behind her ear, trying to look calm. Even though she wasn't the oldest, she still felt like she needed to be the brave one. She knew that all of them, except Cory Ann, were going to be jumping at every little sound and movement. That kind of paranoia was contagious. She saw Katie walking out of the house, so she pushed her uneasiness aside, forced a smile, and got out to greet her.

"I can't believe we're finally here! How is it?" Lizzy hugged Katie while waiting for Cory Ann.

"It's cool. I gotta admit, it's a little spookier than I thought." Katie laughed nervously.

Beautiful architecture and picturesque grounds surprisingly stunned Lizzy masking the dark nature of the old plantation. She'd expected to see an old, dilapidated house with overgrown trees in need of attention, not this massive, almost charming structure that seemed welcoming. This was her first trip to a plantation home and found it a plus that it was supposedly haunted.

The house was even more impressive inside, which added to its authenticity as an antebellum plantation from the 1700s. Lizzy's taste was always more modern, but she found herself captivated by the beauty of the home. They ascended the dark stairway to the bedrooms so they could get settled in their room. She felt odd and with each step came an uneasy feeling in the pit of her stomach. Suddenly, she wished she could turn around and run out the door. She reached her room, and after noticing the half open attic door above her bed, was relieved when the others agreed to go back outside to wait for the rest of their friends to arrive.

They walked out into the sunlight and scoped out the grounds. There were several buildings scattered throughout the property. Restaurant 1796 was operating in one building where they would dine later that evening. She had an early lunch at Gattuso's Restaurant and was feeling the first ping of hunger pains. She had brought snacks, but the thought of going back up those stairs to retrieve them discouraged her, so she decided she could wait for dinner.

Close to the house, tucked under massive oak trees, were two Bocce Ball courts. She didn't know how to play, but it reminded her of shuffleboard and the fond memories of playing with her dad on vacations. She looked down at her phone and typed Bocce Ball rules into the search bar and waited for it to load.

"Anybody know how to play Bocce Ball?" Lizzy was staring at her screen. "Well, anybody?" She finally looked up and was alone. "Hey! Where'd y'all go?" She scanned the area, but there was no one around. "Katie, this is not funny." She felt uneasy and chewed the inside of her cheek. The wind picked up, blowing the overgrown branches of the old oak tree against the plantation house, adding to the eeriness that was already settling deep within her bones. The pranks had begun and not everyone was there yet. She hoped it was a prank because she was starting to panic.

"Katie! I'm not playing! Cory Ann! Hannah? Allie? Come on y'all, it's too soon to start this craziness." The sounds of the wind that howled and the birds that were singing without a care in the world should've relaxed her, but she was still uneasy. She tried to breathe in slowly, and exhale even slower. Her body resisted her efforts and instead of calming down, she felt alarmed. Instead of feeling excited and mesmerized by the surrounding beauty, or enjoying the cool breeze that slapped her face she was tense.

"Katie! I swear I'm gonna kill you!" She heard the soft giggling first, then turned her body to head in that direction. Before she exposed them, they jumped out from behind an old wagon not ten feet away from her. "You're all idiots!" Lizzy was angry, but she felt the relief wash over her body once the joke was over. She yelled a few more choice words at them before letting them off the hook with a smile.

"Lighten up Lizzy. Did you think we just disappeared into thin air?" Lizzy's reaction surprised Cory Ann. "Besides, what was so interesting on your phone that you didn't notice us sneak away?"

Hannah and Katie were still laughing at her expense. She vowed to herself to get revenge later when the night came, and they were more vulnerable. She felt a little guilty because her prank was already in place before they scared her, but now it will be well deserved. She thought back to the smack talking about being brave and who was the bravest, and recalled exactly when she'd devised her plan. It was a brilliant one hatched from hours of searching the internet for the best Halloween pranks. She picked one that promised to be epic. At first, she thought she might include Katie in her plans, but after today, decided that she needed to be taught a lesson. A mighty fright for the queen of the pranksters.

"I was searching for the rules for Bocce Ball. They have several courts over there and I thought we could've played while we waited for the others to arrive. Have any of y'all played Bocce before? Or at least know how to play?"

Cory Ann shook her head no.

"I know you need balls to play. Maybe they have them inside the front office." Allie was googling the rules as she spoke.

The sound of cars approaching snapped Lizzy back to reality. Several cars pulled in at once. They were all looking for the same thing, a spooky evening to kick off the Halloween season. Subconsciously, she glanced back at the house and up to the creepy dormers. She returned her gaze to the parking area just in time to see that Sara had arrived along with Marci and the guest of honor, Millie. Everyone had arrived, so let the party begin.

CHAPTER 3

Hannah

As Hannah and Allie approached the parking lot, excitement took hold because the whole haunted house weekend stay was fast becoming a reality. It wasn't long before a sense of unease filled the sound of their giggles, and instead of joy, reflected the anxiety that was slowly consuming them. For years, Hannah, Katie, and Lizzy talked about visiting the Myrtles and occasionally suggested an overnight stay, but she never intended on actually following through. She didn't know what she believed about ghost and wasn't ready to find out. The old 'Ready or not, here I come' game came to mind. Ready or not, they were going to find out just how brave they were, and Hannah suspected she was not. None of them were.

She stopped giggling and looked over at Allie with a slight smile on her face, hoping to put her friend at ease. Her mood had changed the minute she'd arrived. She opened the car door and realized that her legs were shaking, and her teeth were chattering when she opened her mouth to speak.

"This is ridiculous! My whole body is shaking like I'm freezing, but it's not even cold out here." Hannah looked up at the sun to let the warm rays radiate through her body.

"I can't stop giggling. I guess that's nervous energy." Allie barely got the words out before she started again.

"Allie stop." Hannah's side was hurting from the laughter. "Hey, look at Katie over there. What's she doing?"

They watched as Katie stood still, gazing at an old structure.

"She looks like she's deep in thought about something. Let's go see what's so interesting." Allie reached for Hannah's hand, and they ran toward Katie.

Hannah called out for Katie several times, but she didn't respond. When they got close enough, they could see that something had her attention, and she was clearly oblivious to her surroundings, unaware they had approached her. She called out again hoping to alert her that they had arrived.

"Katie! What are you doing?" Finally, she turned toward them, and Hannah threw her arms around her. Whatever had been holding her attention finally let go and Katie smiled, glad to see them. Hannah found her behavior odd, but the excitement of the weekend events took over and she was looking forward to getting started.

"This place is amazing! I don't know what I expected to see, but it wasn't this. How can something so beautiful be haunted?" Allie was taking in her surroundings. "At least it was rumored to be haunted, and I guess we're gonna find out soon enough."

"I'm not sure, but as pretty as the main house is, there are some really sketchy buildings around the property. Just look at that old storm cellar." Katie pointed, then went on, "But then look how beautiful the restaurant is." Her heart skipped a beat as she stole a glance at the cellar.

Even though something about the old storm cellar bothered Hannah, she was too afraid to investigate. Maybe later. "Let's go get our stuff and check in. How are the rooms? I hope they are at least clean."

"Clean? Yes, the whole place is immaculate. That's not the problem." Katie was walking behind Hannah and Allie on the way to their car to help unload.

Hannah stopped walking. "Wait, what did you say, Katie? Not the problem? There's a problem? What did you mean? Katie, is there a problem we should know about?" She grabbed Katie's arm to get her attention.

"No problem. Just grab your stuff and come on. The rooms are spotless. Nothing to worry about." Katie's voice trailed off toward the end of her sentence.

Hannah had been apprehensive from the start, but Katie's words slammed into her mind and settled, only increasing her anxiety. She wondered if that was just Katie being Katie trying to scare them or if she truly believed there was a problem. Ever since they were kids, Katie would pull pranks, so that behavior wasn't out of the ordinary. But she looked a little disturbed when she said there was a problem, and that caused Hannah concern. She didn't like haunted houses, but she went anyway, always thankful they included her in their plans.

Katie and Lizzy were a few years older than her, and she loved hanging out with them.

They made their way up the stairs and grabbed the first room they came to. Katie was right. The rooms were really clean and smelled fresh. Being worried that it would have that old 'mothball' odor, she was pleasantly relieved. Placing her suitcase on a chair next to the closet, Hannah was startled when the door creaked open. She stood paralyzed and stared into the darkness, waiting for something to leap out at her. Katie and Allie were talking in the background, unaware that she was too terrified to ask for help.

"Hannah, are you ready? Hannah?" Katie jumped off the bed and touched her shoulder.

Hannah let out a blood-curdling scream that echoed around the room and probably traveled throughout the house. She covered her mouth in an attempt to stifle the sound.

"Hannah, what are you doing?" Katie backed up to get a better look. She walked around and swung open the closet door. "Hey, it's just a closet." Katie flipped the light switch, and it flickered before finally staying on. In the back corner, still shadowed from the light, a porcelain doll was sitting on the floor staring back at them.

Hannah was still breathing heavy but had stopped screaming. She gathered herself and tried to find her voice. Her mouth was dry making it difficult.

"That door opened on its own. I swear! And look at that creepy doll. She's staring right at me. Shut the door, Katie! Shut the door!" Hannah pleaded with her.

"It's just a doll, Hannah." Katie was shaking her head as she closed the closet door.

Allie, shaken from Hannah's screams, was ready to run out of the room. Thankfully, Lizzy called Katie to say that she and Cory Ann had arrived. The three of them headed out to meet them when the closet door cracked open again.

"Stop!" Hannah walked back into the room, pushed the door shut, and moved the dresser in front of it. She and Allie stared at the door for several minutes, half expecting it to open again. They stepped back, but kept their eyes on the door. Soon after, Katie went down to get Lizzy and Cory Ann, then came back upstairs.

The laughter coming from outside the room drew her attention, so she and Allie joined the others in Lizzy's room. Hannah was still on edge, but the distraction helped her suppress the terror of looking into the doll's eyes. As soon as she had a chance, she would remove it completely from her room. Maybe she'll put it in Katie's closet since she was so quick to dismiss Hannah's reaction. She wouldn't do that because she wasn't the prankster that Katie and Lizzy were, but she was definitely going to discard the doll.

She wasn't sure why, but Lizzy's arrival put her at ease, if only momentarily. She laughed as Lizzy commented that the slightly opened attic door was a problem, but deep inside her soul, she was crying. Thankfully, there wasn't an attic door over her bed, just a creepy doll that could open doors.

Back outside, the sun was shining, and the warmth calmed her shivers. Lizzy was caught up in her phone and became the target of a prank. Hannah sighed when Katie and Cory Ann pulled her and Allie toward the wagon and then to the ground. She protested, but kept her mouth shut for fear of becoming the next target. It was fun to give Lizzy a taste of her own medicine, even if it wasn't something Hannah would have suggested. Watching Lizzy nervously call out was a harmless prank, but soon Hannah had had enough. She was glad when Cory Ann revealed their hiding spot and ended the prank. Noticing the look in Lizzy's eyes, she knew revenge was coming. She bit her lower lip as she followed them to the parking lot.

The others had arrived, giving Hannah a false sense of security because she'd always felt like there was safety in numbers. Even though they had separate bedrooms, she would make sure she stayed close to the others. Wishing she could get in her car and speed out of there nagged at her and she was certain that feeling wasn't gonna leave her anytime soon.

CHAPTER 4

Katie

As usual, Katie was late to dinner. Knowing that was something about her that aggravated everyone, she really tried to hurry. It didn't matter because nothing ever changed. She made peace with that 'problem' as her dad always called it, and didn't let it bother her. She wondered how she developed that habit because both of her parents were punctual. Something inside of her needed acceptance, as most people did. Katie knew she differed from most, but her mother always told her to "dance to her own tune." Well, that's not all she said. Also in those life lessons was, be kind, be honest, be a woman of your word, and most of all have faith. She'd recently read something on Facebook that made her chuckle–People who are late are happy but not the ones waiting for them.

She looked at the clock while she slipped on her shoes. I'm only 15 minutes late. She'd hoped to go into Hannah's room and move the dresser away from the closet door, but headed down the stairs instead. A noise from behind caused Katie to look back over her shoulder. She recalled hearing that old houses came with unexplained noises. That was definitely unexplainable, but she dismissed the noise and headed to the restaurant.

Instead of being able to slip in unnoticed, her friends all clapped and hollered for her as she approached. She loved the attention, so she bowed and curtsied all the way to the table. It was just the way she liked it–all eyes on her. She did the queen wave as she passed the other tables. She and her friends laughed, ready to have a good time.

"Way to make an entrance, Katie!" Lizzy motioned for Katie to sit next to her.

"Better late than never." Allie was used to Katie's problem with punctuality. "And you look fabulous!"

Katie smiled and took her seat while Lizzy passed her a menu.

"It all looks so good. I want to order everything. Let's do that. Everyone order something different and share." Everyone agreed, even Sara, who was the most particular one.

"Can we order drinks first? It's been a long week and I'm ready to relax." Millie looked at the others. They all agreed, then vented to one another. The waitress came by, and Katie ordered margaritas on the rocks for everyone.

"I want a sugar ring on mine, but salt for the rest of these 'salty' people." Lizzy said that with a straight face.

"Sure, like you're so sweet, Lizzy." Hannah called her out for that comment.

"What do you mean? Admit it, I am the sweetest one here tonight." That drew laughter and kicked off the evening.

They ordered dinner and, like Katie suggested, they all ordered something different and passed it around the table. They also ordered another round of margaritas.

"I love this round table. It's hard to talk to everyone when they seat you at a long one." Katie smiled at her friends. "I can't believe we are finally here. I'm really shocked that Sara and Hannah made it. Proud of my girls. Does anyone want to share their thoughts on the place?" Before anyone spoke, she raised her hand up and continued. "I'll go first. My first thought was that I expected it to look spookier, right? But there are some really old, eerie buildings around the property. And the house itself is sort of creepy. Too many mirrors, for one thing."

"Wow. I never imagined those words would come out of your mouth, Katie. Really, too many mirrors in the house?" Lizzy was teasing her, and the others added their own opinions.

"Yeah, you're right. That was odd coming from me. But they have some creepy mirrors. I'm scared to look into them when I pass by." Katie lifted her glass. "Cheers to us! And here's to those who do not believe in ghost."

The minute she said ghost, a loud crackling sound echoed through the dining room, plunging them into darkness. Everyone screamed, then went silent. One by one, starting with Katie, they reached for each other's hands and held on tightly. The feeling in the room shifted.

"Oh my God, Katie, you made them mad." Marci was so scared she could barely speak.

Katie ignored the comment and looked out the window toward the main house. Everything was in complete darkness. The wait staff rushed to find candles to provide light to the area.

"Do y'all have generators? A place like this should have generators." Katie looked at her friends and saw terror in their eyes. "Look how beautiful this room looks in candlelight." She continued talking, but held on tightly to Lizzy and Sara's hands. She didn't really believe in ghost, but she was as nervous, nonetheless. Winds howled, and the rain was slapping the building. "See, it's just a stupid storm. You all heard the crackling sound. I bet lightning struck something in the area."

Cory Ann was the first one to speak up. She let go of Millie's hand and lifted her drink. "Let's try this again. To us! A long awaited weekend with great friends!"

Everyone slowly relaxed and within a few minutes were back to laughing, eating, and teasing each other about their silly reaction to being suddenly thrust into darkness.

Katie knew there was only one thing to do. "Another round of margaritas, please."

If she was going to deal with a ghost, she needed to be medicated. She excused herself and went to the bathroom. As she passed a mirror, she was startled to see the face of a woman right before it shook and fell to the ground. She ran into the bathroom and locked herself in a stall. She whispered, "We're gonna need a lot of margaritas!"

CHAPTER 5

Lizzy

The entire group was chattering on about their own ghost encounters. The majority were of hearing noises, not seeing anything. Lizzy couldn't recall ever seeing a ghost. She remembered her mother talking about hearing strange noises outside their house and said it was a ghost. Was she just joking, or did that happen? Because she was only about five years old, the memory was fuzzy. Gathering more information would be top priority when she got back home.

Giggles threatened to erupt from her lips as she listened to the breathless ramblings. Most of them were uncomfortable as they spoke about their experiences. She was surprised that she'd never heard any of these stories before. She noticed Millie was sitting quietly and listening as well. Did she not have anything to add to the conversation? Finally, when everyone had their say, the food made its way to the table.

"Hey, where's Katie? She's been gone for a while now." Lizzy looked in the direction that she went. Grabbing her phone, she dialed Katie's number.

"Where are you?" Lizzy waited for her to respond. "Katie! Hello!"

Katie was still terrified to leave the stall. She softly whispered, "In the bathroom."

"What? Katie, I can't hear you. What did you say? Where are you?"

"I'm in the bathroom." She whispered a little louder. "Come get me, please."

Lizzy strained to hear what Katie was saying before the phone disconnected. She stared toward the bathroom, then stood up. Everyone was silent, waiting for an explanation.

"I need to go get Katie. Something's wrong." Instead of moving, she glanced at Cory Ann and was going to ask her to go with her. A strange feeling prickled her skin, and she sat paralyzed. Katie sounded strange. Before she could ask, Cory Ann stood up and volunteered to go with her. Lizzy sighed, inhaled and headed to the bathroom with Cory Ann by her side.

They walked to the other end of the dark restaurant and found a long hallway. A waitress was sweeping up what looked to be glass, but with the dim candlelight, they weren't sure. The waitress looked up and smiled at them as they approached.

"Be careful where you walk." The waitress used the broom to clear a path for them to get by.

"What happened?" Cory Ann saw the broken mirror on the side.

"We don't know. It was just here when I came to the bathroom. Just be careful." The tone in her voice was sharp."

Cory Ann and Lizzy looked at each other and rushed past toward the bathroom.

"Katie! Katie! Where are you, Katie?" Both ran into the bathroom, calling for her.

Stillness filled the room before Katie called out to them from the last stall. The door slowly opened, and there, sitting on the toilet, shaking, was Katie.

Cory Ann reached in and grabbed her trembling hand. "What are you doing in here? Did something happen? Girl, get up! Come on." She led Katie toward the sinks.

Katie paused. She averted her eyes from the mirrors. The last thing she wanted to do was look into another mirror.

"What are you doing? Katie, what's up?" Lizzy's brows drew together in concern.

"I thought I saw a face in the hall mirror, then it fell to the ground." Katie had her hands covering her eyes and her back to the mirrors as she walked sideways toward the door.

Lizzy stood still as she listened. She kept her eyes off of the mirrors just in case. "You're lying! You're just trying to scare us."

"No, I'm not! I wanna get out of here. I really want to go home." Another round of thunder and lightning cracked, causing them all to jump.

At the sound, they latched onto each other and screamed. Lizzy was terrified, but she still thought Katie was pranking them. Regrettably, she looked up at the mirrors and watched in horror as, one by one, they started falling from the wall.

Cory Ann grabbed their hands and yanked them forward. "Let's go, now! Come on!" She used the light from her phone to lead them back to the dining room table. The candlelight was so dim that the color that had drained from their faces was shadowed, but it was clear to the others that they were upset. Katie didn't want to sit down, but Lizzy insisted.

"It's storming out there. Sit down, we need to plan." Lizzy was trying to remain calm long enough to think clearly and make a plan.

Lizzy sat down but was like Katie, ready to go home. She peeked at the windows, watching the rain pound against them with force. The tap-tap sound told her it was hailing outside. Great! Trying to get comfortable, she shuffled in her seat. She stared down at her plate, and it looked delicious, but she'd lost her appetite. Lifting her drink, she raised it to her lips. She'd lost her appetite for food but really needed the drink. When she calmed down a bit, she noticed the fright in Hannah's eyes. She reached over and grabbed her hand to reassure her.

"Everything's okay. A mirror frightened Katie before it fell off the wall. She ran into the bathroom, too afraid to come out. Really, it's okay. Let's finish our meal and head back to the rooms. Come on y'all, we came here to have fun." Her voice shook, but seemed to calm most of them down.

"I did…" Katie wanted to explain.

Lizzy stared at her before saying, "I believe you, Katie. I believe you saw a face. Maybe they have mirrors here that are made to scare us." She gave her a stern look, hoping she would back off and not scare the others. "We can talk about it tonight when we get back to the rooms, okay?"

Lizzy waited for Katie to respond. Relieved that she'd received the message to keep quiet about the incident, Lizzy relaxed. She lifted her drink to Katie and took a sip, encouraging her to do the same. Her face lit up when she saw that everyone lifted their drinks and toasted each other again. This time it was things like, "Here's to getting out of here alive," and another, "Cheers to safety in numbers," and "Here's to our good health. May we grow to be as old as Katie and Lizzy's pranks!"

The table erupted in laughter at the last toast that was delivered by Marci. Lizzy forced a smile, but deep down in her core, she was terrified. Explaining what had happened in the bathroom made her uneasy. Staying the night after hearing about the incident was doubtful. She'd decided that she was heading out of there as soon as the weather let up. She wanted to suggest they get a hotel room for the night. After they found out the truth, she was positive that they would all agree.

Glancing over at Katie and Cory Ann, she noticed they had already slammed back their drinks and had a backup in front of them. She wouldn't say anything yet, but the two of them would need to slow down. She was certain that Katie wanted out of there and although Cory Ann acted tougher than she actually was, she, too, looked scared and was ready to go.

Lizzy looked at the window again and her shoulders slumped at the sound of the pounding rain.

"It's gonna be a long night y'all."

They all tried to settle down and enjoy themselves. Unfortunately, fright had a way of creeping into thoughts and taking over. Lizzy looked around the table and realized that she had to stay focused, so she hid her fear and waited for the rain to stop. Disappointment seeped into her bones as she sat and watched their fun weekend slip away.

CHAPTER 6

Hannah

The weather had turned terrible quickly, which only added to the already tense evening. They were stranded inside the dark restaurant, waiting for the rain to end. Hannah wished she would've stayed with her first instinct and declined the invitation to the Myrtles. All her friends loved to get together at least once a month. They traveled to Austin, Texas, for a music festival. They'd been to Nashville several times and especially loved road trips. When her aunt Lizzy and cousin Katie asked her about a weekend at the Myrtles, she hesitated but said yes and invited her friends to join them. Now, she regretted her decision and couldn't leave even if she wanted to, and she wanted to.

She looked up to see Lizzy, Katie and Cory Ann coming back to the table. They looked upset. Her first thought was, 'they look like they saw a ghost,' but refrained from using the word ghost. She tried to make eye contact with Lizzy, but all three of them were looking at the floor. Their odd display of concern rattled her calm demeanor.

Lizzy spoke first, explaining that Katie was frightened by an image in a mirror that fell and shattered. She still avoided eye contact and was trying to act like it was no big deal. But that was a big deal. Seeing a face in a mirror was a big deal, though. What made the mirror fall off the wall? Hannah had so many questions, but decided she might not want to hear the answers, so she remained silent.

She knew Lizzy wasn't telling them the whole truth. When Katie tried to add to the explanation, Lizzy stopped her with a look. What was Katie going to say? She definitely looked like she saw a ghost. Lizzy tried to distract them by raising her glass and toasting the table, but Hannah was too nervous to relax. She raised her glass but only sipped her drink. A sense warned her that things could worsen, and she needed to be alert. She chuckled to herself as she watched Katie, Lizzy, and Cory Ann slam down their drinks, then order another. Clearly, they're not concerned about keeping their wits. Big surprise.

The lights flickered, then went out again. Everyone clapped, then followed up with disappointing boos. Something seemed different. The entire atmosphere felt different. Hannah wanted to run to her car, but the rain was terrible. Her heart leaped, horrified at the idea that she was stuck.

"I didn't have time to tell y'all, but I had a scavenger hunt all planned out for us." Lizzy was fishing in her purse for papers. She passed them around the table. Hannah took hers and started reading it aloud.

"Aww, y'all, look. This is so cute. Lizzy, did you do this by yourself? Maybe we can do it tomorrow. It looks like fun. I love that we have to take pictures of us doing our activities. That's so cute." Hannah was so caught up with the game that she almost forgot about the weather. A lightning strike brought her back to reality. The distraction was over, and the eerie feeling in the room returned.

"Okay, let's regroup. It looks like we're gonna be here for a while, so let's play a game. What about heads up on the phone? Hannah, don't you have that game on your phone?" Lizzy was tired of sitting there scared and wanted something to help pass the time while they waited out the storm.

Hannah reached for her phone and attempted to open the app. Her stomach flipped when she realized she didn't have service. "Hey, I don't have service. What happened? Y'all, I don't have service, look." She held up her phone to show them, but no one looked because they were too busy checking their own phones. She repeated the process several more times refusing to give up.

Allie had been quiet until then. "This is really creeping me out! Maybe we should make a run for the house, get our things, and get out of here."

Hannah grabbed Allie's hand and said she agreed with her. "I don't care if I get wet. I'd rather go. What do y'all think? Can we please leave?"

Each of them agreed, so they asked for the bill and waited. Hannah felt relief spread over her body at the thought of leaving, but became even more antsy in her seat, waiting to leave. She glanced around and noticed people at the other tables were laughing and enjoying their meals. Didn't they realize that everyone at her table was a frantic mess and was ready to bolt as soon as they could?

She needed to use the bathroom, but decided she'd rather wait. Squeezing her thighs together, she'd hoped to make it up to her room, where she'd use the bathroom, grab her stuff and get out of there. Relief ran through her body when she remembered that they hadn't unpacked yet. The comforting thought of getting to her room safely diminished when she remembered the stupid doll in the closet.

"I should've left when I first saw that creepy doll. Y'all, I swear, the door opened on its own. Twice! Katie, you thought I was overreacting, but how do you feel now?"

Katie laughed and held up her drink. "I'm feeling pretty good, actually."

Hannah noticed that Marci, Millie, Allie and Cory Ann were feeling just as good as Katie. They all laughed at her comment as they took another sip of their drinks. That left her, Lizzy, and Sara to make sober decisions, and Lizzy was questionable. Sara drove an SUV, so she could fit several of them if needed. Lizzy and Cory Ann rode together so they could fit Millie and Marci, leaving Hannah and Allie to ride together. Hannah was angry that they were getting drunk, so she didn't care if they didn't like her plan. They were leaving tonight one way or another.

After paying the bill, they agreed on a plan to make a run for the house. They stood up, making sure everyone could at least walk on their own and, surprisingly, they could. They walked to the door gathering closely, waiting to make a break for it.

"As soon as it lets up a bit, we're gonna run to the house, okay? Everyone got that?" Lizzy looked at their faces and said a quick prayer. "Katie, are you good to go? Cory Ann?"

They both nodded in unison, and Katie held up her thumb. Miraculously, the rain calmed enough, and Hannah shouted, "Let's go!"

They made it out the door and onto the walkway leading to the house. Hannah's eyebrows furrowed in surprise when no one objected to the plan, but she hadn't informed them that the drunk people were not driving their own cars home. She was going to grab their keys first, then tell them the plan. What choice would they have, stay there alone?

Right before they reached the main house, another round of crackling lightning sounded, and an enormous tree toppled over, blocking the driveway that led away from the spooky plantation. They raced inside the door where Hannah and Lizzy stopped, turned and looked back at the parking lot, stunned, unable to move. Sara gasped and followed the others upstairs.

Hannah finally gained her composure and urged Lizzy to go upstairs when a scream traveled from down to them. She closed her eyes and took a deep breath. How much more could they take? Reluctantly, she made her way to the stairs, and climbed each one with a sense of impending doom. She was mentally drained, and they'd just arrived a short time ago.

CHAPTER 7

Lizzy

The storm was relentless. Lizzy was trying to stay focused, but her brain was slowly giving in to the fog of that last margarita. Even with a large amount of alcohol in her system, her body trembled with fear. She scanned the room slowly until her eyes settled on the open closet door in Hannah's room, where the creepy doll now sat at its opening. Noticing the pretty pink bonnet reminded her of the clothes her mom made for her dolls. She attempted to clear her blurry vision by blinking quickly. Someone had to be pulling a prank on them. Hearing Allie's scream forced everyone in her direction, ready to help. She smacked her forehead at the idea of needing help dealing with a porcelain doll.

Lizzy propelled herself forward, even though her legs threatened to give out. "Y'all, someone is playing games here. Look at me. You know that can't happen, right." She looked at the doll again, then back at Hannah. "That's just an old porcelain doll, like the ones Grammy used to make. It's just a doll, Hannah!" Lizzy shook her while spreading out each word carefully to emphasize her point.

She needed Hannah to look at the situation through practical eyes.

Everyone was as terrified as her niece. "Come on y'all, get a grip!" Lizzy kicked the doll back into the closet and shut the door. She reached out and grabbed Hannah's wrist to pull her down onto the bed. Everyone looked horrified but relaxed with the doll out of sight.

The doll creeped her out too, but she had to step up and be the brave one. Stupid doll. Her mother used to make porcelain dolls when she was a little girl, and Lizzy secretly hated them. She never admitted that aloud because she knew her mother loved the dolls. She was grateful that she was only gifted with a few of them, that she gave a proper home on the top shelf of her closet. Her mother never questioned why she put them in the closet, which told her she probably knew she had a distaste for the dolls. Her mother was like that, always able to read Lizzy's thoughts.

She sat next to Hannah and watched as the others relaxed. They were following her lead. "Listen. Everyone needs to calm down." Lizzy couldn't stop her voice from trembling, but took a deep breath to gain control. "Hannah, you know dolls can't move on their own. This place is known all over the world for its 'ghost sightings' and 'strange happenings.' Maybe they added some spooky features, like old porcelain dolls, to enhance the experience." She glanced over at the others. "And maybe someone here is trying to play a trick on you." Lizzy glared at Katie and Cory Ann with a suspecting look.

The rain continued to pound the windows, and the trees continued to knock on the walls. It was still early, so they needed to occupy themselves before they all raced out into the darkness with nowhere to go. Walking to her room, she grabbed a bottle of Fireball. A hand raised to her mouth before a chuckle snuck out. Liquor consumed most of the space in her suitcases. She knew Cory Ann brought an arsenal of liquor as well and would bet that the others had too. The love she felt for her friends bubbled up into her throat. She hated being stuck in a haunted house with no way out, but at least she had them by her side. Lizzy's cold body warmed as her mind flashed lovingly over the women that were there with her, but surprisingly froze when Millie's image appeared. An unfamiliar feeling took over her body, but before it could register in her mind, someone called her name.

Hannah's shaky voice called out for her. She quickly replied. "I'm coming, hold on." Lizzy grabbed the bottle of liquor, and the pack of plastic shot glasses she'd brought for the weekend and headed back across the hall to Hannah's room. The sitting area between the rooms was dark, no doubt contributing to the allure of the house and the excitement of guest possibly seeing ghost. Originally, she was excited, but she was way past that now. Alarm better described what they were all feeling. She quickened her pace, shook off the feeling of dread, forced a slight smile on her face, and walked back into the room.

"Who's ready to play a game?" Disappointment washed over her from the lack of response.

No one answered. No one hollered the usual 'yes.' They were all too terrified and speechless to answer.

"Come on y'all! We can't sit here huddled all night, scared out of our minds? Let's play a game." Lizzy tried to rally the troops.

"I'm not drinking anymore tonight, and I don't think that y'all should either. Something's really wrong here." Hannah's voice trailed off. "We need to be sober just in case."

"Just in case what? What else can go wrong here? We're trapped in this spooky house. The rain is relentless, and our cars are blocked in by a huge tree. We lack power and phone service. What else can we do?"

Katie mumbled, "Call Ghost Bustas?"

Before what she whispered registered with everyone else, Cory Ann put her hand to her ear and yelled, "Who you gonna call?"

This time Katie sang louder. "Ghost Bustas!"

After a moment of silence, Lizzy caught on and joined in.

"When things are bad, and you need some help Who you gonna call?"

Together Cory Ann and Katie yelled, "Ghost Bustas!"

Lizzy shook Hannah's hand and tried to encourage the rest of them to join in. Standing up she continued singing and this time Hannah joined in.

"Ghost Bustas!"

Sara and Marci surprised them all when they mumbled, "I'm not afraid of dem ghost."

They all burst into laughter and continued singing the song and started dancing around the room. Lizzy laughed, admitting that was all she knew.

Allie yelled, "I know some." She yelled out a verse through her uncontrollable laughter."

Then, they all yelled, "Ghost Busters!"

Singing and dancing distracted them for what seemed like hours. They moved on from the Ghost Busters song to Taylor Swift songs and more. Lizzy felt relief and welcomed the distraction from the uncontrollable predicament they found themselves in. Shock flashed across her face when she noticed it was only 10pm. Her margarita buzz was fading, and she worried what sobriety would bring. She willed herself to stop stressing out about what was to come and joined in the fun.

She'd wondered if the other guest staying in the house could hear them. For the longest they were alone while the rest of the guests were still having dinner at the restaurant. A few hours ago, she'd heard people running through the door trying to escape the rain. When they left the restaurant, the skies had calmed but quickly began to roar again. The thought of the tree that fell across the parking lot came to mind. She was surprised that no one had come to check on them. Shouldn't they have reached out to their guests to inform them of the situation? Generators had kicked on and the lights were restored, but the lighting was antiquated and providing little comfort to the spooky atmosphere. Lizzy thought about going down to see what was going on, but looked around the room and reconsidered. Watching them enjoy their temporary escape from reality warmed her heart. She started singing again, happy they hadn't noticed that she was momentarily preoccupied.

An unsettling feeling ran through her body when she looked at Millie and she remembered that she'd had that same feeling earlier. What is it about you that's not sitting right with me? What did she know about her? Maybe it was just the house and its eerie vibes casting suspicion. She tucked the thoughts away and made a mental note to ask more questions as the night went on. Lizzy turned and came face to face with Millie. She forced a smile, grabbed her hand, and pulled her back to the floor to dance.

CHAPTER 8

Millie

She was enjoying her time more than she thought she would. She and Marci had been working together for better than six months now and almost immediately became friends. Marci and her friends had invited her to join them at a local bar, and she had been hanging out with them ever since. They knew that she'd recently ended a relationship, and they wanted to help her through the difficult time she was having. They didn't ask questions, and she hadn't volunteered any answers. She'd decided to let them think she was upset about the breakup, even though it was her idea to end it. It was always her idea.

Millie grew up in the Lafayette, Louisiana, area in a small town called Kaplan and had moved with her family to Baton Rouge when she was in high school. After high school, she came to New Orleans to attend the University of New Orleans, met the love of her life, and never left. The love of her life turned out to be disappointing, just like her past relationships.

She jumped around from job to job, hoping to snag one that she found satisfying. Her degree was in psychology, chosen due to a lack of interest in anything else. She was a smart girl and breezed through all of her classes. It probably helped that her family members were all psychos and provided her with a lot of practice dealing with them. A slight smile caused the corners of her mouth to lift as she thought about her sister Billie, the only one worth thinking about. But she, too, turned on Millie, so she vowed to never look back at the useless bunch again. As far as she was concerned, she didn't have a family. Loneliness set in sometimes, but she forged forward knowing that she was safer on her own.

She refocused her attention back to the room and looked at each of her new friends. She really liked all of them. Aside from a few boyfriends and her sister Billie, she never had friends. When she was young, she'd found girls her own age to be vindictive and spiteful and that hadn't changed as she grew older. College life proved to be just as disheartening with the clicks and sororities claiming their superiority. She'd handled college the same way she'd made it through life, found a boyfriend, and kept to herself. But now things were different. Enjoying her new friends, she let herself feel accepted. Again she smiled, and this time it touched her eyes. She valued these friends and was going to do what was needed to keep them. She'd never regretted the choice she'd made and hoped they wouldn't either. Not that she would ever confide her family secret to any of them. Some things were best left unsaid.

CHAPTER 9

Katie

Things were getting a little spookier than she'd like, but Katie was holding it together. She grew up loving scary movies and playing pranks on her family and friends. She especially enjoyed scaring her mother, who also loved scary movies. Her poor father was sometimes a casualty of their pranks, often stepping right into one in progress. He hated scary movies and wanted nothing to do with their silly games. She smiled fondly as the memories from her childhood years came to the surface. Her mother had documented her entire life, and she often enjoyed looking through the cherished scrapbooks.

She knew Lizzy thought she was behind the porcelain doll scare, but she wasn't. She'd wanted to move the dresser away from the closet earlier, but she ran out of time. Someone else was playing with them and she was sure it wasn't Cory Ann, Lizzy's other suspect. She had to applaud whoever did so, using an old porcelain doll to scare them. Old creepy dolls and clowns were always used to represent horror, and Katie loved it. She was the first one to run out of a haunted house when being chased by a saw wielding clown, but she still loved the scare once she was safe, and it was over. She chuckled when she thought about this weekend, wondering if she was gonna leave with fond memories or never want to look back again.

She had to admit, the mirror thing had her terrified. She saw a face in that mirror right before it crashed to the ground. That might've been a staff prank, but broken glass couldn't be good for business and was probably a liability instead. Maybe it was one of those mirrors you could buy at Michael's Craft Store that switched faces depending on what angle you held it, and it fell on its own. But it wasn't a coincidence that all the mirrors in the bathroom fell to the floor and broke. That was deliberate, but who would want to scare her? It all seemed a little extreme, but Katie felt sure that before long they would find out what was going on, or more importantly, who was behind it.

She looked closely at each of the women in the room. They were dancing and singing at the top of their voices, deflecting the fear that threatened to send them back into a frenzy. Katie and Sara had been friends since pre-k and couldn't be more opposite. Even Sara seemed to be having a good time amidst the chaos. She was absolutely sure she could rule out Sara as a suspect. For that matter, she could also rule out Hannah, Marci, and Allie. That left Lizzy, Cory Ann and Millie. Lizzy and Cory Ann were both strong suspects in her mind, but she didn't know what to think about Millie. What did she really know about her? The only time they were together was when they were out drinking and having fun. Does she like scary movies, Halloween, or pranks? Heck, aside from drinking and clubbing, what were her hobbies? Katie had no idea, and that made Millie suspect #3.

She yelled above the music. "Game time!"

They all ignored her as she walked around the room, admiring the décor. Impressed by how well it represented the era in which the house was built, she wondered if some of the furniture was original. She picked up an old glass bottle and examined it before she got the idea.

"Hey, let's play spin the bottle!" Again, they ignored her, so she grabbed the phone and shut off the music.

"What are you doing?" Hannah reached for her phone. She was angry because she was enjoying the music.

"Look at this old thing. Let's play spin the bottle." Katie held it up for them to see.

"I don't want to drink anymore. And I don't want to play truth or dare, that's for kids." Hannah looked at Lizzy for support.

"We don't have to drink. I know every game we play is a drinking game, but it doesn't have to be. Let's play old-fashioned charades in honor of where we are. We can sit in a circle and spin the bottle and whoever it lands on acts out a charade of their choosing. Come on. We can only dance for so long." Katie was tired of singing and wanted to play a game that would distract her.

"I'm in." Lizzy sat on the floor next to the bed.

"Okay." Hannah agreed and sat next to Lizzy. The rest of them followed suit and grabbed a spot to sit down, forming a circle. "But no scary stuff, okay? I'm already freaked out, so I just want to get through the night in one piece."

Katie laughed at Hannah's comment and shook her head in agreement. "No drinking and no truth or dare, got it." The others agreed to play, but the expression on their faces looked like they were being led to a slaughter, not a fun game of 'spin the bottle.' Katie remained standing and after everyone sat in a circle, she started suggesting some rules.

"Listen! I'll spin the bottle and if it lands on you, go first. After their turn, they will spin the bottle to see who goes next. I think since we are at a scary place, we should play scary movie charades." A few of them protested, but Katie held up her hand and talked over them. "Wait. We all love scary movies, don't we? Actually, Millie, I know the rest of these girls pretty well, but don't know a lot about you yet. Do you like scary movies?"

Millie didn't answer right away, but eventually nodded in consent. Her dark eyes glared at Katie.

"Okay then, it's on." Katie stepped over Millie and into the middle of the circle. Blowing the dust from the bottle, she held it up, then placed it on the ground. She looked around the circle and made a nervous chuckle as she noticed the terror in their eyes. She picked the bottle back up and put her other hand on her hip.

"Y'all gotta lighten up. It's supposed to be a fun game, not a death sentence." Katie waited for them to laugh, but they just sat there with huge eyes staring back at her.

Come on y'all! It's gonna be fun and besides, what else do y'all have to do?"

"Okay. Do y'all want me to go first? I have a few ideas in my head, anyway."

Lizzy spoke up. "No. Spin the bottle. We'll be okay, right y'all?"

Katie didn't wait for responses, but instead leaned over and spun the bottle. She blinked her eyes, trying to clear her vision and get a better look at the bottle because she could almost swear that it was moving in slow motion. Only the hall clock ticked, otherwise the silence was deafening. She felt like it spun around forever before it stopped and pointed right at Hannah. In the silence, she could hear Hannah swallow hard and then watched as she eventually stood up.

Hannah was deep in thought, trying to come up with a difficult movie to stump them. Although they were all terrified, they were also an extremely competitive group, and that trumped their fear. Hannah's facial expressions changed as she contemplated her choices, and her body involuntarily relaxed. Katie recognized the exact moment she'd decided on a movie and watched as she figured out her clues.

"Ok, y'all." She held up her fingers. "2 words, starting with the second word." She looked at the bed, grabbed the pillowcase, wrapped it around her head, and clasped her hands together. She giggled as she walked slowly around the circle. She looked ridiculous but Katie knew that was part of the charm of the game.

The others started yelling all kinds of words.

"Arabian!" Marci yelled.

"Praying? Praying Mantis!" Cory Ann yelled.

They went on for several seconds before Hannah stopped and said, "Come on y'all!" she clasped her hands together again and bowed her head.

"The Nun! The Nun! It's the Nun! Right?" Lizzy was up off the ground yelling her answer, trying to make sure no one else beat her to it. "Am I right Hannah?"

"Yes! It was the Nun y'all. What scary movie has a praying mantis?" They were all laughing and looking at Cory Ann.

"I don't know. It just popped into my head. I knew you were praying, and that just came to mind, girl. Lizzy beat me to it because I realized it was the Nun, but I was too late." Cory Ann stood up and gave Lizzy a shove.

"Okay, okay, okay. Sit back down. It's Hannah's turn to spin the bottle." Katie sat and yanked Lizzy down with her.

Hannah picked up the bottle, placed it in the center, and spun it around. Again, Katie blinked as she watched it go round and round. It was barely moving. Rubbing her eyes this time, she wanted to ask if anyone else noticed anything out of the ordinary, but before she spoke, it stopped. The bottle pointed between Sara and Allie. They both looked up at Katie for instructions. Neither one looked like they wanted it to be their turn. They still looked a little nervous.

"If y'all want, y'all can go together if everyone else agrees." Before she even finished talking, everyone had agreed.

Sara and Allie whispered ideas to each other and finally decided on a movie. Katie mused at the two of them because, out of all of their friends, they were the two more timid and both disliked horror movies. She was going to enjoy watching them act out their choice and had already thought about certain movies that they would've picked. Her gaze moved around the circle, and she could almost guess which movie each one would pick, all except Millie. She stopped when her eyes met Millie's and thought she felt an icy breeze blow through the room. She broke the stare and glanced at the window, even though she knew it was shut because of the rain. When she looked back, Millie was looking up at Sara and Allie, smiling as she waited on the clue. Sara announced they were ready, interrupting her thoughts.

"Okay y'all, one word." Sara and Allie laced arms together and pretended to hold something in their hand. They skipped around and acted like they were knocking on doors.

Everyone started shouting names of movies. They guessed from Werewolf to Nightmare on Elm Street. It was when Cory Ann yelled out Halloweentown that everyone erupted in laughter. Katie knew they were trick or treating and that the movie they picked was Halloween, but she didn't want to answer yet. She was having too much fun and wanted to let them guess a little longer.

Sara acted like she was skating and playing hockey, while Allie pretended to put a mask on. They were working well together.

"Come on y'all! Really!" Katie couldn't believe that nobody guessed it yet. She was trying to be patient, but she couldn't stand it any longer.

"Halloween! Michael Meyers!" Katie stood up. "They were Trick or Treating, and playing hockey, putting on a mask!" She was laughing but still managed to ask how they came up with werewolf?

Hannah said they looked like they were skipping to Grandma's house, and they all lost control, screaming with laughter. Once they settled down, they sat again and waited as Sara spun the bottle.

Around and around, they watched as the bottle turned and landed on Katie. A frown crossed her face because she wanted to go last. What she had in mind would freak them all out, and she wasn't ready to end the game. But she stood up anyway and walked over to the closet. She heard the room go quiet when she touched the doorknob.

"Katie, what are you doing? Don't open that…"

Katie didn't listen, but swung open the door and switched on the dim light. Her eyes grew large as she adjusted to the darkness of the closet.

"No Way!"

Hannah

Dancing always made Hannah feel happy and carefree. It made her feel relaxed and almost whimsical. To her, music was life. It made her feel alive and spoke to her soul. Listening to good music and dancing like she didn't have a care in the world was when she felt most like herself. Like all of her friends, she loved Taylor Swift and knew every word of every song. The terrifying events of the evening were slowly being washed away, and she and her friends began to relax and have fun like they had planned when they arranged this trip.

Recent years have been stressful with school and just life. She'd always thought that post-high school years were supposed to be the best and most carefree, but she found that to be false. And she was certain that her friends felt the same way. Until then, your parents took care of everything, and you just went through the motions that were already decided. After high school graduation, you're expected to know what you want to do for the rest of your life. *How is that fair?* Luckily, Hannah knew what she wanted to do, but that didn't make life easier, just less complicated.

Now, at 24, she felt like her life was finally taking the right track. She was happy with her best friends at her side and living every day to the fullest. Since they all loved music, every chance they got, they went to music festivals and concerts. Life was beautiful, and she looked forward to the coming years. She was so excited for this weekend trip, happy to be making more precious memories.

Initially, her first instinct was to say no when the trip to the Myrtles was suggested, but she eventually changed her mind. She and her friends had always wanted to visit a haunted plantation but never discussed staying overnight. As they continued to sing and dance, she felt panic slowly creep back in. That stupid doll started everything and now she couldn't wait to get out of there. She shoved the unwanted thoughts away and closed her eyes. Swaying to the music helped release the bad energy and replace it with good vibes.

When the music stopped, it took a few minutes to register before she stopped moving. Someone turned off the music. Who turned off the music? Why would they do that?

"Hey, what happened to the music? Put that back on. Come on, y'all, I was just starting to relax."

She'd heard Katie yell something over the music, but didn't bother to listen. She can't be serious. Katie wanted to play spin the bottle. Hannah hadn't played spin the bottle in high school, so why would she want to play now, especially with no boys there to kiss? She listened to Katie explain she wanted to play a charade version of the game, and the theme would be scary movies. Looking around the room, she waited for someone else to say no. Finally, she spoke up and said she didn't want to play. She was tired of being scared and didn't want to play a drinking game. But, Lizzy agreed to play, and the rest nodded.

Watching everyone act out the movies turned out to be fun and almost comical. Sara and Allie had just acted out Halloween and it was hilarious. They were on Katie's turn, and of course, things got tense. She looked like she already had her idea before she spun the bottle and when she headed to the closet, the room suddenly turned cold. Before Hannah could protest, Katie reached out, grabbed onto the doorknob, and pulled open the door.

Hannah's breath seized. She felt like she wanted to jump up and run out of the room. Before she could get up, lightning exploded through the air with the loudest cracking sound she had ever heard. Everyone screamed and Hannah wasn't sure if it was because of Katie opening the closet door or the startling sound of the weather outside reminding them of the predicament they were in and the danger that currently surrounded them.

Breathe! In and out! Breathe! Hannah tried to regain control of her emotions that were racing toward full on panic. She knew that the Myrtles was supposed to be haunted but deep down she hadn't believed it. Realizing there was some truth to the stories frightened her. She glanced at the window and could swear that the old tree was laughing at her. The way the branches swayed in the wind brushing against the walls and the continuous pelting of rain against the windows told her that the house was not going to let them out so easily.

She let out a nervous chuckle at the thought of the forces around her working together. She closed her eyes and tried to think of all the things she'd heard people report happening and couldn't remember anyone talking about porcelain dolls. Maybe the doll was just an innocent decoration representing the era of the house. But that door did open on its own and the doll had moved. Hoping to find some clarity, she vigorously shook her head, but it didn't work. Wishing her mother was there made her feel like a child again. She glanced over at Lizzy for support and although she looked to be just as frightened as the rest, she gave Hannah a reassuring nod right before she jumped up, ran to the closet and slammed the door shut.

A stillness fell over the room because nobody dared to move. Without breathing, they stared at the closet door, waiting to see if it would reopen by itself. Millie was the first to speak.

"What did we expect to happen coming to a haunted house?"

Everyone remained silent for a while longer, still praying that the door stayed shut. Hannah noticed that the weather outside calmed and wondered if it was because the threat was gone. She hoped that was the case.

Finally she whispered, "Not this! I really did not expect any of this!"

Katie looked terrified. No one asked what she saw in the closet and Hannah was too afraid to ask. Maybe when they were safe, back at home, she'd ask, but not now. As if she'd read Hannah's mind, Lizzy came over, put her hand on her shoulder and reassured her they were going to make it home safely. She should've been more comforted by the gesture, but she didn't know if she believed her because at the moment they were still at an old, haunted plantation with no way to leave.

CHAPTER 11

Lizzy

Lizzy was trying not to freak out. She knew she had to pull it together for Hannah's sake. After reassuring her niece, she sat and listed the things that were of concern. The weather was something they were used to living in the south. Thunderstorms often spiked up suddenly and passed through quickly. But before she left home, she checked the weather report for the weekend. It was supposed to be clear, so why all the rain? The fallen tree was common in the area, but it left them stranded. Coincidence? She didn't know. The porcelain doll fit in with the antebellum décor, so why should that scare them unless the closet door opened on its own, like Hannah claimed? Someone had to be playing tricks because dolls don't move on their own. Katie's reaction when she opened the closet door came to mind and caused her to glare at her with suspicion. Katie was also the one who claimed she saw faces in the mirror that fell to the ground. Is she up to something? Across the room, she evaluated Katie's demeanor and had to admit that she looked frightened.

To further add to the suspicious behavior, Lizzy remembered it was Katie's idea to play spin the bottle. In fact, it was Katie's idea to come to the Myrtles. She could only explain the bizarre events as pranking.

Lizzy leaned over and whispered to Hannah. "I believe Katie is behind all of this. What do you think?"

Hannah leaned forward to look at her. She ruled out Katie because of the fear in her eyes.

"I don't know. Look at her. She's really upset. And, when y'all came back from the bathroom, she was definitely upset. Didn't you say she wouldn't look into the mirrors in the bathroom? When did you ever see Katie pass a mirror and not look? I don't know, Lizzy. I think she's genuinely scared. What exactly happened in the bathroom?" Hannah stiffened, bracing herself for information she was probably better off not knowing.

Instead of answering the question, Lizzy called for the others to sit and calm down. They were all losing control while Katie stared at the closet door. Cory Ann glanced at Lizzy, then back at Katie. While everyone followed orders and huddled on the bed, Cory Ann pulled Katie away from the closet. Once everyone calmed down, Lizzy calmly asked Katie what she saw in the closet.

Katie mumbled, "Nothing."

What did that mean? Lizzy asked again and Katie mumbled 'nothing' again.

Katie's frightened demeanor alarmed Lizzy. She motioned to Cory Ann to stay close to her. Losing Katie was not something she could accept when things were racing out of control. Thoughts of being alone in making hard decisions caused her stomach to grumble with fear. She needed everyone to be present, and alert if they were to get out of there safely.

"Katie! Katie! Look at me, Katie!" Lizzy waited until she finally got her attention. "Exactly what did you see in the closet?"

"Nothing!" Katie was almost yelling. "There was nothing there. The doll was gone. The closet was empty." She rambled. "How? Where did it go? I just threw it in there!" Her body shook with confusion.

Everyone was quiet. Lizzy didn't know what to say. She, along with everyone else, sat there staring at the closet door, hoping that it wouldn't open again. She decided not to wait any longer but instead suggested that they leave that room and go to someone else's.

"Wait, what if the door opens and we don't know?" Sara was afraid to stay but also afraid to leave.

"I don't know, but I'm tired of sitting here freaking out. What else can we do?" Lizzy was ready to move.

"Let's go downstairs and find out if anyone else is around. I know it's late, but maybe it won't be as scary down there." Marci tossed her idea at them.

A few of the others agreed with Marci, so Lizzy nodded. "Okay, let's go."

All eight of them huddled closely as they approached the stairway. Reluctantly, Cory Ann pushed her way to the front and mumbled a few choice words as she passed. With a small skip to her step, she made her way down to the bottom. Instead of continuing on into the rest of the house, she hesitated, waiting for the others to join her.

"Come on! What are y'all doing? Hurry up!" Cory Ann yelled up to them.

Lizzy grabbed Hannah's hand and the rest of them buddied up before they started down the stairs. She noticed the creaking sound each step made when they were pushing forward. Poor lighting hindered her sight, only allowing her to find the steps directly in front of her. She could barely see Cory Ann standing at the bottom, and that wasn't sitting well with Lizzy.

"Co? That's you, right?" Lizzy's voice was low and shaky. Silence prompted her to ask a little louder. "Co! Cory Ann, answer me!"

Question answered with the sound of giggling floating up through the air.

Finally at the bottom, Lizzy punched Cory Ann's shoulder! "You idiot! Why didn't you answer me? You know how afraid they all are already."

Cory Ann was laughing louder now. "They? You look pretty terrified yourself. You saw me walk down and stop right here, so who did you think it was?" She shook her head and rolled her eyes at her.

Lizzy waited for everyone to get down, then shushed them. "Listen."

They all stayed huddled and froze. The darkness was overwhelming. Before she spoke, Lizzy took a long breath and listened. It was difficult to recognize which sounds were normal and which ones should be alarming.

"What do you hear?" Katie was impatient.

"It stopped raining or at least has slowed down." She pointed to the front door before moving toward the entrance. Unlocking the door, she pulled it open. She walked out onto the veranda and stared into the dark night. Eventually, they were all standing on the veranda squinching their eyes and gazing across the grounds. Lizzy was pleased to find that it had stopped raining, but thunder roared a warning of more on the way.

"One thousand - one, one thousand - two, one thousand - three." She watched as lightning flashed over the restaurant. "More rain is coming. Let's go back inside and look for someone to help us." Lizzy turned back toward the door. Fear was threatening to take over, but she powered through, refusing to give in.

"Wait. Did y'all see anyone moving around? We can't be the only people upset about the weather, can we?" Sara waited for someone to answer. "I don't like this at all. Something weird is going on. It's too quiet. Where are all the cats that were here earlier? And do y'all hear any wildlife? Birds? Owls? Coyotes?"

Lizzy's spine tingled as she looked around, confirming what Sara had just said. The air felt crisp against her body, and the smell of rain tickled her nose. The sky was heavy with dark clouds that looked to be rolling her way. Glancing down at her apple watch, she wondered how much longer before the storms flared up again. She tried to ignore the fact that she had always hated bad weather. Her mother was frightened of it and unintentionally instilled that fear in Lizzy. She'd never let the fear take over, but her stomach would knot up and her breathing quickened, causing her discomfort every time. She was more afraid of giving into her anxiety than she was of her fear. Anxiety, a monster of its own, if left unchecked, would take down even the strongest. Lizzy had succeeded in keeping her anxiety at a normal level so far.

"I don't see any lights on." She pointed to the downstairs windows. Walking out onto the lawn, she shuddered when she saw one dim light from the same small dormer on top of the roof. She found herself unable to look away, waiting for the curtain to move. Finally, someone spoke, and she shifted her stare back to her friends. Should she tell them about the attic light or keep that to herself? Before she could decide, large drops of rain started striking her, so she bolted onto the veranda. Keeping that bit of information to herself was probably the best course of action, at least at that moment.

They all screamed when the first lightning strike arrived, and Lizzy noticed Katie was staring out into the darkness. She followed her gaze to an old storm cellar that was barely visible except for slight shards of light that peeked through the boards. A nervous chuckle escaped as she thought to herself how that scene screamed 'horror movie.'

Katie

The entire night was quickly getting out of control. From the moment she'd arrived, Katie felt unsettled, and hours later, she was still on edge. She wasn't sure what they expected to find outside, but complete silence never crossed her mind. The old storm cellar that grabbed her attention when she first arrived was again drawing her gaze. Something was calling out to her, playing with her mind. Careful not to react, she welcomed the rain currently distracting her.

The rain started falling again, and their choices were grim. Go back inside or stay outside with no cover amid the approaching storm. When she'd pulled her attention away from the storm cellar, she noticed Lizzy had followed her gaze and was looking at her for answers that she didn't have. Shrugging her shoulders signaled that she didn't know what had her so captivated. She remembered the open lock on the doors and felt the urge to run out into the darkness and swing it open. She wrapped her arms around herself tightly as she fought the impulse. The last thing she wanted to do was enter another scary structure.

The only choice that made sense was to go back inside the plantation home and seek help. She pulled her cell phone out of her pocket, hoping to have a signal, but there were no bars, and her battery indicator light was blinking. She'd brought a portable battery charger, but retrieving it wasn't an option. If she never went back upstairs, she would be fine.

The old storm cellar, the mirrors, the porcelain doll, and the creepy lady from the veranda proved to be a lot to digest. She knows what she saw in the mirror, and it scared the heck out of her. She lied when she confessed to seeing an old woman in the mirror, because truthfully, it was a horrible version of herself. Bile rose in her throat, causing her to gag and swallow hard, pushing it back down.

"We better go back inside because that storm is coming in fast." A bolt of lightning launched them all into action. Once inside, they crowded close to the door, afraid of the unknown waiting for them in the darkness. Thankfully, there were a few dim lights that helped them see, but the halls were pitch black and completely silent. Suddenly, seven cell phone lights turned on and pointed toward the darkness. They all looked at Katie, surprised that she hadn't turned hers on.

"What? My phone's about to die. Do any of you want to run upstairs and grab my portable charger? I didn't think so. Besides, we don't need everyone's phone lights on at the same time. We need to save some batteries, in case."

Lizzy announced that her phone was fully charged, and she would keep her light on.

"Okay. Who else has a full charge?"

Millie said that she did.

"Everyone else, turn off your lights and save the battery. We'll take turns using the flashlights."

"How can everyone be sleeping? Are we the only crazy ones? I'm just saying something's wrong here." Hannah ended her statement with a mumble.

"We can't stand here all night, can we?" Allie kept her voice low.

"Y'all. I have to go to the bathroom. Is there one down here?" Sara was hoping there was because she dreaded going back upstairs.

"I don't know, but I think we should go down the hall in search of someone to help." Lizzy waited, but no one volunteered. Once again, Cory Ann raised her hand and switched on her phone light. She was turning out to be the only person ready to approach everything head on and Lizzy was grateful for that.

"I'm not comfortable staying here without you and Cory Ann. Just saying." Hannah was too nervous to have the group split up, especially Lizzy and herself.

Katie didn't want to be alone and felt safest closer to the door. She remembered the hallway was short, so she opted to stay put.

"Hannah, you go with Lizzy and Cory Ann if that makes you feel better. I'll stay right here and wait if anyone wants to join me." Katie hoped that at a few of them would.

Katie with the group, aside from Lizzy, Cory Ann, and Hannah, gathered close to the door again and, as if on cue, the wind picked up and rattled the windows, causing them to squeeze in tighter together. She welcomed the sound of the rain because it broke the monotonous sound of silence that was driving her crazy.

She watched as Lizzy and her crew started down the hallway. Lizzy tapped lightly on the first door she came to, and Hannah pointed her light on the door with a sign that read 'Ladies.' Lizzy turned the knob and evidently found the bathroom.

"Sara, here's a bathroom."

They left the door open and continued down the hall, so she and Sara entered the bathroom. She didn't close the door, but instead they took turns standing in the doorway. There were several other doors on both sides of the hallway, and she could hear Lizzy tapping on each one. After a few minutes, she heard them knock a little harder and still no one answered.

"Do you think these are guest rooms? I wonder where the staff sleep, or do they leave at night? Someone has to be here, right?" Lizzy was rattling on as she approached each door. The idea that the staff left their guest by themselves at night still bothered her. That was unacceptable.

Katie watched from the door as they reached a sitting area at the end of the hallway and stopped, deciding what to do next. The sound of the toilet flushing made them all gasp, including her. She suggested they come back and join the others.

A loud tapping sound hit the window next to the door, forcing them all to run away from the sound and up the stairs, searching for safety. Katie was the last one to make it to the stairs and she could swear she saw eyes peering at her from down the dark hall. Someone was in the house with them, but she wasn't going back to see who it was. She thought there was something odd about the eyes, but wondered if she was just so freaked out that she imagined the whole thing. She hoped for the latter, but the way the night was going, she knew that wasn't the case.

They were all safely upstairs and crowded on the sofa in the sitting room. Everyone was too afraid to go into the rooms, even though their current location was as spooky. The tapping sound was repeated, louder this time.

"Someone's out there! What are we going to do? I don't want to go back down." Marci covered her eyes and rocked back and forth with anxiety.

Katie rubbed her forehead, then her eyes, while she was thinking. She didn't want to go back downstairs either, especially after she saw their eyes staring at her. She tried to reason with herself by thinking out loud. "Maybe it was just a tree branch scraping the house. Strong winds remain. That could explains it, yes?"

"No!" Hannah almost shouted. "No, Katie. The veranda is too wide. There's no way a tree branch could reach in and touch that window. No way!"

"Okay, okay. There has to be an explanation. Why wouldn't they just knock on the door?" Lizzy's reasoning didn't have the effect she'd hoped for.

A loud banging on the front door rippled up the stairs and answered her question.

"Maybe it's the police, since the lights are out, and the tree is blocking the driveway. Certainly, someone called that in when it happened. We have to go answer the door." Katie sighed.

No one moved. No one made a sound.

"Fine, I'll go. Besides, if it were a ghost or a serial killer, would they be considerate and knock before coming in to haunt or kill us?" Katie was up and headed down the stairs before her comments had time to sink in.

By the time she reached the bottom step, she regretted her decision but decided she needed to follow through. Her friends were all terrified and if help had arrived, then they could all relax. She walked slowly toward the door and contemplated looking through the curtain first, but another burst of pounding on the door erupted. Reaching for the handle, she turned the lock and flung open the door.

After the initial shock wore off, Katie asked, "What are y'all doing here?"

CHAPTER 13

Lizzy

All of her senses had heightened as she walked down the hall of the plantation. Her eyes were adjusting to the darkness just enough to see the surrounding area. The air was chilly against her skin and normally she welcomed the cold, but there seemed to be something dark looming around in it that grew stronger as she ventured further down the hall. A slight shiver made it all the way to her toes this time. When she touched each doorknob, there was an electrifying feeling that shot through her fingers, reminding her of static electricity, but different. Even the smell in the air was a peculiar mix of cigar smoke and Old Spice scented cologne. She remembered that the whole establishment was non-smoking, aside from a small, designated smoking area that was on the other side of the house, but the smell was so strong she could swear she saw smoke floating up through the air in front of her. Maybe someone was vaping right outside the doors, and it was lingering in the air. She looked at Cory Ann and Hannah to determine if they were smelling the same thing, but they didn't seem to notice. After knocking on the last door without a response, her mouth grew dry, and that made it hard to swallow. They were all alone.

She wondered if anyone had read all the information on the website when they booked the rooms. Wasn't someone supposed to be on the premises at all times, or do they go home in the evening? Those were good questions to know before something like this happens. Maybe one of them had the printed out reservation and they could see if it had a phone number on it in case of an emergency. But a lot of good that would do. The phones were down. The sound of a toilet flushing put her back in motion.

"I think we should just go back and join the others. I wish we would've become familiar with the place when we first got here. Did either of you print out the reservations with all the information on it by chance?"

They both shook their heads no. Hannah reached for her phone to go pull it up online before remembering she didn't have service. "How did people live without the Internet? This is so hard and frustrating."

Deep down, Lizzy laughed, but it fizzled out before it reached the surface. She pointed to the front room, directing Hannah to make her way back to join the others. As soon as they were all reunited, a loud tapping sent them barreling up the stairs and away from whoever was out there. She was breathing deeply from sprinting up the stairs and wondered what happened to the smoke and Old Spice smell that was in the hall. She wanted to mention it to the others, but decided it might freak them out. Besides, if someone else noticed the smell, they would've said something.

She started to suggest everyone regroup and grab their purses, keys and battery chargers, just in case they have to leave the premises in a hurry. Right now, that was a real possibility. But before the words left her mouth, there was a loud pounding at the front door. Everyone's eyes grew large with fear. Lizzy could feel the sofa she was sitting on shake from their trembling bodies.

Surprisingly, Katie jumped up and volunteered to go down to see who was at the door. She moved so quickly that no one had a chance to go with her. Lizzy stood up and walked over to the edge of the stairwell, trying to hear what was happening. She heard Katie fling open the door, then she was silent. Lizzy's heart stopped and she couldn't breathe. Did something happen to her? Oh My God! She opened her mouth to call out to her, but then she heard Katie say something. She was talking to someone, but she couldn't make out what she was saying. She waited a few minutes more than heard laughter.

"Katie! Are you all right?" Lizzy walked down a few steps as she spoke.

She could hear talking, and it sounded like there were several people in the house now.

"Katie! Answer me!" Lizzy demanded a response as she made her way to the bottom of the steps.

Through the darkness, she could see several bodies, and they were all hugging and greeting Katie. She knows them. It was definitely not the police. She stepped into the room and immediately recognized the first face she saw. Demi. What is she doing here? The panic she was feeling lifted, and suddenly she didn't feel the need to know why she was there anymore, because she was just so relieved that it was someone alive and not a ghost. Not a ghost or a serial killer.

She joined in with the southern way of greeting people, hugging and kissing. After she hugged Demi, she noticed she had Brittany, Savannah and Stephanie with her. She made her round, greeting them all before remembering her group upstairs patiently waiting for answers.

"Hey, y'all come on down. It's okay." Lizzy ran to the bottom of the stairs to make sure they heard her. She assured them it was safe to come down, then laughed at how a few newcomers had changed the whole dynamics of the terrifying evening they were having. What happened to the threat that they all felt since they'd arrived? Her stomach did a somersault when the realization creeped back in that nothing had changed and the threat was probably still there alive and well, well maybe not alive.

"What are y'all doing here?" Lizzy looked at Katie. "Did you know they were coming?"

Katie was still chatting up the others. "No. I did not. Did you know?"

"No. Of course not. But I am so glad to see y'all." Lizzy turned to Demi. "How did y'all get here in all this rain?" She noticed the blank look on her face.

"What do you mean?" Demi looked confused.

"The storming rain. How did y'all drive through that? It was crazy. The lights are out, and the phone service is down. Didn't you see the enormous tree blocking the parking lot? Where did you park?"

Demi still looked confused.

Lizzy ran to the front door and swung it open. She ran out onto the veranda to confirm that it was still pouring down raining, but it wasn't. It had stopped completely.

"I don't understand! It was just storming, and the wind was shaking the windows." She looked back at Katie for confirmation.

"Rain was coming down like a deluge and the wind was beating the house. It must have just stopped when y'all arrived. It's been on and off for the past few hours, so I'm sure we're in for another round soon. Weren't the streets flooded?" Katie was sure they had to be.

"First off, it wasn't raining when we got here, and it hadn't rained at all today. Not at home anyway." Demi's words confused Lizzy.

"Wait, the streets aren't flooded. Yes! We have to get out of here before it flares up again. Please tell me you came in your van. I think we could all squeeze in just to get away from here. We'll sit on each other's laps if we have to, but we gotta go. Thank God you came when you did. I don't think we would've made it through the night. Come on y'all, let's go grab our stuff before the rain starts again. We can come back tomorrow for our cars."

She was running toward the stairs when Savannah yelled, "Wait! We don't have a vehicle. My mom dropped us off. They were on their way to Natchez, Ms., to meet up with your parents Katie, so they dropped us off. They were going to pick us up on Sunday on their way back home. Is something wrong?" Savannah sensed the dread in the room.

"Yes! The lights are out, there's no cell service, the mirrors are falling off the walls, and there's a creepy porcelain doll that keeps moving on her own and opening doors and we're here all alone. We really need to go!" Hannah was hysterical.

Everyone looked at Katie for an explanation.

"Right before we ran up the stairs, I saw glowing eyes down the hallway."

"What do you mean, glowing?" Brittany asked as she grabbed onto Savannah and Demi for assurance.

"Just what I said, glowing. It may be the stupid night lights making them glow, I don't know, but they were glowing." Katie was positive about what she saw.

Lizzy believed Katie. They all stared down the hall, praying that the eyes were gone, and they were.

"Thankfully, whatever or whoever it was is gone now. Demi, do y'all have rooms reserved? Why are y'all so late? No one's here to do a check in."

"We were supposed to be here around nine, but the traffic was terrible, because of a wreck on the Interstate over near the spillway, and it's backed up for miles. I'm sure there's someone here. Someone must be on the premises for emergencies, right?"

Everyone fell silent when the realization hit that they were still stranded and were probably all alone. She watched as Demi walked over to the desk and hit the small silver bell on the counter for service. The sound vibrated and then echoed throughout the house before a bolt of lightning lit up the veranda, followed by thunder and the pity pat sound that rain made when slapping a window.

"Here we go again. The next round of storms has arrived." Lizzy looked around the room and saw raw fear on everyone's faces. Everyone except Millie. The word 'annoyed' came to mind when she looked at Millie's face. She was glaring at the new arrivals as if they were enemies. To Millie, they were strangers, and maybe with all the chaos, the look on her face was of concern rather than annoyance. Whatever it was, disappeared, replaced with a faint smile - the same faint smile they were all trying to force just to keep it together.

Guilt set in when Lizzy felt relieved to see the new arrivals. She and Demi were old school friends and sometimes still got together for events. The others were always with Demi, so they were familiar too. Savannah's parents had been friends with Katie's since they were young. Lizzy trusted all of them and was happy for the extra support.

CHAPTER 14

Katie

Things were getting out of hand quickly, and Katie didn't know how to rein it all back in. Everyone was on edge and ready to bolt, and now there were four more people to worry about. It wasn't her job, but she felt responsible since it was her idea to visit the Myrtles.

Apparently, the staff was gone, and they were left to fend for themselves. No one would be sleeping anytime soon, so she offered for the new arrivals to join them upstairs. There was more than enough room for all of them. She chuckled because she knew that her group was going to stick together even if they'd have to jam onto one bed.

Katie's thoughts turned to her own life and level of happiness. Currently single, contentment thrived because of her animals and her friends. After a few recent catastrophic relationships, she needed time to regroup and focus on herself. She had a dog and two cats, and they were her babies. She almost brought her dog with her, but decided it would take time away from enjoying her friends. Her thoughts continued to ramble on before the sound of thunder jolted her, bringing her back to the present.

"Hey, y'all are welcome to stay with us until someone shows up." Katie watched Demi as she looked behind the counter.

"Thanks. I know we booked a Suite on the ground floor. Shouldn't there be a key here with the name on it?" Demi was behind the desk searching. "The key hooks are all empty." Feeling frustrated, she said, "I guess we better go upstairs with y'all for now."

Katie encouraged everyone to go back up.. The last thing she wanted to do was go back upstairs, so she understood their hesitation. Aside from the rain and occasional thunder, there was a low hum of a generator somewhere in the distance. The house was still so dark, but she was grateful for the one small light showing them the way up. Without saying a word, they all went to their respective rooms, grabbed pillows, blankets and even a mattress and drug them into the sitting room. The tension was so high it was almost unbearable.

Katie plugged in her phone and prayed that the outlet was connected to the generator and almost smiled when the charging circle started to turn. She searched her phone for Spotify and put some jam on, hopefully to calm herself down, as well as everyone else. She was sitting still on the floor when she thought she heard a noise. Hannah was leaning against her and jumped, apparently hearing the same sound.

"What was that?" Hannah barely whispered the words. She looked terrified, and Katie felt her whole body tense up in response. Hannah asked again, louder this time. "Y'all, what was that noise?"

The others quieted as they strained to listen. The faint sound was coming from Hannah's room. Unless someone came in when they were all downstairs, it should be empty. As much as she didn't want to, she stood to investigate the noise. She figured she was on her own, but surprisingly, Millie stood up and said she would go with her.

She reached for the doorknob, with Millie right behind her. She looked back for confirmation that her partner was ready, then slowly pushed open the door. The room was dark with only the occasional lightning strikes lighting it up. Again, they heard a noise coming from the closet door that was slightly ajar. Katie gasped, startling Millie.

"What's wrong? Do you see something?" Millie grabbed onto Katie's arm.

"No. Yes. I mean, the closet's open and I know it was shut before we left the room. I know it was!"

"You're right. I remember watching Lizzy jump up and shut it, so how could it be open? Did Hannah open it when she came in to get the pillows and blankets?"

"Hannah didn't come in here, Allie did. And I doubt she went anywhere near the closet, not since that dumb porcelain doll was in there." She and Millie stared at the crack in the closet door.

Katie squeezed her eyes, hoping to see a little clearer in the darkness. She was almost afraid to look into the opening of the door, fearing that a pair of eyes might be glaring back at her, but she looked anyway. She squeezed Millie's arm against her body and pulled her forward, deeper into the room. Every step was hard, as if her body was trying to keep her from getting any closer to an un-foreseen danger. Millie didn't fight her as they grew closer, but Katie could feel her body tense with unease.

When she reached the closet, she let anxiety take over and moved quickly to end the suspense. This time, Millie gasped. Katie stared at the back of the closet at what seemed to be another open door, but this one smaller. Millie turned on her phone flashlight and pointed it to the open doorway.

"What is that? Was that there before? Did you know there was another doorway in here?" Millie was afraid to look away.

"I don't know. I don't remember seeing a door, but I was so focused on the doll that I could have missed it. I don't know." She looked at Millie, who was standing still beside her.

"What should we do?" Katie wanted to run out of the room and slam the door shut behind her.

Millie didn't answer because she didn't know what they should do, either.

Katie inhaled deeply, then, holding her breath, pushed forward. Millie's phone light was shining all over the place in different directions because of her shaking hands. The small closet grew shorter and tighter the deeper they went in. Katie wasn't good at math, but she guessed the closet to be about fifteen feet deep and probably ran the length of the sitting area all the way to the next room. She felt relieved by the last thought that it was probably a door that lead to the next room.

She whispered to Millie. "It probably goes to the next room, right?" She was looking for encouragement to continue on.

Millie just shrugged her shoulders while still clinging to Katie's arm.

"Alright. Let's do this. Are you ready?" Not waiting for a response, she moved to the door. She screamed when a hand grabbed her and started pulling her toward the darkness. She yelled and kicked, but the hold was too tight. Millie leaped forward and scratched the arm, trying to remove the grip it had on Katie. All at once, the grip on Katie's arm was released, causing her to fall backwards to the ground. When she looked up, she heard Millie scream and then watched her disappear through the door that slammed shut behind her.

"No!" Katie scrambled to her feet and raced to the door. She clawed at the closed door, searching for a knob. There wasn't a knob. She felt around frantically trying to find a way in, a way to Millie, but there wasn't one. She felt a hand on her shoulder and shrieked in terror. The others stumbled into the dark closet to find her screaming for Millie and clawing at the door.

She yelled for everyone to back out of the closet. She was shaking and scared, but she refused to leave Millie.

"Someone grabbed me, and Millie helped fight them off. Then they grabbed her and pulled her through that door. We have to find her." Tears were running down Katie's face. "We have to find her. She saved me. We have to go back and save her."

Cory Ann looked back toward the closet. "Who has their phone with them? We need some light." Sara offered her phone. She took the phone and stood at the edge of the closet. "I hate dark places! Why am I here?"

Katie shouted she would go back in, but Cory Ann told her to calm down and moved into the closet before she lost her nerve. Katie watched as she took her time and right as she approached the door, it slowly eased open. She looked back at her friends, who were wide eyed watching and then waited as Cory Ann pointed the light down to the floor.

Everyone screamed at the same time.

CHAPTER 15

Millie

When Katie stood up and volunteered to go investigate the sound coming from Hannah's room, Millie was surprised. Katie didn't strike her as being too brave, but she was stepping up, and that impressed her. No one else volunteered so she jumped up and said she would go too. She didn't consider herself particularly brave either, but she'd been through enough in her short life to realize that having courage and standing up for what's right was important. Her family was a big disappointment in that area, and she refused to follow their lead. She'd wanted to break the cycle of evil that her family had going on for generations and at one time even thought her sister would've been the one to join her, but in the end, she too chose the dark side.

She felt alone in the world, unsure who she could trust. Eventually she'd have to take a more aggressive approach in her search for others with her abilities. But for now, her new friends were an important part of her normal life that she'd come to rely on. Her fondness for each of them grew every day. Millie was going to do whatever was needed to keep them safe. This weekend offered harmless fun, but things re-channeled, and now she could sense the danger.

Something didn't feel right but Millie didn't know how to relay that concern to Katie without drawing unwanted questions. So, she followed her into the darkness and kept her eyes peeled for any signs of trouble.

Katie gasped, bringing her attention to the back of the closet. She could've missed it earlier, considering she didn't go all the way into the closet. She tightened her grip on Katie's arm refusing to lose sight of her. Once she saw the door, she knew the danger was behind it.

Her heart pounded, wishing she could run out of there. She wanted to pull Katie out of the room, but how would she explain her reaction? They were all scared, terrified to be exact, but they were also willing to face danger head on. The evil that was lurking in the darkness would eventually find them.

Katie's dash for the door proved too swift; she was already gone before her intentions were clear. Millie hung on and allowed herself to be thrust forward. The hand that now gripped Katie's was so tight that Millie felt helpless as she tried to loosen the hold. Finally, she exerted enough force to break the hold, but the same hand grabbed hers pulling her into total darkness. She screamed for help but knew immediately that there was nothing anyone could do. The door shut behind her and she found herself all alone in total darkness. Before she could react, she felt something cold on her neck then a fog began to fill her mind. A slight smile crossed her lips because she knew she'd just saved Katie from the danger. She would find her way back to save the rest of them, too. She had to save them because they were her friends and without them she would be all alone. She closed her eyes, giving into the sudden allure of sleep.

CHAPTER 16

Katie

Katie ran screaming back into the closet. She shoved Cory Ann, who was too stunned to move, and plopped down to the floor. Instinctively, she opened the door, reached into the darkness, and with both hands around Millie's shoulders, pulled her back into the closet, slamming the door shut. Securing the door with her body, she leaned down to check Millie for a heartbeat.

"She's alive!" Katie put her hand in front of Millie's nose and felt the air exhaled from her body. "She's breathing! Somebody help me. Cory Ann jumped into action and helped Katie pull Millie into the bedroom.

"Should we move her?" Sara's knowledge of first aid was limited, but she knew you shouldn't move someone that was injured.

Katie ignored everyone's concerns and instructed Cory Ann to help get Millie out of that room and onto the sofa in the sitting area. She checked her phone to see if by some miracle she had service, but it was still offline. Unsure of what needed to happen next, Katie looked at the others for ideas. Marci and Allie ran to the bathroom and brought back a wet towel for Millie's head. A somber mood filled the entire room while they prayed Millie would wake up. And she did.

"Oh, my God! Millie, are you okay? Are you hurt?" Katie was relieved to see her eyes open.

Stunned, Millie lay still, then let out a low groan. She touched her head and then, as if she had just woken up from a bad dream, bolted upright. Her eyes were wide, looking around, trying to figure out where she was.

Katie grabbed the wet towel that had fallen and assured Millie she was safe.

"Hey, are you okay? You're safe now, but are you hurt? Do you know what happened? Do you remember?" She waited for a response. Millie just shook her head.

"Do you know where you are?" Marci looked concerned.

"Yes." Millie answered them in a whisper. She took a deep breath, ran her hand through her hair, then stood up. Louder she said, "Yes, we're at the Myrtles. I'm okay." Then, as if suddenly remembering the incident, she reached for Katie and asked if she was okay. "Are you hurt? Did she hurt you?"

"She? Who are you talking about? Did you see the person who grabbed you?" Katie asked again. "Millie, did you see something?"

Her expression changed from frantic to calm, and she stumbled over her words. "No. I didn't see anything. Nothing. It was dark. I don't know why I said 'she' because I didn't see anything. The hand wasn't big, so I guess I assumed it was a woman's hand." Agitated, she walked in circles while she explained herself.

"Look, we're all spooked here tonight. Let's settle down and talk this through. Obviously, things have taken a turn from spooky ghost stuff to an actual assault from a human threat. That wasn't supposed to be part of the weekend. None of us should be alone, so let's make sure we stay together. Any ideas about getting out of here?" Lizzy was trying to sound calm, but her voice cracked as she spoke.

"We could just walk out of here." Allie wanted to do just that.

"And go where? What time is it anyway? Is anything open?" Katie wasn't against the idea, but they needed a solid plan before they acted. Millie seemed unusually quiet, which was to be expected if she was traumatized, but she didn't look distressed. She looked like she was concentrating on something or maybe devising a plan herself. Forcing her attention back to the group, a slight shiver ran up her arm. Everyone was throwing out different ideas and talking over each other. She sat down to take a minute. Something was different. She felt the shift in the room, unaware where it was coming from.

Her thoughts went back to the closet and the fact that she was almost pulled into the darkness when Millie saved her. The girl risked her life for Katie, so why the skepticism? She wished she knew Millie better. Where was she from? She talked about being estranged from her family, but why? What happened? There were so many unanswered questions. She knew all the other's well. She knew their history. Even Demi and her group. Katie's parents were good friends with Savannah's parents. Millie was the only one she didn't know, and that caused her to feel uneasy. She made a mental note to talk to Marci since she works with Millie. Maybe she could shed some light on more of her past.

Katie guided her attention back to the ideas flying all over the place. Everyone had formed different groups to bounce their ideas off of, trying to make a case for their own plan. Millie and Marci were off to the side having their own brief discussion, except Millie was the one doing all the talking. She wasn't being quiet any longer. Walking over to them, she leaned in to ask for their ideas. Millie smiled and suggested that they do nothing but sit and wait until someone comes back in the morning.

"I'm not a big fan of walking in the dark on a rainy night along a deserted highway looking for help. I just feel like we would be safer staying here together." Millie looked at Marci, who nodded her head in agreement.

Before she could ask Marci anything, Sara grabbed her arm and pulled her in to her conversation. Out of the corner of her eye, she watched as Marci and Millie joined in with Allie and Hannah.

"I think we should go." Sara nudged Katie, who was staring at the other groups. "Hello! Katie, come on. I really want to leave."

Katie heard what Sara said and agreed, but she couldn't help but notice Millie doing all the talking in the other group. She wondered why all of a sudden she was being so vocal. Didn't the rest of them have any suggestions? They were listening to her talk and no one added anything to the conversation. She grabbed Sara's hand and marched over to the other group, asking for everyone's attention.

"Listen up. We need to decide what to do quickly. My guess is another round of storms is about to fire up again. Who wants to leave?" Katie watched, and only she and Sara raised their hands. "Who wants to stay here until morning?" One by one, the other ten raised their hands. Even Allie, the one who suggested they walk out of there, voted to stay. She looked to be unsure but raised her hand, anyway.

She felt deflated but went along with the majority. Katie didn't want to make a scene, but something bizarre was going on. No one shoveled out their usual complaints about the situation. Everyone just accepted the decision and found a place to sit and relax. She doubted anyone was going to relax, but at least they could get some much needed rest and take time to pray for daybreak to get there. She settled in between Sara and Lizzy and debated whether she should share her concerns with either of them. Lizzy was tense, but she agreed to stay. Sara still wanted to leave.

"I need to go to the bathroom. Sara, come with me, please." Katie hoped Sara didn't put up a fight because she really wanted to talk to her alone.

"Okay. I need to go anyway."

Millie stood up, but Katie cut her off and said, "Let's go to the restroom in two's since we have 12 of us. That way, everyone will have a partner. We can all go now, then settle in for the night." Before anyone objected, she and Sara headed to the bathroom and shut the door.

"Sara, something's up. Have you noticed anything strange about Millie? I can't put my finger on it, but she's giving me a bad vibe. She's different somehow."

"I haven't paid attention to her with everything going on. Do you think she's still traumatized by the attack? She doesn't seem to be too distraught. I'm traumatized, and I wasn't even in the room. Who was in that closet space? That's creepy. I think staying up here is a mistake because they could come back. I know you feel the same way I do, so why do you think the others voted to stay?"

"I agree with you. Whoever grabbed us is most certainly still here in the house. I was upset, but I wasn't the one being pulled through the dark closet door. Maybe she's in shock, I don't know. How did she persuade all of them to side with her? That's a good question, and one I don't have an answer for. All Allie wanted to do earlier was bolt! What made them agree? Did she try to talk to you?"

Sara shook her head no. "The only person I talked with was you until you joined their group, and I was right beside you, listening. What do you think she's doing? She never left the room, did she? I agree it's weird that Allie was so quick to agree and even the others who were ready to leave hours ago, but what would be her reason to stay?"

Katie used the facilities, then Sara did the same. "I know I sound crazy, but just please stay clear of her, or at least keep your eyes open. I'll do the same."

Katie and Sara finished and agreed to stay close to each other. She reached and pulled open the door, finding Millie and Marci standing right outside. Sara yelped. She was startled to see them there, but quickly recovered and smiled. Were they loud enough to be heard through the closed door? She'd purposely kept her voice to a whisper and was glad she had. Millie was acting sketchy, and she was glad that she had Sara to share her concerns with. Together, they'd make it through the night in one piece and alive. She was gonna to make sure they all did.

CHAPTER 17

Katie

Katie sat still, too afraid to move. The rest took their turns going to the bathroom, then found a space to sit down and wait. Wait for what? She wondered what was going to happen next. The whole night seemed so bizarre. Not real. Feeling like they were making a mistake by staying, she searched for a way to convince them to leave. The idea of her and Sara sneaking out by themselves sent another round of shivers through her body. Distant sounds of crickets made its way into the room. The rain had stopped, and the winds had died down as well. Timing was important because leaving while the weather was quiet would be more desirable than when it was storming.

She closed her eyes to recap the night while things were quiet. She squirmed, unable to forget the mirror incident confirming that ghost and spirits scared her as much as the person trying to hurt them. The alive human threat could still be lurking in the house. Pulling the blanket tighter, she thought of what could've happened had Millie not intervened. The thought caused her to glance at Millie and hated herself for her suspicions of someone that saved her life. But she could feel the threat lurking, waiting, and Millie was the only one behaving differently.

Katie recalled the earlier event step by step. It all happened so fast. Finding a doorway in the back of the closet was unexpected. It bothered her they hadn't noticed the doorway before. Was it some kind of trick? From what she'd heard and read about the Myrtles, it was a legitimate haunted house. She'd watched the Ghost Hunters episode where they featured the plantation and had concluded that the Myrtles was "One of the most haunted places in America." Everyone she spoke to that had visited talked about doorknobs rattling and images showing up in mirrors and ponds. A few said they witnessed objects moving by themselves. No one she talked to or anything she'd read suggested that mirrors crashed to the floor, and creepy dolls moved on their own.

Katie leaned forward. The doll! Where was the doll? Was it still in the closet? She didn't see the doll. Or did she? She can't remember seeing the doll. She was too focused on discovering the new door. Her heart pounded faster with each thought. Was it the doll who tried to pull them into the darkness? Katie jumped up and covered her mouth to keep from screaming out. Frantically, she looked around the group, happy they were finally settling down. She didn't want to alarm them, but she had to know. The urge to locate the doll was too strong. She had to go back to the closet and check and satisfy the drive growing inside her.

She looked at Sara, who had terror in her eyes. Reaching out, she squeezed her hand in comfort, but knew nothing would help while they stayed trapped inside a haunted house. Millie, who was also watching Katie's every move, met her eyes. Katie nodded toward the bathroom, hinting that she wanted to talk to her.

"I need to go to the bathroom." Katie declared in a whisper.

Millie stood up and offered to join her. "Gotta go in two's, right? I'll go with you."

They both left the group, heading to the bathroom.

Katie waited until the door shut, then swung around to Millie with terror-stricken eyes.

"The doll! Where was that porcelain doll? Did you see it in the closet?" Katie was shaking.

Millie paused before answering. "I don't know. I don't think it was there. Everything happened so quickly, I don't remember. I know I was expecting to see the dumb doll. I think we all thought the doll was the source of the noise. But when we entered, the first thing I saw was the door. The doll could've been there, but I don't know."

Katie noticed Millie was shaking as well, which, surprisingly, comforted her. Her body slacked as she sensed she was just like the rest of them, petrified. Maybe she was wrong about her and the changes she saw were caused by trauma. For a moment she felt horrible, but deep down inside she knew that wasn't the case. She didn't know what Millie was up to, but she was sure it wasn't anything good.

"We have to go back and see if the doll is there." Katie couldn't believe she said that. "We need to know what we're dealing with if we're going to stay here, which, for the record, I disagree with." She hated to ask her next question, but she had to. "Do you think it was the doll that grabbed us?"

Millie looked at her like she was nuts. Katie had expected that response, but she had to ask.

"What? I know it sounds ludicrous, but nothing here would surprise me. I know they think I was behind moving the doll to scare them, but I didn't do it. I thought about it, but circumstances got in the way. Again, are you sure that it wasn't the doll that grabbed your arm?"

Millie grabbed onto Katie's hand before she spoke. "I don't remember seeing the doll in the closet and I didn't see who grabbed me, but I can't believe that a small porcelain doll could've grabbed on to me that tight and then pull me into the darkness. Do you?"

"I'm unsure what to believe, but I have to know if the doll is still there." Katie softened her voice. "I can't ask you to go with me after what happened to you the last time. When we go back, I'm going straight to the closet to see if it's there." Katie held up her hand to Millie's protest. "I'll be okay. Trust me, I will not get too close. Promise me you'll look after them if something happens." Katie thought about her friends and smiled. She couldn't lose any of them. The thought caused her to shudder.

"Let's get back before they worry." Katie grabbed onto the doorknob but didn't turn it. Instead, she looked up at Millie. "Why don't you want to leave? Why stay here with someone or something that wants to harm us? How did you persuade them to agree with you?"

"I don't want to stay here, but I thought it was too dangerous to go out in that weather. Ans I didn't persuade anyone. Something bizarre is happening, so I was afraid that if we left... I don't know." Millie held Katie's gaze the whole time.

Katie stayed silent as she turned the handle and walked out. She wasn't sure how she felt about Millie's answer because, of course, what she said was true, but she still wasn't ready to let go of her gut suspicions and trust her 100%.

Returning, Katie bypassed the group, heading straight to Hannah's room where the closet door was still closed. Before she lost her nerve, she swung open the door and pointed her phone light into the darkness. Once her eyes adjusted to the darkness, she looked for the doll. Her neck extended, searching the closet, and when the light reached the small door, she jerked back. Sweat had formed over her brow, sending a drop into her eyes. She swiped her face, then continued searching for the doll, the doll that wasn't there. It wasn't there. She knew it. Her body stiffened, paralyzing her until someone touched her shoulder. A scream she'd been trying to suppress escaped.

CHAPTER 18

Hannah

Hannah sat on the floor, trying to keep her wits in check. Staying near Lizzy and Katie was her new aim. She couldn't remember ever being this scared. A trip to the Myrtles promised to be so fetch but now she wished she'd stayed home. Brave would never describe her and admitting that she was the opposite came easily. Terrified, she wanted to go home. Regrettably, she raised her hand when they asked who wanted to stay because she really wanted to leave. Fear of what's lurking outside just makes little sense because the real threat was inside this house. Changing her mind without explanation suggested someone had compelled her to do so.

Katie and Lizzy's faces showed no signs that things were going to be alright, but looked as terrified as the rest of them. She checked her cell phone again, praying that she would have service. One bar appeared, but when she attempted to dial, it wouldn't go through. Her trembling fingers turned off her phone to save the battery and then slid it into her pocket.

Hannah tried to manage her thoughts by turning her focus to all the babies in the NICU that she had been taking care of at work. They were the cutest little things, some of them just a few pounds. She'd loved her job because even though it was heart wrenching at times, it was so rewarding at others. Working a lot of hours exhausted her mentally and physically, so she was ready for the weekend break. Now she wished she could just go back and work. Exhaling loudly, she caused those sitting next to her to look up with concern.

"Hey, are you okay?" Sara noticed a sadness in Hannah's eyes and understood exactly why she was upset.

"No. I'm not okay. None of us are okay. Sara, we need to get out of here."

"Wait! What? You raised your hand to stay, and now you want to leave. I want out too, but aside from me, only Katie raised her hand to leave. You all overrode our vote, so here we are." Sara's voice raised some as she tried to grasp what Hannah wanted.

"I know. I have no explanation, and I don't care about that now. We just need to grab our stuff and leave."

She glanced around the room and shuddered in fright. The old house was the perfect setting for a horror movie. The decor seemed hauntingly beautiful, and the few dim lights being powered by the generator made it difficult to see clearly. They'd closed all the bedroom doors and were hanging out in the sitting area right by the stairs. Hannah leaned forward, trying to look to the bottom, but the lighting was so bad that all she saw was a big black hole. Chills ran up her spine at the thought of going down those stairs to get out of the house.

She had settled down, feeling defeated. Katie had suggested they go to the bathroom in two's, so she obediently waited her turn. Once they were all done, they found a place to sit and wait. That's what she found so unnerving, waiting. What were they waiting for? The rain slowed down and there wasn't anyone coming for them. She wondered if anyone was aware they were stranded and without electricity. Had someone called the outage into the electric company? Something was very wrong with this entire picture, and Hannah was ready for answers. She craved answers that no one could supply, or maybe just wouldn't.

Surprisingly, a few of them fell asleep, and the others tried to close their eyes and relax. Katie announced she needed to go to the bathroom again and, of all people, Millie volunteered to go with her. She watched as the two of them disappeared behind the bathroom door. She tried to close her eyes and relax, but the scary stairs had her on edge and she couldn't get the dark black hole out of her mind. Instead, it went on a tangent, and thoughts of someone watching her from below caused her uneasiness to spike. Unable to stop herself, she leaned forward again, only this time she thought she saw a pair of eyes staring back at her. She jerked away and covered her face with both hands. When she removed them to look again, there was nothing there. Had she imagined what she saw because Katie had mentioned seeing glowing eyes downstairs in the hallway? She felt like she was going crazy and was having trouble deciding what was real and what was not.

The movement coming from the bathroom distracted her, and she was glad to see Katie and Millie heading back to the group. Her eyes trailed them all the way, and her heart leaped when Katie didn't stop where they were. Where is she going? What is she doing? Her eyes widened as she watched Katie open the door to her room and enter the darkness.

Hannah shook Lizzy, who was already watching intently.

"Where is she going? Go stop her, Lizzy." Hannah was so scared. She didn't want anyone to go back into her room.

"I don't want to go in there." Lizzy called out to Katie and looked at Millie for answers. "What is she doing? Millie, where is she going? What did she say in the bathroom?"

Millie answered right away. "She couldn't remember seeing the doll when we were grabbed earlier. She needed to know if it was still there. Neither one of us remembered seeing it, but I told her that didn't matter because there was no way a doll could've pulled us like that. She didn't care. She was so fixated on locating the doll."

Hannah watched as Lizzy stood up and inhaled deeply. Going into that room was the last thing she wanted to do. Hannah stood up to offer support, but Lizzy shook her head and motioned for her to stay put. She kept her eyes glued to the doorway until Lizzy entered the room and faded into the darkness. The next thing she heard was a blood-curdling scream and then silence.

Lizzy came bursting out of the room with Katie in tow. Hannah was on edge and glad to have Lizzy back. Concern poured through her as Katie just stood in place, wide eyed and staring. She'd never seen her speechless, and that scared her. Tears rolled down Hannah's cheeks, slowly at first but then faster, like someone opened flood gates. Slowing her breathing by inhaling deeply helped regain her composure. Guilt seized her because she found comfort in knowing that everyone else was on the verge of tears as well. The desire to reach up and pull Katie into a hug was abandoned because she was too terrified to move. She didn't enjoy seeing her like that, and the sight of Katie's crumbled face tugged at Hannah's heart. Instead of moving, she tried to attract her attention.

"Katie. Katie, what are you doing? What's wrong?" Hannah wanted her to snap out of it.

She looked down at Hannah and, without emotion, said, "It's gone."

Katie

Calming down took longer than she wanted, but she wasn't surprised because of the stress they'd been under since arriving. So much had occurred. It was difficult keeping up with the details. One disturbing detail was the missing porcelain doll she'd personally thrown into the closet. It was gone! Disappeared. It was difficult to see all the way to the back, but she refocused her eyes, revealing a completely empty closet. The rack lacked coat hangers, the shelf, blankets. Did she believe the doll had attacked them? That possibility frightened her. But why would someone take the doll? More importantly, why had someone attempted to grab them? Was it a prank? Katie had so many questions she felt dizzy. Finally, she sat down on the sofa next to Hannah and placed her head in her hands. When she looked up, faces were staring back at her.

"I don't know what to say. I know that doll was there because I threw it in the closet myself." She paused to choose her words carefully. "What do y'all think is going on here? Does anyone have an idea or at least suspect something?"

The room was silent while each of them tried to come up with a thought to add to the conversation.

"I don't know, girl." Hannah wrapped herself around Katie and looked into her eyes. "Are you okay? I need you to be okay." She chuckled lightly as she finished her sentence.

Katie put her hands on Hannah's arm giving her a re-assuring squeeze.

"Right now I'm good, but we need to get out of here, so I'll ask again. Raise your hand if you want to leave this pl..." Before Katie could finish, they all raised their hands, stood up and started grabbing for their phones and purses. She watched Millie closely and was relieved that this time, she was just as eager to go as the rest of them.

Everyone huddled together, waiting for guidance from her. Katie giggled to herself because she never imagined, in any circumstances, that her friends would look to her for leadership. She was no follower, but not a leader, either. The middle ground was where she was most comfortable, and having fun was top priority. They often teased that she was a 'Hold My Beer' kind of girl because she was daring and up for almost anything. Living by the seat of her pants was the philosophy that worked for her, but for her mother, not so much.

She pulled herself from her thoughts and looked at the group. Panic tried to crawl up her spine, but she knew she could do this, so she straightened up and forced a smile. Her friends were depending on her and she would rise to the task.

"We can do this. The rain stopped, so all we had to do was get out of the house and make our way to the highway. That's not that far, but it's dark outside, so we have to be careful and stay together. Let's form groups of twos again, like we used to do in school. Hey, who knew that preschool training would come in handy one day?" A few of her friends chuckled, but the tension in the room was so high that it wasn't heartfelt. Not even close.

"We don't need the jokes, Katie. We just want to get out of here alive." Cory Ann was done with it all. "You lead, and Lizzy and I will take up the rear." She looped her arm through Lizzy's and waited for everyone to move. "Can we please go now?" Cory Ann's words were sharp.

Katie was grateful for Cory Ann because she needed a little push and who better than her to give it? Unlike Katie, she was more straight forward and said whatever was on her mind regardless. She grabbed Sara's hand, who reluctantly accepted it, and together they peered down into the darkness. She glanced back one last time and noticed that Millie looked more disturbed than scared. Emptying her mind of all thoughts, she yelled out, "Let's go," and moved forward slowly. Her legs were shaky, so she leaned on Sara for support. She half chuckled to herself again because poor Sara was probably struggling to hold her own self up. Katie squeezed tighter, pulling her down the long stairway, stopping on each step, then moving on until they finally reached the bottom.

The sound of everyone exhaling echoed through the empty house. She couldn't accept that they were there all alone. She made a mental note to know the rules next time she planned on staying somewhere besides a hotel.

Once everyone was downstairs, they adjusted their eyes to the dim lights being fueled by the generator. It wasn't enough light to read a book, but it let them see the room, and locate the door. It seemed further than her twenty foot assessment. A noise from behind the front reception desk caused her to jump. They all did.

"What was that?" Allie whispered almost too low to hear. "Did y'all hear that?"

"It sounded like papers being shuffled, right?" Demi answered while standing up against the desk with Savannah. They quickly scooted away. "Hello? Is someone there? Hello?" Demi continued to call out, but everything was silent again.

Katie nodded, encouraging her to look behind the counter. At first Demi shook her head, then moved toward the desk. She looked over, then back to the group, specifically at Katie, and with a small toss of her head, showed there was no one there.

Her small group of eight friends, that had grown to 12 since Savannah and her crew had arrived, were once again waiting for guidance. So much pressure. Katie rarely felt pressure like everyone else, but that's because she was usually only worried about herself. She loved these girls, even the new arrivals, and felt protective of them. That level of emotion felt strange, even unwelcome. A few of other friends were getting married and talking about having kids, but she wasn't sure she wanted either. She frowned when she thought about the anguish she put her own mother through and how she prayed and worried about Katie all the time. Maybe that's why Katie was always so laid back and feared little, except now ghost, porcelain dolls and falling mirrors. She visualized the bubble her mother constantly prayed for that was supposed to surround her and keep her protected.

She shook her thoughts free and geared up to move again. The longer they waited, anything could happen. The night provided uncertainty, and they needed to go.

"It's so dark y'all!" Hannah shouted out as they ran toward the parking lot leading to the highway. "I can't see where I'm going."

Katie put on her flashlight, but it didn't do any good. A light drizzle fell and then lightning lit up the sky, followed by the loudest boom she'd ever heard. They all stopped and screamed. Some wept and Katie understood, wanting to cry, too. How were they going to stay out there in the thunderstorms? The thought of going back into the house terrified her. She looked around and her gaze landed on that cellar she'd found earlier. Her stomach flipped at the idea of going down there, so she searched for other options. The only other one that would have been safe was the restaurant. The same restaurant where the mirrors on the wall had shown her a horrible version of herself. Where she watched as they crashed to the floor one by one. The thought made her cringe, but she knew there was no other choice.

"Come on! Hurry! This way!" She ran toward the restaurant, but felt like someone brushed past her as she approached the steps. She hesitated, then dashed to the door, praying it wasn't locked. Everyone shoved forward to get in and out of the rain. Turning the handle, she opened the door, and a sense of doom filled her body. Her mother's bubble would come in handy right then, and she prayed for it to be thick enough to protect her through the night.

CHAPTER 20

Lizzy

Leaving the house behind should've brought relief, but that didn't happen. Even with the threat inside the house, Lizzy couldn't shake the desire to stay put. She and Katie had agreed to monitor Millie because something peculiar was going on with her. It was the brief expressions that were concerning. Also, the willingness to leave now but not before when she swayed the others to agree with her to stay. She was flip flopping and Lizzy wondered why and what she was up to. Maybe she overreacted, but she didn't trust her. Not one bit.

It was of no consequence what had happened before since they all agreed to leave now. All they wanted to do was get out of there. Cory Ann had just volunteered her to stay in the back of the group, but that wasn't a surprise, because Cory Ann was tougher than the rest of them. And by tough she meant that she usually met adversity head on and just dealt with it while the rest would've preferred to cower from things.

They made it out the door, but then the rain came again. The flash of lightning backed them into the restaurant. The place was pitch dark. Apparently, the generators that had kicked on when they were there earlier had been shut off once they closed up for the night. The air seemed thin, but she figured it was because she was so unhinged with anxiety. They all were.

Lizzy switched on her light and walked around the restaurant, calling out for anyone there. It was so eerily quiet it was creepy. She imagined living in the country without all the noise of the city and didn't find it appealing at all. In fact, she found that when she was in complete silence, it wasn't silent at all but instead filled with a ringing in her ears that drove her crazy. Thankfully, she could hear the crickets chirping outside in the distance. Usually, she was annoyed by the deafening sound but was surprisingly comforted by it now.

"Does anyone want something to drink?" Lizzy looked at Katie. "Not liquor, but a coke or water." She was by the wait station, so she reached for a glass, filled it with ice and coke. The others made their way to her and fixed themselves something as well. Not wanting to leave a mess, she wiped down the area and removed the ice that had overflowed. A slight feeling of anger welled up in her throat because it wasn't her job to fix her own drink or wipe down the counter afterwards. How could they just leave them there all alone?

"We can square up with them in the morning or whenever they decide to show up. I still can't believe that no one stayed here tonight." She walked back to the table they'd sat at for dinner and took a seat. "We might as well get comfortable because it sounds like the rain will be here for a while."

Everyone got a drink, then settled down. After her earlier scare in the closet, she'd started counting heads to keep track of everyone. As she sat down, she counted and realized someone was missing. Fearful that she was correct, the color drained from her face and her eyes widened, horrified!

"Hey y'all. Somebody's missing! There's only eleven." Quickly recounting caused her heart to sink when she came up with eleven again. There was supposed to be twelve. She jumped up frantically. "Where's Marci? Y'all. Where's Marci? Is she in the back? The bathroom? Who was her partner? You know, her two-by-two partner." Lizzy, along with everyone else, started calling out for Marci.

"I was her two by two, but when it started to storm again, she let go and ran after you." Millie looked distraught. "She has to be here. I was the last to enter, so I know she wasn't left outside. Maybe she's in the bathroom." Millie headed to the hallway that led to the restrooms. "I'm sure she's here somewhere."

Lizzy froze, remembering the earlier scene. She wasn't surprised when Cory Ann, without hesitation, tore through them to join Millie in the search. Lizzy instructed everyone to search the rooms for Marci but to stay with a partner. She knew this time they were going to listen because if Marci was missing, they were all in danger. And her gut told her she was missing. Going anywhere alone was too dangerous, and Marci knew that. She would've asked someone to go with her if she needed to go to the bathroom.

Everything was happening so quickly. Demi and Stephanie searched the extra dining area while Brittany and Savannah went to look on the front veranda. The others were calling for Marci while searching under tables and behind counters. She'd simply vanished. There was a slight chance that she ran back to the house, but Lizzy didn't think that wasn't the case.

Lizzy prayed they had found her in the bathroom, but Cory Ann and Millie resurfaced and confirmed that it was empty. Deep down she'd expected that, but it still felt like someone gut punched her.

"Do you think she fell running over here? She might've hit her head and is laying out there unconscious."

"We looked. Lightning is illuminating the sky, allowing us to see all the way across to the parking lot." Brittany yelled convinced, "She's not out there."

Lizzy looked back at Millie. "Do you remember seeing her enter the restaurant?"

Millie shrugged her shoulders. "I don't, but I don't remember seeing anyone enter except Demi because she was right in front of me. We all bolted for the door when that last bang of thunder hit. I feel so bad. I should've never let go."

"It's not your fault. I did the same thing to Hannah." Allie felt sorry for Millie.

"Does anyone have phone service yet? Check your phones. We need help." Lizzy was up again and pacing. She paused and her face twisted into total confusion. She returned to the table and grabbed something before turning around and yelling at the group.

"Who did this? Hello! Who is doing this?" She had the porcelain doll in her right hand and was shaking it above her head. "This is not funny, y'all!"

Hannah stared back at Lizzy.

"Where did you get that? Where did it come from, Lizzy?" Hannah was crying.

"It was right there on the chair I was just sitting in. Someone here is playing pranks, and I think we are beyond that, don't y'all. This is serious! Marci is missing! I was assaulted, and then Millie! Not the time for pranks!" Katie's voice was loud, but shaky. She was trying to understand how someone could be so inconsiderate when someone was missing. It was downright rude, and she was pissed.

"Maybe that's a different doll. We're in an old plantation home that's probably filled with them. Are you sure that's the same chair? Maybe some kid left it here earlier." Allie attempted to convince the other's as well as herself that it could be true.

"I'm 100% positive! I sat right there in the same chair I sat when we had dinner. The doll was definitely not there." She was still waving it in the air. "And yes, it's definitely the same doll because I remember the pink bonnet."

Lizzy chose a new chair and placed the doll on the table. Its eyes appeared to be following her, and they looked like they were scary black holes that could reach into her soul. Her bottom lip quivered, but she fought the urge to cry. She calmed herself enough to speak without yelling.

"So, no one wants to admit to the prank?" They all stared back at her.

"Sorry, but you are on top of that list. You and Katie." Hannah hated to say it, but it was the truth. "So I guess we're looking at y'all for answers. Did either of you do it?"

"It wasn't me." Katie declared her innocence and threw up her hands. "I was going to do something, but the crazy unexplained things happening prevented me from acting. And y'all know that I like to take credit for all my pranks."

Lizzy watched as they all turned their attention back to her.

"Nope! I didn't do it either. So what, the doll can move on its own?" A chill raced up her body as she spoke the next thought out loud. "Or is someone else here with us?"

CHAPTER 21

Hannah

Hannah was struggling with the disappearance of Marci, yearning for things to calm down. She immediately began to search the area, but after everyone looked inside the restaurant and outside on the front veranda and lawn, it was determined that she was gone. Gone! Gone? That didn't make sense. She was just with them, so where was she? They were all trying to come to terms with the situation when Lizzy started screaming at them while holding that creepy doll.

Hannah's heart felt as if it were in her throat. She had grown to hate that doll and yet, there it was, sitting on the table, staring back at her. She sat down in a chair at the next table. Everyone was finding some place safe to sit and wait out the storm. The dining room was big but, without the air conditioning, it had felt stuffy. Taking a sip of her drink, she kept her eyes on the doll, determined to put an end to the pranks. Lizzy plopped the thing down on the table, apparently thinking the same thing.

"What do we do now?" Savannah asked, knowing that they didn't have an answer.

"We have to wait out the storm, again. Don't y'all find it funny that our cell phones aren't working? I have Verizon, but I know Lizzy has AT&T. I guess it's possible they would both be down at the same time. And what about Demi's claims that it wasn't raining until they got here? Y'all know me and know that I always look at the weather forecast. There was no mention of rain. None for the entire weekend." Katie was rattled and it could be heard in her voice..

Hannah glanced down at her phone. She had AT&T too. She believed Katie was on to something because usually one network or the other would go down. Sure, during a major hurricane, when trees and cell towers go down, they might both be out, but this situation was a little odd.

"Maybe there's interference with the signal." Hannah asked.

"No. I used my cell phone when I got here. I think everyone did because when we arrived, we texted or called each other. And maybe the storm did interfere, but it stopped several times, and I know I checked my phone for service every time." Katie assured them it wasn't the rain.

"What are we gonna do now?" Hannah asked.

"We're going to stick to the plan. As soon as the weather lets up, we'll run out toward the highway and get help. Does anyone know the time?" Katie hated waiting and her patience was being tested like never before.

"It's after midnight." Sara looked at her watch. "Twelve ten, to be exact."

The lightning outside was putting on a show, providing much wanted light in the restaurant. Hannah focused on the doll, only glancing out the window a few times. She looked up from the doll to Lizzy. Sitting in the chair with her head against the wall, she kept one hand on the doll. Millie had sat down next to Lizzy and offered to keep watch, but Hannah was thankful to hear Lizzy decline.

"No offense, but I'm keeping this doll with me. If someone is pranking us, they'll have to find another way. I'm done with all the jokes." Lizzy sounded angry.

The rain outside pounded the window, and the wind howled, announcing it was far from done. Hannah hated they were now stuck inside the restaurant. At least they had drink and food. Well, crackers and butter anyway. Nobody went searching for anything else because they decided it was best to stay together. She wished she would've eaten the food they'd ordered earlier but with all the chaos, she'd lost her appetite.

Time was crawling by. She was so tired, but was determined to keep an eye on the doll. Her lids were heavy, and she fought to keep them open. Several of the others had their eyes closed. Staring at Lizzy, she noticed that Millie's head was down, and she appeared to be sleeping.

Hannah nodded for Lizzy to notice because she knew she was leery of Millie. She hated to admit it, but now she was, too. Millie and Marci worked together and now Marci was gone. Thinking back to the times she'd gone out with the group, Millie included, she couldn't remember anything that would cause distrust. Of course, she was either related to or had been friends since childhood with everyone except Millie, so it was understandable that she trusted them. But even though Millie had done nothing to cause doubt about her intentions since things started happening, her behavior was concerning.

Hannah thought she saw movement by the drink station. Looking that way, she noticed a waitress from earlier and froze before calling out to her. Then she was gone. Just as quickly as she appeared, she disappeared. Her call for help woke the few that were sleeping, and everyone was staring at her.

Lizzy jumped up just as the blood drained from Hannah's face.

"Hannah, what's wrong?" Lizzy followed her gaze to the other side of the restaurant. "Did you see something? What's wrong Hannah?" Lizzy could see she was upset about something."

"Y'all, there was just a waitress standing by the drink machine. I saw her, but then she was gone." She sat stunned as Cory Ann and Katie ran to the area and called out for help. Everyone else was up and moving around, trying to draw attention to themselves and feeling more optimistic.

Her stomach tossed a few times, and her words caught in her throat. She was sure that she saw a woman standing there, but it was so quick, then she was gone. Hoping to trigger her memory, she replayed the scene in her head over again. She must've walked through the doors to the kitchen, but Hannah didn't see her move. She was just there and then she was gone.

Almost out of habit, she glanced at Millie and tried to read her emotions. She didn't look optimistic or sound as excited as the others. Feeling alarmed, she tried to categorize the look on her face. Maybe it was concern or possibly even anger, but it was so slight. Then, when she noticed Hannah looking at her, she shifted and forced her tight lips into a smile. If she wanted to be trusted, it was going to take more than that.

Once again, she waited while they searched the entire restaurant before it was determined that Hannah must've imagined seeing someone. Lizzy told her she was probably dreaming because of the lack of sleep and the stress she was under. That was not the case. She was not dreaming!

Hannah didn't respond. She was positive that she was not dreaming. Although she'd been looking at Millie right before she saw the movement, it happened so fast it was confusing.

"I know what I saw. I saw the waitress from earlier and she was standing by that drink machine. Then she was gone. Yes, I'm tired. I'm extremely tired. And yes, I'm stressed out. We all are. But y'all, I know what I saw." She was quiet for a moment, then went on. "Y'all stressing me out! Quit looking at me like I'm crazy. She was there!" Hannah got up and walked over to the drink station.

Looking around, she opened the door to the kitchen just enough to call out, hoping someone would surface. Letting the door close, she turned to look down the long, dark hall that led to the bathroom. Staring into the darkness felt like a slap in the face, waking her up and warning of danger. She hadn't noticed that Lizzy, Cory Ann and Katie had joined her, so when she turned back around, she jumped.

"Y'all scared me. Look how spooky that hallway looks. Guys, I know I saw a woman, so aside from scary hallways and dark rooms, there are apparently ghosts." She directed her next question to Lizzy. "Do you think I saw a ghost? It looked so real. No, that couldn't have been a ghost because it was the same waitress from earlier. Unless something happened to her." Hannah slapped a hand over her mouth in shock.

"Hannah?" Lizzy was worried.

"Guys, what if she died? What if that's why there's no one here? They all went to the hospital with the woman." Her words sounded silly to her even as she spoke them. But there had to be a reasonable explanation.

Hannah went to the drink machine and grabbed another glass to get a coke. She asked if anyone else wanted one and Lizzy stepped over and grabbed a glass, too.

"Stop!" Lizzy yelled at Hannah, who was about to fill her glass with ice.

She noticed a confused look on Lizzy's face.

"Did you already get ice and poor it out?" Lizzy didn't wait for an answer. "Look, there's ice all over the top again. I definitely cleaned that up after we finished getting our drinks before. Hannah, did you get ice yet?"

"No. Y'all were standing right here with me." She looked down at her empty cup.

"I know. So where did that ice come from?" The tension in the room was so high because Lizzy just gave them an answer. "I know this sounds crazy, but if Hannah said she saw a waitress standing here, and now, there's fresh ice, I have to believe her." She looked at Hannah and added. "Not that I thought you were lying. It's just I know how things can seem so real when you're exhausted and tired. Even dreams sometimes feel real when you wake up. Ugh! I am so tired myself and I just want to go home. I can't believe that someone is pranking us, not to this extent. And where is poor Marci? Maybe we should've gone out to look for her."

"There's no way we can go out in that weather, Lizzy. As soon as it lightens up, we'll look for Marci and then get to the road for help. There's nothing we can do now but wait." Cory Ann hoped they didn't decide to go out there now because the rain was coming down sideways, creating a dangerous situation.

Hannah's body slumped from the stress and her feet wobbled as she made the walk back to the tables, joining the others. She was saddened, because instead of a fun-filled weekend, they were trapped in an unescapable nightmare.. She'd even considered maybe she was having a nightmare, but knew that wasn't the case. One thing after another was keeping them from leaving, and she prayed that would change soon. It had to, right? Because how much more could they take?

"Hey guys, I need to go to the bathroom."

CHAPTER 22

Lizzy

Still reeling from the idea that someone else was in the restaurant and that they had put the doll there to scare them, Lizzy's mind was exploding with 'what if's?' What if they were secretly being watched? Her skin crawled at the thought of a stranger observing their every move. What if they try to grab someone else? As upset as she was that Marci was missing, something happening to Hannah or Katie would be unbearable. What if they come in shooting? What if they go outside and are attacked out there? The darkness make it the perfect canvas for an attack because they were at a disadvantage without light. She smashed her hands against her ears to stop the chaos. She was driving herself crazy, but didn't know how to stop all the different scenarios from playing out in her mind.

They were all settling down when she noticed Hannah's face pale. Her heart dropped. Then Hannah yelled out to someone at the other end of the restaurant. Did she see Marci? Had they found Marci? Before she could ask, Hannah explained that she saw a waitress at the drink machine.

Thank God. Relief covered her face because someone was finally there to help them. Exhaustion set in, and she wasn't sure how much longer she could stay strong and keep everyone calm. She felt like a child who wanted to run to her parents instead of someone the others could look to for comfort. The realization that mothers must feel that type of responsibility every day once they have children was unsettling. Butterflies fluttered in her stomach because she'd always wanted children, but she wasn't so sure anymore.

Relief quickly turned into panic because Hannah's next words were, "But then she was gone."

Lizzy watched in disbelief as Katie and Cory Ann jumped into action and ran toward the drink station. She stood up and, once the shock wore off, started searching the restaurant for the now missing waitress. Where could she be, but more importantly, was she real?

She hated the emotional roller coaster she was on and was ready to get to the docking station to get off. Once again, the restaurant was empty, and they were all alone. She'd almost forgotten that it was storming outside, but as if on a timer, the rain slammed against the windows. The more she thought about it, whenever they were dealing with a crisis, which was way too often, the rain picked up and intensified their anxiety, making everything that much worse.

It took a while for everyone to give up on the idea that help had finally come. Lizzy settled back down with the rest of them, feeling defeated and waiting out the weather.

Chills ran up her spine when she thought about the ice in the tray. She was certain that she had cleaned up after the others got their drinks. She was almost convinced that Hannah had seen the waitress, and that she had made the new mess. A nervous giggle released because something strange was going on and they were being sucked into playing the game. She thought about one of their favorite shows, "Stranger Things" and half expected to see the lights blink to spell out words of warnings. She loved that show but wasn't particularly fond of living it in real life.

"Hey guys, I need to go to the bathroom."

The thought of going down that long hallway terrified her and, from the responses around the room, everyone else too. Of course, she wouldn't let Hannah go alone, but she did not want to go back into that bathroom. As if on cue, thunder rumbled loudly, cutting off her thoughts of running back to the main house and using the bathroom there.

"I really need to go, too." Sara said nervously.

"I think y'all have a serious problem and need to get checked out when we get back home. Too many bathroom trips!" Lizzy was shaking her head.

She figured at that point they all had to go to the bathroom. Especially after getting drinks from the drink station that was being operated by a phantom waitress. Safety in numbers. She wasn't sure that was true, but figured it was their best option.

"I'm guessing we all need to use the bathroom, so let's go together. Safety in numbers, right?" Lizzy stood gearing up to face the dark hallway and the mirrors. She couldn't forget about the mirrors, and she wasn't sure which one scared her the most. The dark hallway was unusually long and while it was probably only a few seconds to get down, it seemed like forever.

Lizzy grabbed onto Hannah and Cory Ann while the others latched onto each other, but no one was moving. Finally, Cory Ann let go of Lizzy and said she would go first. Her friend was not that brave, but always stepped up anyway, and her heart swelled at the thought.

She met Cory Ann's eyes and nodded her gratitude. Next, Millie said she would cover them on the backend. A twinge of mistrust shot through her, but she kept quiet. This time, her gaze met Katie's eyes and saw the dread that filled her normally bright, beautiful eyes. Katie let go of Sara's arm and stepped back to join Millie. Lizzy knew that after being victimized, the last place Katie wanted to go was back into that bathroom. Joining Millie was a good idea, even if it was only to delay the inevitable. They were probably wrong about her anyway, but it didn't hurt to be cautious.

She poked Cory Ann's shoulder, prompting her to start walking because Hannah was dancing in place, trying to hold it in at that point. The more she thought about it, the more urgent she had to go. Why is it that the closer you get to the bathroom, the more desperate you need to get there?

They reached the wait station and paused to see if the waitress would resurface, but it was dark and empty. The whole restaurant appeared to be one big Haunted House.

Cory Ann had her light on and headed slowly down the hallway. The light barely lit the area, but it landed on something shiny by the wall. Lizzy focused her light on that spot and noticed a shard of glass on the ground. She ran the light upwards to a space on the wall that was empty. That was where the mirror hung that Katie said fell to the ground, so that confirms they weren't completely delusional.

Lizzy glanced back at Katie and nodded. "Are you okay?"

"No. But I have to pee too, so let's go." Katie's voice was squeaky and unsure.

Lizzy nudged Cory Ann forward and this time, they moved a little faster. She just wanted to run there, use the bathroom, and get back out without incident. When they reached the bathroom, Cory Ann opened the door and Lizzy held her breath. Her mouth was tight, and eyes were wide open, waiting to see if the mirrors were there. The light hit the first mirror, and she almost screamed. It was still hanging on the wall. She grabbed for Cory Ann to stop her from going any further, but she was already darting into the stall. She didn't want to look at the wall but couldn't help herself. Her shoulders lowered in relief at the sight of the missing mirrors. Apparently, the mirrors falling to the ground had happened. She didn't waste time darting into one of the stalls. The air felt a little lighter, and she filled her lungs quickly, something she hadn't been able to do lately.

After she was done and finished washing her hands, she moved closer to the door to wait for the rest of them. If it hadn't been for the toilets flushing, there would be complete silence.

Lizzy heard a clicking sound outside the door.

"Did y'all hear that? Did anyone hear a noise, like a clicking sound?" She stood by the door, almost too afraid to open it. As much as she wanted to get back to the tables, she felt safe right where she was.

She reached for the door and pulled, but it wouldn't open. She yanked again, this time harder, and still it didn't open.

"Oh my God! Y'all, it's stuck! The door won't open." Cries and yelling replaced the silence in the room. She tried again, but finally stopped.

"It's locked."

CHAPTER 23

Katie

Going back into the bathroom from hell was the last thing Katie wanted to do, but she did need to go. Hannah was positive that she saw a waitress, spreading hope of a rescue. Disappointment loomed heavily in the air across the whole room. Options were running out while danger lurked all around, terrifying her. But the memory of the monster she saw in the mirror was scarier than anything else because the monster was her.

The brief moment she'd looked into the mirror would forever be etched in her mind. The image reflected back to her was a distorted figure of herself. Her eyes were sunken with black circles all around and her nose was nothing but bones. Her hair was wild and frayed and her teeth were chipped and missing. She was unrecognizable except for her red plump lips. She wanted to scream but the words jammed in her throat. Why did she look like that? A part of her was afraid that the mirror was predicting the future. That was probably one of her greatest fears. She didn't want to think about it much less talk about it, so she kept it to herself.

Katie considered herself a good person. All of her friends were, well, most of them. The jury was still out on Millie. She was kind and accepting of all, hence why Millie was with them. But they all had their own insecurities and were vulnerable because of them. Sometimes, she felt out of place but usually faked her way through the situation. Other times, she felt like she needed attention, and her god given beautiful features made her feel good.

Once, when they were drinking around a campfire, she'd brought up the subject and was surprised to hear Lizzy and Cory Ann had similar feelings. That was several years ago, but Katie never forgot it but instead tried to remember to be accepting of all because you never know what someone else was going through.

She wondered if that was what she saw in the mirror earlier, her insecurities shining through. She sucked in air along with her fear and moved forward with the group. Thankfully, the mirror had fallen and shattered, so she didn't have to worry about that one. The hallway was so long, and darkness enveloped them as they walked. Even with the phone lights on, it was difficult to see right in front of her face. She was thankful for that, too. She kept her head down and prayed to get in and out quickly.

They all stumbled into the bathroom, darting for the stalls, heads low. The mirrors in the bathroom had fallen to the floor too, but she wasn't going to take a chance and look up. She didn't want to see that image of herself again. Earlier, she'd acknowledged that it could've been a prank, but something deep down told her that it wasn't.

Once everyone safely used the bathroom, the tension lightened, and small chit chat started. It wasn't laughter, but the sound of relief filled the air and even optimism creeped in and sounded cheerful. Until Lizzy pulled the handle of the door.

Katie was not claustrophobic at all, but she'd suddenly found it difficult to breathe. How could the door not open? After a few more tries, Lizzy announced it was locked. She'd heard a clicking sound. They all had, but never dreamed that they were being locked in the bathroom.

Katie made her way to the front and banged on the door. She yelled for help and was quickly joined by everyone. She beat on the door and cried out for help until her fist hurt.

"That must've been the waitress. Hannah was right, she was still here. She's probably locking up the building for the night." She banged once more on the door.

"Why would she lock the bathroom door? That makes little sense if she was going to lock the building." Lizzy spoke her thoughts out loud.

Katie looked around the group, and her eyes landed on Millie. She noticed she appeared calm, unlike the rest of them, but then again, she wasn't a very emotional person.

"Millie, do you know what's going on here?" Katie came right out and asked what a few of them were already thinking. She wanted answers and she felt like Millie had some.

When Millie's eyes met hers, she immediately regretted the choice to corner her. The piercing look was intimidating, forcing her to take a step back. But then Millie frowned and shook her head.

"What? Why would I know what's going on? I've been stuck with y'all the whole time." Millie kept her tone light.

"I don't know, but you are the only one I don't really know, and it seems like someone is always one step ahead of us. And you were away from us in the closet." Katie's voice shook as she questioned Millie.

Katie felt bad because Cory Ann, along with a few others, mumbled their concerns as well. She hadn't wanted to attack Millie, but things were getting serious, and that scared her. Their voices were getting louder, echoing through the bathroom, and everyone shook in fear.

"Stop! Please everyone, stop! Lower your voices." Hannah was yelling at them while covering her ears.

Everyone became silent. It wasn't often that Hannah raised her voice, so it caught their attention quickly. Katie looked around the oblong bathroom. There were several stalls lining one wall and sinks lined the other. They were trapped. Her eyes searched the room for a window, but there wasn't one. Her pulse raced once reality set in. Stuck inside the bathroom, they would have to wait until morning to be let out.

She watched as the same realization hit her friends. They all exhaled and looked defeated. Millie was the only one that didn't look beat but seemed to still be looking for a way out. She frantically pushed each stall door open and then moved to the next. She reached the end of the row, then stood staring blankly ahead.

"Hey Guys." She continued to stare. A little louder this time, she called for the group. "Guys! Come here, hurry." She finally broke her gaze and looked back at them.

Katie stared back into Millie's eyes and saw hope radiate from them. She ran to the back of the bathroom, where Millie stood and looked up to find a door. At first it looked to be a closet door but had turned out to lead to another larger room, and it had windows. She hurried in and tripped over a mop bucket that was left in the middle of the floor. The others flooded in behind her and pointed their cellphone lights at Katie sprawled out on the floor. The prospect of getting out of the locked bathroom had lightened the mood enough to allow the giggles to start. That turned into full-blown laughter from everyone, including Katie.

Sara bent down while still laughing. "Are you okay?" She reached out her hand to help her up.

"Yeah. Thanks, Sara." Katie grabbed the extended hand and stood up. She was grateful that she had just peed because she was laughing so hard. She moved the mop bucket to the side and looked around before she took another step. The room was enormous and filled with all kinds of restaurant items. Extra tables and chairs lined one wall, and supplies stacked high on another. Everyone walked around the room, trying to get their bearings.

"Look at that." Sara pointed to a small mattress laying on the floor behind a shelf. Next to it stood a few water bottles and some snacks. A large flashlight sat on a chair beside it. Katie grabbed it and prayed it worked. Cheers erupted when it turned on and lit up the room. After a few minutes of celebrating, they came together and devised a plan to reach the high windows. As if on cue, lightning flashed through the window, reminding them that the weather was not cooperating.

They started to push a table under the window when Lizzy called out. "There's another door y'all."

Katie ran to where Lizzy was standing with her hand on the doorknob. The rest crowded in from behind and breathlessly waited to see if the door would open. Lizzy turned the knob and pulled with more force than needed and the door swung open wide.

Hannah exhaled and said, "Great, another dark room!"

CHAPTER 24

Lizzy

Lizzy was so over the whole weekend. If she could go back in time, she would not agree to a visit to the Myrtles. She chuckled inwardly because she knew that wasn't true. If asked again, she would definitely say yes. She'd always wanted to spend a night in a haunted house. Ironically, she still hadn't spent a night in a haunted house because they had yet to sleep, and she doubted they would anytime soon.

All eyes gazed into the darkness of yet another room. The whole place reminded Lizzy of a Halloween corn maze. Maybe that was all part of the illusion to make the place appear haunted, but she figured it was likely just how old houses were built. Whatever the reason, she didn't like being thrust from one scary room to the next.

Lizzy motioned for Katie to go first, since she had the flashlight in her hand. Katie attempted to hand it to her, but she refused, pushing it back.

"Why do I have to go in first? You saw what happened to me the last time. I don't think I'm the wisest choice here." Katie pleaded her case with seriousness.

"You're fine. Stop whining and just go into the room. I really want to get out of here." Lizzy knew Katie was right, but she didn't want to go first.

"Okay. If I fall again and break the flashlight, it's not my fault. It's gonna be on…"

"Give me the flashlight!" Cory Ann grabbed the light from Katie and took the lead. "Y'all are all such babies. Come on. One of these rooms has to lead outside, or at least back into the restaurant."

Lizzy looked at Cory Ann, grateful that she was stepping up, even though she knew she wasn't that brave. She figured she was acting on adrenaline and at the moment had a little more left than the rest of them. She noticed the room was smaller than the last one and not as overcrowded with stuff. The flashlight that Cory Ann now held flickered, and the light was dancing around the room, blinking on and off. When it was off, total darkness consumed them, confirming the absence of a window.

The group squeezed tighter together and inched forward behind Cory Ann. After the last person passed through the door, it slammed shut behind them and the light went out.

"Wait! Open that door!" Sara yelled to the back.

"Come on, someone open the door." Lizzy sounded impatient. "I can't see anything, not even my hand."

Lizzy found the pounding noise of the rain outside to be comforting because there was nothing worse than complete darkness and dead silence. She could feel the tension in the room rise even in the darkness.

No one moved, apprehensive about opening the door again.

Frustrated, Lizzy whispered, "Go Cory Ann. Keep walking forward. The door is straight ahead of us. Keep moving."

The walls were closing in, feeding her anxiety and making escape crucial.

Millie yelped. "Did y'all hear that?"

"Yes, what was that?" Demi's voice floated from the back of the group.

Everyone strained to listen and heard a faint cry that was coming from behind.

"What is that?" Savannah and Brittany asked at the same time.

Lizzy hated to say it, but it sounded like a cry - a baby's cry. Chills surfed up and down her body as images of an abandoned baby crossed her mind.

Instead of saying her first thought out loud, she threw another one out.

"It could be a cat. Right? Don't cats sound like babies sometimes? Or maybe another kind of animal, like a nutria or opossum." Instead of reassuring the group, she just made things worse because they liked the thought of an animal in there even less than a crying baby. Scared voices broke the silence, yelling to get out. The whole situation was already getting out of hand when Hannah yelled that something touched her leg. Terror erupted and instead of staying together, they all bolted forward toward the door. Or so they thought. The darkness made it difficult to see which way was forward, especially after they let go of one another.

Lizzy held onto Cory Ann and screamed for her to shake the flashlight and for everyone else to put their phone lights on. Amid the chaos, everyone was running around in the dark and apparently forgot about the phone lights.

She reached into her pocket and grabbed her phone while Cory Ann shook the flashlight forcefully. Her hands were shaking so violently that she was having trouble fishing it out of her pants pocket. Afraid she would drop it; she squeezed it tightly in her hand. The flashlight flickered a few times but wasn't on long enough to get their bearings. Another scream that something touched their leg added to the panic in the room. Everyone was scrambling to get out.

"What is happening? Something's in here with us!" Lizzy tried to calm down as she reached for her phone to tap the flashlight icon. Thankfully, she was familiar with the phone so that she could activate the light even in the darkness. The first thing she did was shine it on the surrounding ground to make sure there was nothing there. Relieved, she pointed it up at Cory Ann to see her face because earlier, she'd had a fleeting thought that maybe it wasn't Cory Ann's arm she'd grabbed on to and wanted to dismiss that thought. Satisfied that there was no immediate threat to herself, she started shining the light around the rest of her friends.

She screamed, "Hey, y'all. Come this way."

Instantly, all of her friends ran toward the light and squeezed tightly amongst each other once again. The screaming stopped, but the sounds of everyone's deep panicked breathing still filled the room. Lizzy tried to listen for the crying, but heard nothing. Once everyone was secured, she moved the flashlight toward the back of the room but was unprepared for what she saw. The screaming started again and this time they all ran away from the door they'd just entered.

"Run! Hurry! Get to the door!" Katie was pushing them all forward and looking back, screaming at the same time.

The sound of a baby crying intensified now and instead of one cry, it was several, and it was growing louder. And even though she couldn't believe what she was seeing, it was babies crying.

While Cory Ann reached for the doorknob, Lizzy danced around in suspense. She held her breath until the door opened and they all piled through it, slamming it shut behind them. She bent over to catch her breath, but before she could gain control, there was a loud bang on the door. Her breath caught again, forcing her to stand up and wait, knowing that it wasn't over yet.

CHAPTER 25

Hannah

Tears were steadily rolling down her cheeks, and her breaths were coming quickly. Things were getting really scary. The whole situation was so surreal. A bunch of porcelain dolls, crying and banging on the door, apparently trying to get to them. She knew what she saw, but her mind couldn't comprehend. How was that possible? But it was happening, and the group feared the door would not keep them out for long.

Hannah rubbed her eyes on her sleeve, trying to clear her vision. To keep them out, the others jammed against the door. Hannah, at the back of the group, looked around the room for an escape. There were windows on the far wall that gave way to light from the storm. The room was still dark, but her eyes had adjusted enough to see what was around there. Her eyes darted downward, making sure there wasn't anything by her feet. She relaxed slightly, but marched in place just in case. Her hands were over her ears, trying to drown out the pounding sounds.

She reached around, grabbing Lizzy's arm to get her attention because she didn't think she'd hear her over the noise.

"Look." She pointed to the windows. "I think we need to get out of here."

She waited for a response. She followed Lizzy's gaze to the room that had a door. They locked eyes and, without words, Hannah made her reservations clear. She didn't want to continue to go into dark room after dark room. She wanted to get out of that building as soon as possible.

Lizzy walked toward the door. "I'm just gonna go see if it's open and where it leads. Stay right here."

"No way!" Hannah latched on to Lizzy and reluctantly followed her to the door.

The others were frantically trying to hold the other door shut. They didn't realize she and Lizzy had left. They reached the door and paused to gather their thoughts and courage to brave the effort after so many setbacks.

"Are you ready, Hannah?" Lizzy already knew the answer.

"No! Come on, Lizzy, what if there are more of those creepy dolls in there? We won't be able to hold this door closed for long." She pointed back to the window. "Why can't we just go out the window? I know it's raining, but I'd rather take my chances with the storm rather than what's in here with us. Please Lizzy. I don't want to go in there."

"I'm scared too, but let me just see if it's locked." She turned the handle, and it wasn't.

Lizzy stared at Hannah for a second, then glanced back at the window.

"I have to know where this leads. Sorry."

Before Hannah could voice her concern, Lizzy opened the door and walked through. She followed.

When Hannah saw the dining room, she rushed in, throwing her hands around Lizzy's neck. She wasn't completely happy about being in the restaurant, but glad they weren't locked in a room with no way out. The dining room sported large windows that someone could easily break. She visioned herself throwing one of the chairs right through the glass. But then what? Resigned to the fact that outside was dangerous, she walked to the doorway, pulled up a chair and sat down, feeling defeated again.

"Hey. We have to go back and get the rest of them. Do you want to stay here? I'll go by the doorway and call them. I won't be long."

Hannah stood up but didn't move. "I don't know what to do. I'm scared, Lizzy, and I don't want you to leave me alone." She took a long, deep breath and waited.

Realizing that she was sounding like a baby, she nodded her head for Lizzy to go. From where she was, she could see the edge of the doorway. Her mind went crazy thinking of all the things that could happen, but the one that rocked her to the bone was if Lizzy didn't come back, she would be all alone.

Thankfully, Lizzy shouted to the group from the doorway reassuring Hannah that she was still inside the dining room. Hannah felt horrible that she was being so selfish. She was worried about her friends but let her fear get the best of her. Relief spread across her forehead when she saw Katie and Sara race through the door, followed by the rest of her friends. They were all safe. And the pounding sound stopped.

Everyone rallied around Hannah, celebrating that they made it back into the dining room. She recognized the irony; they were right where they started and no closer to getting out safely. They were simply happy to be together and away from imminent danger.

Everyone was hugging and cheers erupted, expressing their relief to be out of the locked bathroom and back in a safer area. Excitedly, Hannah jumped up and down, until she realized that something was wrong. She stopped jumping and tore through each person, one at a time.

"Where is she? Y'all, where is she? She's not here. Where is she? Allie! Allie! Where are you? Allie!" Hannah was moving in circles, calling out for Allie.

Everyone froze around her. Disbelief filled their faces, replacing the joy that was just there.

"No! No! No! Allie, where are you? Come on. Answer me! Allie! Y'all, where is she? We have to go back to find her." She was reeling in desperation.

"Did anyone see Allie? Did she make it to the dining room?" Lizzy tried not to sound as frightened as she truly was. She prayed that Allie wasn't taken like Marci was. They had to find her.

"No! This can't be happening!" Hannah was almost hysterical as she called out for her friend again. "Allie please! God no! Please, someone find her!"

She was shaking and sobbing uncontrollably, so she plopped down in the chair by the door to steady herself before her legs gave out.

She listened to the claims about where they last saw her and then called out for Allie to answer. She was gone. Just like Marci, she was gone. Hannah knew that if she could answer, she would. She was gone.

"I'm going back to look for her." Cory Ann started toward the door. "If we hurry, we might find her before..."

Hannah looked up, knowing that Cory Ann didn't finish her sentence on her account. She didn't want to be a burden to anyone, and she knew that Cory Ann was tiptoeing around her. Lizzy and Katie were too. Thay thought she was too fragile to handle things and maybe she was. Losing Marci had devastated her, and she was hanging on by a thread. Her friends meant the world to her because they made life worth living. How could she go on if something terrible had happened to Marci and now Allie? The more she thought about the situation, the angrier she got. She wasn't fragile, she just was a very compassionate person. She tried to stay upbeat avoiding anything that would stop her from enjoying life and that sometimes came off as fragile. No she wasn't fragile, and it was time they understood her. She wasn't the only one hanging on by a thread, they all were.

"Before what? Do you think she could be hurt or worse? Marci too? Don't hold back on my account."

"No. I think someone is playing with us, and I've had enough! Lizzy, come by the door and keep watch for me, please." Cory Ann tried to smile at her friend, but it was weak and didn't reach her eyes.

"Sure." Lizzy answered her with a trembling voice.

Savannah stepped forward, announcing that she was joining the search for Allie.

Hannah stood up and walked toward Lizzy, but was stopped before she reached her.

"You're not going with them." Katie put her hands up in front of Hannah. "You are in no condition to go with them." Hannah protested, but Katie continued to argue her point. "You'll only slow them down, and this needs to happen quickly. Hannah let them go look for Allie. They need to hurry. Let them go."

Hannah nodded and backed away from Katie. "Y'all, please find her. I need y'all to find her."

She watched the selected group head to the door and then disappear.

"Wait! I thought Lizzy was going to stay by the door. Why did she go in?" Hannah was up out of the chair again. "Lizzy!"

"I'm okay. I'm right inside the door with Millie. Cory Ann and Savannah are at the other door now. Just wait."

The restaurant was quiet with anticipation. Even the storms outside seemed to calm to support the mission to find Allie. She wondered where the dolls went. Were they still there? She will never look at another porcelain doll the same again. Maybe they were possessed. Hannah looked around the room and remembered seeing the wait-ress. So much had happened since then, it seemed surreal. Was the waitress a ghost or was she possessed by one? Trying to shake off the unwanted thoughts, she shook her head. Until she'd arrived at the Myrtles, she hadn't be-lieved in ghost. She wished she'd gotten back into her car when she first arrived, when her legs were shaking so badly that she had trouble walking. Why hadn't she lis-tened to her body and responded accordingly? If she had, then Allie would still be by her side and not missing in some creepy freak show.

She cupped her hands together and placed them over her mouth, inhaling deeply. Her nerves were shot, and calming down was vital because she didn't want to cause more problems for her friends. They had enough to deal with, so she kept taking deep breaths, waiting patiently for Cory Ann to call out that they had found Allie. She prayed for that to happen, even though she knew it wouldn't.

CHAPTER 26

Lizzy

Alone, isolated, and terrified with no cell service or electricity made the situation feel perilous. Lizzy was beating herself up for not doing a better job of keeping the group together. She blamed herself for Allie and Marci's disappearance. They should've stayed put where they were in the house instead of trying to leave in the dark stormy night. She thought it was the right decision, but it turned out disastrous and she was sure there was still more to come.

Who would be next? Why did they take Marci and Allie? Were they targeted, or was it random? Originally, when Marci went missing, she suspected Millie had something to do with it, but she'd done nothing since then to validate that suspicion. Actually, she was doing the opposite, trying to help as much as she could. But was that a ploy to throw them off her trail, or was it genuine?

Lizzy watched as Savannah and Cory Ann explored the area by the door. Out of the corner of her eye, she kept watch of Millie. Until they were all safely back home, she wouldn't be able to trust her.

"I think we need to go into the next room." Lizzy heard Savannah reasoning with Cory Ann. "She might still be in there."

"Yeah. I know." Cory Ann hated going back into the room where the creepy dolls were last seen but knew she had to.

Lizzy saw Cory Ann pull open the door and peeked inside, looking back at her occasionally.

"The dolls are gone, and the room is dark and quiet." Cory Ann sighed in relief as she felt Savannah come up behind her and they both shined their lights around the room.

"Nobody's in here." Savannah told Lizzy that they were moving to the next door, then she disappeared through it back into the first supply closet that led to the bathroom. They kept yelling back to Lizzy, keeping the lines of communication open while they continued their search.

Lizzy and Millie stood waiting at the doorway to the restaurant. They were both tense waiting for good news that probably wouldn't come.

"I can't believe this is happening. Where could Marci and Allie be? I mean, why would someone take them? What do you think about all of this, Millie?" Lizzy watched for any signs that she was involved.

"I don't know. I wish I did. It makes little sense."

"What doesn't make sense is, where is everyone? The hotel staff? The other guest? Did they all just leave? It's not very professional to just leave guest stranded in a thunderstorm without electricity or cell service. Someone has to still be here." Lizzy paused, then went on. "Do you think Hannah really saw a waitress? I know I cleaned up that ice and wiped down the area. I'm not sure what's going on, but I believe Hannah saw her and that she was probably the person who locked the bathroom door." She ran her hand through her tangled hair and rocked back and forth in anticipation.

"I don't know about the waitress, but obviously someone locked us in. I had no idea this place would be this creepy. Where I come from, we have haunted houses at Halloween, but they are all fake. I knew there were a few Plantation Homes, but I haven't been, at least I don't recall going to one. But then again, we didn't go too many places. My family didn't have a lot."

Lizzy waited for her to finish. "Where are you from again?"

Millie took a moment to answer, which was a red flag for Lizzy. That was a simple question and if you had nothing to hide, you would answer automatically.

"I'm from Baton Rouge. Well, really, I was born in the Lafayette area in a small town called Kaplan, but we moved to Baton Rouge. What do you think's taking them so long?" Millie stretched her neck to look further into the room.

"Hey y'all! What's going on?" Millie called out into the darkness.

Lizzy felt like she was trying to dodge the question and the whole subject by turning her attention back to Savannah and Cory Ann and their search for Allie.

"Do you have a big family? Any brothers or sisters? I have two brothers and a sister. Our house was never quiet."

Millie didn't look at Lizzy when she finally answered. "Yes, I have a big family."

Lizzy felt like she was having a one sided conversation because Millie was giving short answers.

"Brothers or Sisters?"

"There are 9 of us kids." Again, she tried to divert the conversation. "I wish they would hurry." Millie was tapping for foot anxiously.

She kept her eyes glued to Millie to watch her while she answered the questions. She looked like she was about to go off the deep end. Lizzy wondered if she was overreacting because they were all on edge, letting nerves get the best of them. But she couldn't help feeling that she didn't want to talk about her family and was acting like she had something to hide. When Lizzy was nervous, she talked more, not less. She should've asked questions before in a more relaxed setting, but the opportunity never came up. And she wasn't much on talking anyway. They'd usually meet out somewhere or at dinner as a group and never one on one. She made a mental note to ask more questions and get to know her better if they got out of there and she wasn't some sort of serial killer.

She reached over and placed her hand on Millie's arm to soothe her.

"Hey. Are you okay?"

Millie jumped when she felt the contact and pulled away from her. Her eyes were wild and, for a moment, almost demonic. Her expression quickly softened as she looked back at Lizzy and halfheartedly smiled. She was definitely hiding something, and Lizzy wanted to know what it was. Cory Ann yelled again that they were headed back to them.

"Millie, why don't you want to talk about your family?" Lizzy pushed a little harder. She didn't know what she'd expected to find out but knew that Millie was involved somehow.

Her eyes shot back to Lizzy like daggers. "What did you say?"

"Every time I ask about your family, you give me quick answers, and it seems like you don't want to talk about them." Lizzy wasn't backing down.

"I'm sorry, but no, I don't want to talk about my family or any other chit chat right now. All I want to do is find Allie and Marci and get out of here. Besides, what do you need to know right now about my family? Shouldn't you be worried about finding them, too?"

She was trying to turn the tables on Lizzy, and she wasn't having it. As much as she hated confrontations, she knew this one was necessary. Even though she worked in a bar, Lizzy avoided talking to people all together. It wasn't that she didn't like people, it was conversations she hated. Too often people would divulge way too much personal information and who really cared. She was always of the opinion that less talking was better and normally she wouldn't dig into the personal life of someone else, but they were in real danger and Millie was getting under her skin.

"Yes, I am worried about them, but the only person here I don't really know is you and I'm sorry, but that raises suspicion. I really believe that someone is behind everything that's happened and, aside from you, I trust everyone else. I'm not accusing you of anything, but I would feel better if I knew more about you. Basic things like your family and friends."

"My family life is complicated. I don't have much to do with them. I don't like to talk about them, so I don't. Sorry." Millie backed through the door, still talking. "Guess you'll just have to trust me."

A flash of anger shot through Lizzy because she wasn't just going to trust her. In fact, now more than ever, she was convinced that Millie was not to be trusted. She'd calmed herself down enough to respond, but before she did, Savannah and Cory Ann appeared empty-handed.

"No luck?"

Cory Ann shook her head. "No sign of anyone. Even the dolls are gone. I thought maybe we'd see one or two lying around, but we couldn't find any. The bathroom door is still locked, though, so I'm gonna go back around and unlock it." She started toward the hallway.

"Wait. Don't go by yourself. I'll go with you." Lizzy didn't want to go back to the group just yet. She wanted to gather her thoughts on Millie and maybe share them with Cory Ann.

"Do you want me to go with y'all?" Savannah asked.

"No, you don't have to." Lizzy gave her a hug. "Thanks for coming with us to search for Allie."

"I can't believe she's gone. I think we need to all stay together, so hurry and get back to the group." Savannah walked back into the dining room.

When Savannah was far enough away, Lizzy told Cory Ann about her conversation with Millie and waited for her reaction. Cory Ann was usually pretty laid back about everything and wouldn't normally think Millie's reluctancy to talk about her family strange but giving the circumstances, she might not brush it off so easily. At least Lizzy hoped she would validate her feelings and back her up.

"That's kind of messed up. I don't particularly like my family either, but if you asked me a question about them I'd straight up tell you that. But some people don't like to share their private stuff, ya know. You of all people know that. Not everyone is an open book. Aside from that, though, I do get a bad vibe from her, always have." Cory Ann just shrugged her shoulder.

Lizzy grabbed her arm and stopped her from walking. "Wait! Why didn't you ever say anything? That would've been nice to know before we invited her to join in our friend group. Why do you think you feel that way? Did she say something you didn't like?" Lizzy was grasping for answers that would confirm her suspicions. She hoped Cory Ann could pinpoint why she didn't trust Millie.

Cory Ann shook her head. "There wasn't any one thing, Lizzy. She just rubbed me wrong from the beginning. I chalked it up to being new to the group and maybe a little dry humor. She's just not fun. Have you ever seen her laugh? Like really laugh like we do. Something is really wrong with that girl, but I don't know if that makes her dangerous. But maybe she is."

They had reached the bathroom door. Lizzy was relieved that their conversation had preoccupied her as they walked down the long, dark hallway. Sure enough, the dead bolt was turned to the locked position. Cory Ann unlocked it and asked Lizzy if she needed to use the bathroom since they were already there.

"I do, but I'll wait until we all come back so that some of us can guard the doors. You never know who's waiting to lock us in again."

They both chuckled, then headed back to the dining room to join the group.

Lizzy wasn't finished with Millie yet, but she would not start an argument in front of everyone. She was just going to keep her close and watch her every move until she was sure she wasn't a danger to them. Even if it took all weekend.

Katie

K atie was feeling like a sitting duck waiting to get picked off. She felt safer being all together in a group, but wondered what was coming next. Millie had just returned, sporting a scowled look on her face. Something must've happened because she looked furious. Katie watched as she grabbed the nearest chair and pulled it to the edge of the group before folding her arms and plopping down on its seat. Katie was staring right at her, waiting to hear if they found anything, but she just ignored everyone and sat in silence. She debated whether she should ask how things went, but thankfully, Savannah walked up and announced that the rooms were empty.

Hannah let out a loud sob while the rest looked like they were ready to lose it at any moment.

"Where's Lizzy and Cory Ann?" Demi asked with concern.

"They're coming. Cory Ann went to unlock the bathroom door and Lizzy followed her. The rooms were all empty. We looked in each room, expecting to at least come across one of those stupid dolls, but they were all gone. We looked around the area to see if we could find any clues as to what happened to Allie, but we found nothing. I don't know if that's a good or bad thing." Savannah sat down next to Brittany.

Katie knew what she meant. There were no signs of an attack, such as blood on the floor. At least if there was no blood, she might still be alive and alright. But where could she be? Where could they be? She tried to make sense of it all but was failing. Why would anyone want to take them? Were they caught up in some sick game where they were being hunted one by one? This was all too much to process. And scenes from all the scary movies flooded her mind and weren't helping.

She was reminded of the game Clue or that movie about some rich guy inviting a group of people to an old mansion and murdering them one at a time for sport. She'd even thought of the Halloween movie where they were filming several thrill seekers spending the night in Michael Meyers' old house and he showed up and started killing off the actors. Halloween: Resurrection was the name of that movie. The Halloween movies were her favorites, but she never dreamed of reenacting one.

Her mind was running wild and imagining all sorts of scenarios, but none of them were realistic. She'd always believed that there were very evil people in the world and recently found out that human trafficking was rampant in the United States and around the world. She'd watched a movie about human trafficking and was surprised to learn that it was a major problem here in the United States because she'd always thought that it was most prevalent in third world countries. If what the movie reported was true, then the United States was top on the list because it was so profitable. The idea made her want to throw up. How could people be so cruel when it came to human life? She didn't want to think that maybe someone had kidnapped both Marci and Allie for that reason, but it was possible.

Katie stood up and looked around the room. She needed something to occupy her mind before she recalled every bad thing she'd ever heard of. Lizzy and Cory Ann were walking toward her and looked like they were whispering about something. They didn't appear to be scared or upset, but they were definitely discussing something they didn't want everyone to hear. Of course, that immediately peaked Katie's curiosity, so she met them before they reached the group.

"What's up?" Katie stared them down waiting to be included in the conversation.

"Lizzy confronted Millie about not wanting to share anything about her life and she got mad. Now Lizzy believes more than ever that Millie is not to be trusted and is definitely hiding something." Cory Ann kept walking and sat down next to Hannah.

"Did she say anything? I don't trust her, but I'm not sure she has anything to do with what's going on here. I mean, how could she? We planned this trip at the last minute and whoever is behind things had to have time to set it up." Katie was baffled.

"I don't know, Katie, but I'm keeping her close to me from now on. I hope I don't end up regretting it though. Let's go back and talk about what to do now. Say nothing about Millie, okay?"

"I won't."

Katie followed Lizzy back to the tables and sat down. She looked around and was heartbroken because everyone looked so tired and uncomfortable. She wondered if they should just go back into the house and try to get some sleep. Of course, they would have to take turns keeping watch, but there was no reason for everyone to stay awake.

"Hey. Anyone have any new ideas of what to do now?" Katie almost yelled the question.

All of her friends stopped talking and stared at her while thunder grumbled in the background, refusing to leave the party.

After a pause, Katie announced, "Since no one has anything to say, I thought that maybe we should go back to the house and get some sleep."

"Yeah, right." Sara spoke up, followed by a chuckle. "Oh. You're serious. Absolutely not. There's no way I can sleep, not when there are a bunch of creepy dolls after us. I say we just stay right here and wait until the morning. Somebody has to come back by then. And right here we can see when they do."

"It's still only 1 o'clock in the morning. I hate to say it, but a lot of things can happen before daybreak, Sara. I don't want to go back into the house either, but what are we going to do? And I know y'all feel safe sitting here by the windows and front door but look out there. Anyone could be watching us right now. We're like sitting ducks." Katie looked at the faces of her friends and saw the fear rise from her last comment.

She didn't want to scare them, but she was scared and staying in front of the window made them vulnerable. So far, they were attacked when things were chaotic, but who's to say they won't step up their game and come for them all? That was what had her worried the most. What if they weren't done with them yet and they were all in danger?

The small comments started, and soon the room was full of loud voices, expressing their own concerns. It was apparent that no one agreed with her to go back into the house to get some sleep. That suggestion was now off the table, and most of them wanted to just stay put. Katie couldn't blame them because so far, every decision they made hadn't gone well. She just had an eerie feeling she couldn't shake and didn't know how to protect her friends from the danger. The right decision was unclear at that point.

"I want to know what everyone thinks about the dolls." Stephanie was trying to sound calm. "How were they moving like that? That was the freakiest thing I have ever seen, and I just can't get it out of my mind. They looked alive. How were they so lifelike? And the pounding on the door, do y'all think that was really them? How could that be? I never thought I'd hear myself say these words, but I think there's something supernatural going on here and I'm terrified."

Demi put her hand on Stephanie's shoulder to show support. Katie was glad they were there because she felt there was safety in numbers. If they hadn't come, then it would only be six of them left. Her stomach sank when she thought about poor Marci and Allie being missing and prayed that they were okay. She also said a quick prayer that help would come soon, but she wasn't too hopeful because the weather was still so bad.

Katie glanced over to Lizzy, who was glaring at Millie. Millie was looking at the ground in front of her and hadn't said a word since she rejoined the group. Katie could swear she almost saw smoke fuming above Millie's head, but knew that wasn't possible. About to turn away, she noticed a small lift of the right side of Millie's mouth and her lips pursed together, forming a smirk. The look of evil on her face caused Katie to shiver as she contemplated. She looked away in time to see a brick fly through the glass door, just missing Hannah by mere inches.

Everyone screamed and jumped out of the way. Innately, she knew that something dangerous was coming and now she was back in panic mode. Everyone was except Millie, who still sat in the chair fuming with anger.

What just happened? Millie didn't look fazed at all by the flying brick. Was she responsible in some way? It wasn't just a coincidence that she smirked right before. Was that a victory smirk? Katie was sure she was behind it all.

CHAPTER 28

Lizzy

Was it a coincidence that right after Katie had warned them about being sitting ducks in front of the widow, a brick came crashing through it? Immediately, Lizzy looked over at Millie and saw that she wasn't as fazed as the rest of them were. After a few seconds had passed, she jumped into panic mode with everyone else. She was pretending to be scared, but why? Lizzy glared at her for a few more minutes, then she turned her attention to the brick. They all moved to the back wall of the restaurant where the table they had originally sat stood empty except for the porcelain doll that Lizzy held on to earlier.

Surprise struck her when she saw the doll still there and wondered if it was there the whole time. Hoping to find an explanation why the other dolls could cry and move, she picked it up. Looking for a for a battery pack, she lifted the dress but there wasn't one. She shook it next to her ear, not knowing what to expect. Finally, she glared into the eyes and aside from being creepy and dark; it appeared to be just a normal porcelain doll. She tossed it back onto the table, frustrated.

The weather outside was terrible again and she could only speculate if that was what caused the brick to fly. Admitting that someone threw the brick through the window was accepting that they were being watched. Placing the responsibility on the weather was easier to accept.

She really hoped that was the explanation because if not, then someone is outside watching their every move and that sent waves of terror through her body.

"Maybe it was the wind that picked up that brick and sent it flying. I know I just said that we were like sitting ducks, but why would someone do that? Do you think they are just playing with us? Trying to scare us?" Katie was throwing out her thoughts to her friends.

"The wind is pretty fierce and capable of picking up a brick, but with everything else going on, I believe that someone is trying to scare us. And we are sitting ducks. Maybe we need to gather in the hallway away from the windows now that we know we have two ways out. The only problem would be that its pitch dark without windows. Do we have enough battery left on our phones to at least provide some light? I don't know what would be the best course of action to take, but I do know we need to move out of plain sight." Lizzy was thinking to herself that this was the longest night of her life, and it wasn't over yet. She was exhausted and wanted to go to sleep.

Cory Ann stood up and grabbed a chair. "Let's go. Grab a chair and we can line them up in the hall because I'm not sitting on the floor for hours. In fact, grab two so you can put your legs up if needed." She grabbed another chair and walked away.

Everyone agreed and followed Cory Ann to the dark hallway. They lined the chairs up, starting from the entrance of the hallway. Strategically, this was their best option because they were shielded from the rest of the restaurant by the wall of the drink station, and they were in the perfect position to see someone coming. Lizzy glanced down to the end of the hallway that led to the bathroom and shuddered. She could barely see the door as she peered into the darkness. That was the only drawback, and she prayed they would at least hear the bathroom door open if someone came from there because they wouldn't be able to see them until it was too late. She wished they'd left it locked.

She looked around for Millie and wasn't surprised that she placed her chair at the back of the group closest to the bathroom. Maybe she wasn't doing these things herself but instead had help. That new revelation sent shivers to Lizzy's toes and back up again. That could be it! She was not working alone.

She continued to stare at Millie, waiting to meet her gaze, but she never did. She'd kept her head down and seemed to be indifferent to what was going on, while the rest of them were a ball of nerves. Lizzy was sure that something was up because, in the beginning, Millie seemed quieter and more reserved. Before they came to the Myrtles, she was a little odd but always friendly. But something had changed. She wasn't even trying to hide her anger and unwillingness to share information about herself.

Lizzy continued to study Millie and her body language. She pondered the behavior change and suddenly thought of another reason her demeanor shifted. Was she possessed? Earlier, she had a thought that maybe the waitress and the porcelain dolls were possessed. She had never believed in ghost, or someone being possessed, but now she wasn't so sure. What if the woman she'd seen earlier was a ghost and she'd possessed Millie. She hated not knowing what kind of threat they were facing.

"I remember seeing some blankets and tablecloths we could use in that storage room. I'm going to run and get them." Millie disappeared down the dark hallway before what she had said registered.

"Wait. Don't go by yourself." Demi jumped up and pulled Brittany along with her.

Before Lizzy could object, they were all swallowed into the darkness. Lizzy was filled with anger because Millie had now separated the group again. She hated not to go after them, but they were already too far ahead, and she didn't want to drag any of the others back into danger. She would just have to wait and pray that they all come back safely.

"Lizzy, calm down. There are three of them. Safety in numbers. Do you want me to go by the bathroom doorway and keep watch?" Cory Ann had volunteered again.

She was always volunteering to put herself in danger. A red flag waved across Lizzy's mind as she wondered about her motives. Cory Ann was always the one to take chances, but she had to be just as afraid as the rest of them, unless…. She didn't finish that thought because she couldn't believe that Cory Ann was the one behind all the terror. They'd been friends since grade school, and she refused to think she could do anything so sinister, on purpose at least.

She dropped her head into her hands and tried to shake some sense into her thoughts. Her mind was off on a tangent, and she needed to reel it back in and think clearly. Sensibly. That was the problem. Nothing made sense since they'd arrived at the Myrtles.

She had been so deep in thought that she hadn't realized she was holding her breath until Cory Ann snapped her fingers at her, demanding a response.

"No! Absolutely not. We have to stick together if we want to get out of here, and Millie knows that. Why would she do this?" Lizzy didn't wait for an answer.

Noise from the end of the hallway silenced them as they waited with baited breaths to see who was coming toward them. Their voices reached the group identifying who it was before they became visible, and with a sigh of relief, everyone exhaled and silently cheered.

Millie came into view first, carrying an armful of tablecloths. She seemed to be in a better mood and even sounded a little cheerful as she conversed with the other two. Demi and Brittany had their arms full too and when they reached the group, tossed the blankets and tablecloths they had to the others.

"Did y'all see anything back there?" Katie hoped the answer was no.

"I didn't notice anything, but I grabbed the tablecloths and got out of the room quickly." Demi laughed. "I did not want to find anything!

"Yeah, Demi moved so fast I had trouble keeping up with her." Brittany nudged Demi's shoulder. "I was afraid you were going to leave me."

There were a few nervous giggles as they watched them tease each other.

"The mattress was gone." Millie didn't even look up as she spoke.

Katie gasped. "What? Millie, are you sure?"

"Yes, I'm sure. I was going to drag the mattress out here, but it was gone."

"That means someone is still in here with us." Sara looked terrified.

"I did grab these." Millie held up a broomstick that was broken and a few bottles of Clorox cleanup. "Just in case."

Why hadn't she thought of that? They should've looked around the restaurant for things to use as weapons to protect themselves. Knives. Restaurants should have plenty of knives. And they probably have them at the wait station so that the wait staff can set the tables. She started to share her idea, but then doubt set in and made her pause. Would she be able to use a knife to stab someone? She wasn't sure if she could do it, but she'd rather have the option than be unable to defend herself. The other dilemma was Millie. Was it a good idea to arm her? She was already armed with a broken broomstick, so she guessed it didn't matter.

"Listen. I think we should check out the wait station to look for knives. Even forks would do if that was all they have. We are clearly in danger, so we need a way to defend ourselves." She watched as her words dug in. "I know it's a scary thought, but we really need to be able to fight back, and I know personally that I'm not strong enough to fight off an attacker. Let's just go see if we can find some, just in case. If you don't want one, you don't have to take one."

Reluctantly, they all went to the wait station and grabbed the whole container of forks and knives and brought them back to where they were held up for the night. Lizzy hated to be the one to suggest it and she prayed they didn't have to use them. They needed to get out of there in one piece and that included mentally.

CHAPTER 29

Hannah

Hannah's body was twitching as her frazzled nerves took over. They were held up inside the restaurant with a dangerous psychopath. She tried to stop her body from shaking, but was unsuccessful. Lizzy had suggested that they arm themselves with knives and forks just in case they had to fight. Her hand subconsciously touched the knife she had hidden in her pants pocket. She'd slipped another one into her sock just in case. She leaned back in her chair and closed her eyes. She didn't want to sleep, but she was so tired. They all were.

With closed eyes, she imagined being at home in her soft, comfortable bed. Possibly engaging in a self-defense fight for her life never occurred to her, until then. The idea that she could actually stab someone even in self-defense was inconceivable, but possible. She recalled a few hunting trips she made with her dad. Even though it wasn't her favorite thing, she had shot a deer and helped clean it. But that was different than stabbing a person. Would she be able to do it? She shuddered at the thought.

Her eyes opened as anxiety crept in, sleep was no longer an option.

Finally, they agreed to take turns standing guard while the others tried to sleep, or at least get a nap. Usually, Hannah hated bad weather, but she'd come to find comfort in the steady sound of pelting rain hitting the restaurant. She wondered if it was hailing because the sound was so loud. She couldn't remember it raining for such a long period except for a tropical storm or hurricane. The wind howled, causing the doors and windows to shake and the old bones of the building groan.

Naturally, Cory Ann volunteered to take first watch. Hannah had suggested that maybe two people should keep watch, and Lizzy agreed it was a good idea.

"We can start with two of us for the first hour, then we can swap out one person each hour. That way there will always be two people awake." Lizzy hoped they would agree. "I'll stay up with Cory Ann first, then Demi, you can take my place after an hour. Next, Stephanie can relieve Cory Ann and so on. Please try to sleep because you'll need to be rested. If we make it to… At first light, we are running out of here no matter what."

Hannah wanted to believe that they were going to make it, but daylight was still hours away. She opened and closed her eyes for the first few minutes, unsure that she should actually go to sleep. Just trying to relax and calm down allowed unwanted images of the porcelain dolls and anxiety about what had happened to Allie and Marci. They were two of her best friends, and she didn't know what she'd do without them. Every time she closed her eyes, happy memories of Allie and Marci flooded her thoughts. Then a cold darkness took over and her eyes flew open. Eventually, she gave in and closed her eyes, praying for sleep.

Hannah bolted upright and looked around the room in a panic. After she remembered where she was, she reached into her pocket, powered up her phone to see the time, then powered it back down. It was 3:45 in the morning and the room was quiet. Hannah looked around at each of her friends sleeping. Lizzy had settled down next to her, and Katie was on the other side. Her panic eased, and she leaned back down on the chair, ready to go back to sleep.

An odd noise roused her, and she stared into the darkness. Again, she raked her eyes over each of the others and landed on the two lookout chairs at the edge of the group. She sat up and refocused her eyes, rubbing them to get a better look.

Demi was slumped over and apparently sleeping while the other chair was empty. No one was watching. No one was keeping guard. Alarm took hold of her, but she didn't want to react before she was sure. With shaking fingers, she took count of the sleeping group. Nine. That can't be right. She recounted and came up with nine again.

No, no, no, no, no! She cringed at the thought of someone else missing. She guessed it was possible that no one was missing but was just walking around checking out the place. Lizzy and Katie were safe because they were next to her. She could see Sara, Brittany and Savannah too, but there were two that had their faces covered and Demi was sleeping in the chair. That left Millie, Stephanie, and Cory Ann. Oh no, Cory Ann. Hannah covered her mouth in horror. She knew they needed Cory Ann and if she was missing, someone else would have to step up.

"Lizzy," Hannah shook her quietly. "Wake up. Lizzy, wake up."

"What time is it?" Lizzy grumbled and went back to sleep.

Hannah shook her harder this time. "Wake up! Something's wrong!"

Hannah was relieved when Lizzy finally sat up rubbing her eyes.

"Somebody's missing. Look. The chair next to Demi is empty and there are only eight of us here sleeping. Somebody's missing." Hannah's stomach felt like it was in her throat. This can't be happening again!

She watched as Lizzy jumped up and ran to the chair to wake Demi, who was in a deep sleep. The rest of the group woke up because of the commotion. Hannah quickly took another head count and then ran through the faces. Stephanie was missing. She made another pass over the crowd to confirm and when she was sure, she yelled out. "Y'all Stephanie is missing."

Panic erupted and everyone raced around the area like mice going in circles, looking for a way out or waiting for instructions about what to do next. They searched the immediate area but came up empty. She wasn't there.

"Demi, wake up! Demi!" Lizzy shook her several times, but she didn't budge. "Demi!"

"Something's wrong with her. She never sleeps like that. Demi, wake up!" Brittany had made her way over and shook her. "Demi!" She felt for a pulse and was relieved to find a strong one. "Thank God, she's just sleeping." Brittany continued to yell for her to wake up.

Hannah watched as Brittany shook Demi and tapped her on the face several times. Eventually, a groggy Demi opened her eyes.

Hannah was clinging to Lizzy, afraid to let go. If someone came for either of them, they'd have to battle both of them because she wasn't letting go. Not until they were far away from the nightmare they'd found themselves in.

Hannah felt sorry for Demi because she was devastated when she realized that she'd fallen asleep and blamed herself for Stephanie's disappearance. She explained she was wide awake and unable to sleep, then the next thing she knew, she heard everyone yelling for her to wake her up.

"It was difficult to wake you up. We tried for several minutes. Do you normally sleep that sound?" Hannah was sitting next to Demi trying to determine what had happened. "Are you a heavy sleeper?"

Hannah looked down at the floor and noticed an empty glass. She reached for it and asked if it was Demi's.

"Yes. I was thirsty, so I went right there to the wait station and got some sprite." Demi's words were a little slurred, and she seemed confused. "Stephanie had one too."

"Did the glass of sprite ever leave your sight?" Lizzy took the glass from Hannah and smelled it. "I only smell sprite but of course I have no idea if you can smell a drug."

"No. Wait, yes. I got my glass right before Stephanie relieved Cory Ann. When Stephanie sat down, she said she was thirsty, so we both went to the station to get her something to drink. I left my glass on the floor by my chair, but I was only gone for a couple of minutes." Demi seemed to still be groggy. "Oh my God! I can't believe Stephanie's not here. Wait, do you think I was drugged? Do you think Stephanie was drugged?" Panic took over and Demi was sobbing.

"I don't know about Stephanie, but I think you were drugged. How do you feel now?" Lizzy waited for an answer.

"I feel loaded, actually, and ready to go back to sleep. Y'all don't let me go back to sleep, please." Demi reached for Brittany's hand and pulled her into the empty chair next to her.

"Maybe we should look around the area for Stephanie. She might just be in the bathroom." Hannah wasn't sure what to do and felt more helpless by the minute.

Everyone agreed to go as a group to look for Stephanie. Hannah nudged Lizzy, trying to get her attention quietly. When Lizzy looked at her, she nodded toward the chair that was closest to the two chairs that were used for the lookouts. The person who had been sleeping in that one was none other than Millie. Hannah wasn't surprised because she knew that Katie and Lizzy didn't trust her and, as time went on, she trusted Millie less and less herself. Now she believed Millie was most likely to blame for drugging Demi and that was alarming. She wanted to confront her but knew that would be a bad idea since they still had several hours until daylight. Until then, she'd just join Lizzy and Katie in keeping a watchful eye on her and try not to be alone.

She fell in step next to Lizzy to join the search for Stephanie. She was thankful that Katie stayed back by Millie to keep watch, because she really didn't want to be near her. She hoped they would find out that they were wrong about Millie, but until then, she was considered to be the enemy. A quick mental note to be careful who they invite into their circle of friends was quietly tucked away for later.

CHAPTER 30

Katie

Things were way out of control and even though they stayed as a group, a group of 9 now, they were still vulnerable. Sitting Ducks. Those two words had crossed her mind way too much lately. Even Cory Ann was no match for whoever was after them because they didn't know what was coming next. When Marci and Allie went missing, it was during a moment of chaos, and no one noticed. Then Stephanie disappeared while they were all sleeping. How was that even possible? Katie couldn't believe that they all slept right through Stephanie's abduction. She must've been drugged too, otherwise, she would've put up a fight. Nothing made any sense, especially the spooky porcelain dolls.

Katie was deep in thought when she noticed a pair of eyes staring back at her in the dark, only this time, they were attached to an entire face. It belonged to a young dark complected woman. She was staring right at Katie with deep sorrow in her black sunken eyes. She blinked, then the vision was gone.

Her body trembled. She realized she had just seen a ghost, but refused to believe her own eyes. She didn't want to, but what other explanation could there be? She just vanished. But a ghost. What if it's true? What if all the stories about ghost were true? She moved closer to Millie for protection, without even thinking. When she realized she was squeezing Millie's arm, she met her eyes, then loosened her grip. Millie had a questionable look on her face. Katie didn't want to say anything to Millie about the ghost. She just apologized and moved away without explanation. Admitting that she saw a ghost was not something she was ready to reveal, especially to Millie.

She could feel Millie's eyes on her, but she didn't look back. The search for Stephanie was moving slowly, with everyone feeling as though they were walking on eggshells, afraid of what they were going to find, or not find. The unknown was difficult to accept. Her mind was on overload with all the unexplainable things that had happened to them and there was more to come.

Katie was curious about the ghost. Her first reaction was to be afraid, but she soon realized that she wasn't afraid at all. She was more afraid of the girl next to her than she was the ghost. It was normal that as a first instinct we were to be afraid of ghost because we see them as a threat, but that was because of our own perception of them, not necessarily the reality. Maybe she was a friendly ghost. She looked sad, not angry. Was she trying to communicate with Katie or possibly trying to help them? Perhaps she knew where the missing girls were and who was responsible for their disappearance. Or was she responsible for their disappearance? She had so many questions.

She refocused her attention and noticed that they were in the back of the bathroom and headed to the door that led out to the first room from before. Her eyes widened as they filed into the dark room. She needed to be sharp and alert, not preoccupied with a ghost that may not even be real. Now and then, she looked over to watch Millie. As far as she could tell, Millie looked just as nervous as the rest of them and maybe even a little worried. Could she be wrong about her? Feelings of guilt washed over Katie, but she shook them off and stood firm. She honestly believed that Millie was hiding something and had played a part in the disappearances.

Goosebumps ran up Katie's arm as they crept through the dark room to the next door. She was grateful that someone left it open because slices of lightning helped guide them. The few phone lights were barely enough to see right in front of their feet, so the rest of the room was in total darkness. She was never fond of the darkness.

A muffled sound made its way to Katie's ears, but she couldn't identify what it was or even where it came from. She glanced over at Millie for her reaction and was positive she'd heard it too. Fear spread like spilled paint all over Katie's body, rendering her speechless. Once she found her voice, she whispered to Savannah, who was right in front of her, asking if she'd heard anything. When Savannah turned back to Katie, her eyes grew wide, and she screamed.

Katie turned right when Savannah yelled the word dolls. She could barely see a few dolls crawling toward them from behind. It was another ploy to get them in a chaotic state and grab someone else. It was working because everyone became frantic and ran toward the door.

"Wait! Don't let go of your partner. Y'all listen! It's a ploy! Don't let go!" She tried to reason with them, but everyone was already in full panic mode.

Realizing that Millie had let go of her and was running toward the door,. Katie quickly grabbed onto Savannah for support. There was no way they were going to get to her. She was on to the game and as long as they stayed together, they should be safe. That's what she was telling herself anyway.

They all rushed through the door and into the other room. Katie and Savannah, who were still holding onto Demi and Brittany, came in last and shut the door behind them. She looked around to see if everyone was safe. She counted heads and there were 9. She exhaled slowly and took a moment to regain her composure before she lit into Millie.

"You let go! Why did you let go of me? Did you want them to take me? Was that the plan to get rid of me because I'm on to you?" Katie was eye to eye with Millie and yelling.

She felt hands grab onto her arm and she stepped back. Lizzy was trying to calm her down, or at least stop a fight from happening. She knew she was out of control, but she didn't care anymore. She just wanted Millie to admit that she was behind all of it. She needed her to confess. Maybe that wasn't the brightest idea she'd had yet, because what would she do if she was cornered with no way out?

"Listen. We are all on edge, but at least we're all here together and safe. Katie, please calm down. I know you're upset. I would be too, but there's nothing you can do right now. We're all stuck here together. We need to move before that army of creepy dolls decides to march on and attack us again. I can't believe I just said that. How could that even be possible?" Lizzy shook her head.

"That's not the only thing we have to worry about." Katie stared at Millie. "I saw a ghost back there." She was done with all the secrets. She did see a ghost and needed them to know.

A few of them gasped, but none louder than Sara and Hannah. They were completely terrified and had started to cry. Katie wanted to cry herself, but anger helped her fight back the tears. She was angry at Millie. She was angry at herself for losing control, which was probably what Millie wanted her to do. She was angry that three of her friends were missing and there was nothing she could do to help them. The list went on and on and she was angry about all of it.

Millie started to answer, but Katie just put her hand up to stop her.

"Stop. I'm sorry I snapped at you, but right now we have to move on, like Lizzy said. There are nine of us left, so instead of paring up in twos, let's do threes." She glared back at Millie. "That way, if someone lets go, you'll still have another person in your group to hold on to.

Again, Millie started to talk, but everyone grabbed on to each other and headed toward the next set of doors. This time Katie grabbed on to Millie and Cory Ann grabbed onto her from the other side. She was flanked between them, and they were not letting her out of their sights. Guilty or not, she was considered the number one suspect. Actually, she was the only suspect they had. As they moved, Cory Ann turned toward Katie and said, "A ghost? Really?"

Katie shook her head and left it at that.

CHAPTER 31

Lizzy

Everything was quiet except for the sounds coming from the old structure, probably trying to warn them of the impending danger that was lurking indoors with them. Lizzy tried to remember what she was told about the age of the old plantation house and restaurant. She thought it was built around the 1700s, however, her memory was unclear. She would bet all the old buildings had a lot to say if they were permitted to speak freely.

Her mind drifted to her first impression of the house and grounds and the old, weathered dormers she'd noticed. At first, she wasn't positive that the curtains moved, but now she was convinced someone was up there. Was that the ghost Katie claimed to have seen? They were in the restaurant, not in the house. We're ghost allowed to roam free. She'd always thought they were trapped in one place until their souls were set free. Actually, that's what she'd seen in the movies, but in real life she didn't even believe in ghost.

Her thoughts shifted to her friends and family, who were there with her. She loved them all so much — well, most of them. This was the first time they'd experienced anything so bizarre and dangerous. They'd gone on a bunch of adventures and traveled quite a bit together, but always had fun, and everyone survived. She prayed that Marci, Allie and Stephanie were stashed somewhere still alive. She'd even accept this being a sick joke that they were all part of because then they would be safe in the end. Her anger would eventually subside making way for forgiveness and they'd still be around.

Her mind felt like a pinball machine bouncing from one thought to the next. The creepy dolls popped up next. If that was a prank, then someone was really good. They were so realistic and were definitely moving and talking. Lizzy's thoughts were interrupted by the feeling of something on her foot. She looked down, but it was too dark to see anything. She shuddered at the thought of it and stopped walking.

"Something was on my foot." Lizzy's voice squeaked. Images of every kind of animal and insect slithered across her mind.

Cory Ann was behind Lizzy and pointed her phone down to the floor. "I don't see anything. Keep walking. We need to hurry."

The sounds of thunder roared, one clap after the other as the storms raged up again. Lizzy picked up the pace and actually started to tiptoe across the room. She hated to think about what might be down there. She shuffled forward, trying to ignore it when someone shrieked.

"Something just crawled across my foot y'all!" Sara was bouncing up and down, attempting to keep whatever it was, off of her feet.

Right after Sara's shriek, Hannah let out a scream. Her throat was scratchy from all the screaming she'd done since she'd arrived.

"No Way! Sorry, but I'm getting out of here." Hannah pulled Sara and Lizzy to the next door and didn't stop there. Lizzy yelled back for everyone to keep holding onto their partners and run. By the time they crossed the short distance back to the dining room and into the hallway, she was out of breath.

"What was that? When we get out of here, I'm calling the board of health." She was livid. "Y'all, I think that was a rat! Really. It felt like something slid across my foot, like a tail."

"Maybe it was a snake." Millie sounded indifferent when she threw that out there.

"Thanks Millie. That really helps." Lizzy's tone dripped with sarcasm. "Way to be encouraging."

Lizzy felt bad about being so mean, but exhaustion stopped her from being nice to her number one suspect. The thought of creatures crawling around the floor was unsettling. Mice were the likely culprits, since most restaurants too often dealt with that problem. She'd originally thought of those large cockroaches when she felt something crawling across her foot. To her, that was just as bad because they could fly, and she hated that about them.

Demi's soft cries caught Lizzy's attention. She felt bad for her because she knew how she felt. They were all in the same mess. Everyone had blood shot puffy eyes from crying about all the missing girls and the situation they were in. Surprisingly, even Millie's eyes were red and puffy. Was it real or was it just for show? She never saw Millie cry but maybe she had, and Lizzy hadn't noticed.

Lizzy was deep in thought when Millie charged over to where she was and started pleading her innocence, but before she reached her, she tripped over the leg of a chair and fell to the ground. A loud thud sounded when her head hit another chair on her way down. Katie leaped forward to help her and noticed that she wasn't moving. Sara yelled out that there were lights on in the main house. Everyone else ran to the edge of the wait station where Sara was standing and saw that the main house was completely lit up. Every light in the house was on. Millie groaned and brought the attention back to herself. She was trying to sit up, but Lizzy warned her to stay still for a moment. She was sure that the fall had knocked her out, and she probably had a concussion.

Sara yelled again. "It's dark again! Y'all saw the lights, right? I know I saw the lights on, but now the house is completely dark again! That makes little sense." She whimpered as absolute darkness swallowed the house again. They were never getting out of there.

"Maybe the electric company is working to restore the lights, and they flickered. I don't know, but yes, I saw the lights too!" Brittany was now standing in the doorway staring at the house.

Lizzy was concerned about them standing out in the open again. She didn't want to tell everyone what to do, but she truly felt like they needed to stay out of sight until daylight. She was grateful that Hannah and Sara were clinging close to Katie and Cory Ann, and they were all still behind the wall of the wait station.

Lizzy helped Millie up into one of the chairs, then shouted for the others to back away from the door, reminding them it was still dangerous. Lightning crackled, forcing the rest of them to run back. They all huddled together, waiting out the darkness and wondering the same thing. When will this nightmare end? How will it end? That last thought was even more frightening. Before arriving, she'd made plans for the following week and to have dinner with her parents on Sunday evening. Would they come for her if she didn't show up? The thought of enduring this chaos until Sunday sent into a tailspin and knocked the wind out of her lungs.

Lizzy sat down next to Hannah and Sara, watching Sara fidget with the hem of her shirt. They were sitting on the edge of their chairs, ready to bolt at any moment. Whispering about something that was upsetting both of them, wasn't helping. They were about to come unglued, and Lizzy wasn't sure she could stop it.

"What are you two up to?" Lizzy asked accusingly.

She watched as they exchanged looks, then Hannah spoke up. Her face morphed from a nervous, jittery mess to a calm, firm expression before she started to speak.

"Sara saw movement in the house when the lights came on. Someone else is here with us. I think we should go to see if they can help us. It's probably the night manager. They can tell us what's happening and when help will come." Hannah waited for Lizzy to respond.

"Are you sure it was a person? Did you see someone specifically or just movement?" Lizzy thought of the dormer curtains. "It's so dark and if we go we need to be sure. My mind had been playing tricks on me all day."

"There were shadows in the front room, and then I saw the curtains move in the upstairs window. Someone is there, maybe the entire staff. We need to hurry because I don't want to miss him."

Lizzy's blood ran cold. Maybe it was the staff, or the person who grabbed Katie and Millie in the closet. Even the ghost that Katie saw earlier could be trying to lure them back into the main house. She had no idea what to do. What she didn't want to do was have a discussion with the entire group because that would be too many opinions to deal with.

"We need to think about this before reacting. We don't know who's over there or if they are friend or foe. Let's talk to Cory Ann and Katie to see what they think." Lizzy hoped they would settle down and be patient.

She jumped when Cory Ann walked up from behind and touched her arm.

"Jeez Lizzy. It's just me. What's up over here? You look like you saw a ghost." Cory Ann sat down in an empty chair. Lizzy's reaction told her that she was scheming something she didn't want to share with everyone.

"Funny you should say that. Sara said she saw movement in the main house when the lights flickered on. Also, the curtains moved in the upstairs dormer. They think it might be the staff and want to go for help. Personally, I think it might be the ghost Katie said she saw. Or possibly the person who grabbed Katie and Millie in the closet. Heck, it could even be the person messing with us over here. Someone threw that brick through the window. I say we stay put until daylight. What do you think?" Just as Lizzy finished, Katie walked up.

They brought Katie up to speed and let the information sink in before asking her thoughts. Lizzy insisted that they all agree before they made a move. And after they had decided what to do, they would include everyone else and take a final vote. She'd preferred to have a solid plan in place before presenting it to the group.

She watched closely as they contemplated their options. She'd had a fairly good idea what Cory Ann would pick, but wasn't sure about Katie. They all knew Cory Ann was all guns blazing and full speed ahead, but this could be costly if they made the wrong decision. Going to the house for help and finding danger was not something she wanted to do. She wanted to wait for first light and run as fast and far as she could away from the house and grounds. The question was, could they wait it out or would they be forced to react? Only time would tell.

CHAPTER 32

Katie

Lizzy had thrown some pretty heavy decisions on her and Cory Ann. How was she to know what to do? She wasn't a leader or the most levelheaded person there. Lizzy must've hit her head too. Or at least she'd forgotten all the times Katie made the wrong decisions over the years.

She tried to reason out the things she knew to be factual. Like, the fact that someone had tried to grab her, and had successfully grabbed Millie, in the closet. They searched a good part of the plantation and couldn't find anyone. There was a slew of creepy dolls in the restaurant that seemed to be after them, along with someone that had snatched three of her friends. And last but certainly not least, there were ghosts. She decided that neither place was a good option. She was leaning toward agreeing with Lizzy that they should just stay put until daylight.

"I think we need to stay put." Cory Ann had decided. "It's already 4am so it should be light soon. We made it this long. What's a few more hours?"

The sun should rise around 6:45 am, so that meant holding on for almost 3 more hours. Alot could happen in just a few hours. Katie hoped they could stick together and not lose anyone else.

"I agree with Cory Ann. I don't think either place is safe, but we're out of the weather and safe for the moment. That's my vote." Katie forced a smile, then stated why she felt the way she did.

"Hannah and Sara, now that you've heard Katie's reasoning, what do you think? You know, I think we should stay put." Lizzy added, not wanting to dismiss their votes.

Hannah said that she was willing to wait until daylight, and Sara nodded in agreement.

"I think that someone is in the house that could help us. Just saying. But you're right, it could be the person who has been stalking us, so we'll wait." Hannah wanted to be on record that she had reluctantly conceded to them. But in reality, she couldn't decide which option would be better, so took the easy road and just agreed with the others.

The memory of the woman Katie noticed on the veranda when she'd first arrived skated across her mind. She wondered if the vision was a ghost or a real living being. She looked very old, and her clothes were dated, but she could've been an employee playing a role to enhance the experience for the guest. So many unanswered questions had Katie's mind spinning out of control. She reasoned that there had to be a logical explanation for everything that had happened, but at the moment, she was having trouble finding one.

Katie looked at Millie, who was now up off the floor and sitting in a chair.. She looked a little disoriented, but at least she wasn't still unconscious. When they'd made the final decision to vote, Millie hadn't taken part. She watched as Millie struggled to stay awake. Her expression seemed dark and even dangerous, causing her to look like the real psychopath Katie had come to suspect she was.

The room grew quiet, and the thunderstorms had settled. She was exhausted and just wanted to go to sleep, but that would not happen. She wondered where the dolls went. Not only that, but she also needed to know how they had chased after them in the first place. Why haven't they followed them out into the restaurant? Katie sighed in desperation for answers.

A sudden feeling of anxiety came over her, along with an image of that old storm cellar she'd seen earlier. She was drawn to it from the moment she'd noticed it, but didn't know why. She'd never seen it before. And this was her first time visiting The Plantation House. The tug started slowly, with images of the storm cellar randomly coming to mind. Thoughts of what might be down there and the need to find out nagged at her to make a move. But now, the pull had intensified, causing her to experience physical symptoms. Her body was literally shaking with anxiety, and her stomach was in knots. Was this what withdrawal symptoms felt like? Her curiosity had peaked, but she knew it wasn't the time to act. She'd wondered if there was a link to the ghost she'd seen earlier. Once again, she tucked the thoughts to the back of her mind and tried to refocus on the threat at hand.

Katie stared out into the darkness. The stillness of the night should've been calming to her, but she was robbed of those feelings the minute she'd arrived. If Hannah had seen lights on and movement in the house, there was no evidence of it now. The small lights that were generator produced inside the house were so dim that seeing inside was impossible. Still, Hannah wouldn't make something like that up, so she must've seen something.

She continued to stare out into the darkness, trying to determine what their next move should be. They had agreed to stay put, but she was afraid that something or someone could push them into changing that decision and they'd have to act fast. Her eyes were tired, and the monotony of the darkness was making them heavy and difficult to keep open. She vigorously shook her head back and forth and lightly taped her face. She squeezed her eyes shut and then popped them back open, hoping to energize herself.

Katie jumped out of the chair and glared into the night. Someone was on the veranda staring back at her. They were standing in the corner, leaning against the house. At first, thoughts of the ghost from earlier had come to her mind, but this person was much taller and heavier. She crouched behind the wait station just enough to be out of sight. She looked around and noticed that the others had settled down and were quietly chit chatting as they passed the time waiting to fall asleep or for dawn to arrive. Keeping her eyes glued to the veranda, she tried to get a better view, but she was just too far away.

She knew she should tell them what she was seeing because they were probably in real danger, but she hated to overreact. She looked again, squinching her eyes to see. They were still there. He was still there. She was positive that it was a man, a really big man. Her stomach was jittery as she sat there, trying to see his face. What could he possibly want from them? He was definitely outnumbered and unless he had a gun, what was he going to do? A cloud of smoke loomed above his head. Was he smoking?

Lizzy came up behind her and she almost screamed out of surprise.

"You startled me! Why are you up?" Katie looked back, noticing that a few of them had dozed off. Even Millie's eyes were completely shut. She looked smaller than Katie remembered, but maybe it was just the position she was scrunched in. Could the feeling of intimidation she felt when she looked at Millie be what disturbed her?

"Sorry. I didn't mean to scare you. I thought you saw me coming. What are you looking at?" Lizzy looked out into the darkness. "It's so dark I can't see anything."

Katie didn't want to scare her, but she needed to tell someone about the man on the veranda. She reached up and grabbed Lizzy by the arm, pulling her down behind the counter. She put a finger over her lips, showing that she needed to be quiet.

"There's someone on the veranda." Lizzy rose, but Katie pulled her back down. "Wait. He's leaning against the corner of the veranda, trying to hide. I don't know what to do. I don't want to scare them when they are finally getting some rest." Katie and Lizzy both looked back and saw that they were all sleeping.

Katie stood a little taller so she could make sure that the man was still in the same place. They both gasped when they saw lights on in the house. Every room was lit up providing a perfect view inside the house.

"Oh my God! What do we do?" Lizzy whispered, because she didn't know what else to do.

"Look, there's the man. He's smoking a cigarette. And look, there are others inside. We gotta go over there and get help. Should we wake them?" She glanced at the group. "I don't know what to do. They are finally resting so I hate to disturb them." Katie waited for an answer.

"I'll go with you. Let's go. We can run over and get help quicker if it's just the two of us, but we need to hurry. What if he leaves? Come on Katie, let's go."

"Wait!" Katie grabbed onto Lizzy's arm. "I'm scared. What if he's the man that pulled us into the closet? He might be the one who threw the brick through the window. Look, he's smoking on the veranda and that's against the rules. Maybe he's a serial killer and not someone we can go to for help." Every single word that came out of her mouth sounded so crazy, but unfortunately, they were all possibilities.

"Man Katie, I don't know. But I think we gotta take a chance. We can run over and go straight into the house. We'll let them know we're in the restaurant and in need of help. I'm scared too, but we need help, and I agree not trusting the guy on the veranda, but I'm praying there are staff members inside that could help us. Right?" Lizzy grabbed Katie's hand with her own and tugged her forward.

"Okay. You're right. We need to get help. Even if he's not a good guy, he probably wouldn't try to do anything with the other people around. My legs are shaking so badly right now. And I gotta pee." She made a funny face at Lizzy and they both released a nervous giggle.

"When don't you have to pee? Come on, lets…"

"What are y'all doing?"

They both let out a quick shriek, but then covered their mouths.

"Hannah! You scared the heck out of us! Why are you up?" Lizzy was trying to keep her trembling voice low.

"Look! I told you there were lights on earlier. Look!" Hannah pointed at the house. "Do you believe me know?"

"I never said I didn't believe you! Of course I believed that you saw lights on and someone moving around. I just needed to be sure you saw a person, a live person."

"Shh! Don't wake them up. We see the lights and the movement inside. We were just going to run and get help." Lizzy wasn't happy that now Hannah was going to go with them.

"Listen, there's movement in the house, but there's also a man standing in the shadows of the veranda smoking. He's been there for a while, just staring this way. We don't know if he is friend or foe, but we decided to run past him and into the house for help." Katie watched as Hannah's eyes grew wide when she noticed the man on the veranda.

"Y'all I'm scared." Hannah grabbed onto their arms." "Is he watching us? Maybe he's the lookout for someone?"

"Hannah, you don't have to come. Stay here and wait for us to come back. We're gonna run in and out quickly because we don't want to leave the group alone for long." Katie waited for her response.

"No way. I'm not staying here by myself." Hannah latched onto Lizzy and Katie's arms, refusing to be left behind.

"You're not by yourself. There's six other people here."

"No way. I'm coming with y'all. But it's sort of creepy that he keeps staring right at us. He looks like he's daydreaming or in a trance. Maybe he doesn't see us."

Katie opened the door and walked out onto the veranda. Lizzy and Hannah followed right behind, and they all kept their eyes glued to the large man across the lawn. Katie moved slowly, then stumbled on the last step, almost tumbling to the ground.

"Why are you in the front?" Lizzy brushed past Katie and took the lead.

"Y'all, I gotta pee." Hannah hadn't had time to say that was why she was up.

Lizzy shook her head. "I can't with y'all! Come on. We are supposed to run there and back, not walk at a snail's pace." Lizzy picked up the speed and dashed across the lawn, dragging Katie and Hannah behind.

As they were approaching the veranda and stepping into the light, the man caught sight of them. He jumped like he had just seen a ghost and followed that with a few choice curse words. Katie didn't wait around to listen, but instead swung open the door and ran inside. There was a woman behind the front desk and as she looked up to see what the commotion was about; the lights went out and everything went silent. She was gone.

The three of them stood there shivering in the middle of the deserted room, wondering what had just happened. Katie raced back to the veranda, but the man was gone too. They were all alone. Katie was about to say something when they heard a noise. She closed her eyes, too afraid to see what was there. Her mind was reeling with confusion. She ran back to Lizzy and Hannah, and they all held their breath, waiting for what was to come.

CHAPTER 33

Lizzy

She had to admit that when she saw the lights on in the house, she was surprised. Katie was suspicious of the man on the veranda, but she found everything about the situation suspicious. If there were staff running around the house, why didn't they notice that twelve of their guest were missing and do the natural thing and search for them? But she agreed that they needed to take a chance and go for help. And the man on the veranda scared her too, but he didn't appear to be staring at them after all. He was definitely startled when they came into the light from the darkness of the lawn between the house and the restaurant.

After they made it into the house, the lady disappeared. She was definitely there and then she was gone. How could that have happened? She'd originally thought that someone was behind all the craziness, but when people started disappearing, she doubted herself. There was something else going on there, and Lizzy shuddered at the thought that they were going to find out soon enough.

She stayed glued to Hannah and Katie, keeping her eyes alert. A sound reached them, but they were unsure where it came from. They huddled closer and waited.

Not surprisingly, the weather had picked up again, and the thunder grumbled.

"Maybe that's what we heard. Thunder?" Katie hoped that was true.

"That was not thunder we heard. It sounded like it was coming from the hallway." Lizzy averted her eyes, refusing to look in that direction.

"What are we gonna do? We can't stay here like this. Maybe we should go back to the restaurant. That was the original plan right, stay there and wait until daylight. I think we need to go back." Hannah made a move toward the door.

"Hannah wait. We don't know where that man went. He could be on the veranda waiting for us." Lizzy was worried. He couldn't have just disappeared into thin air, could he?

"I looked. He wasn't there." Katie moved past Hannah and went out onto the veranda. She wanted to make sure he was gone before they all went back outside.

Lizzy called for Katie to stop, but her voice was drowned out by thunder and the scariest lightning strike she'd ever seen. The whole area was lit up and that's when Lizzy heard the scream. There was so much chaos that she wasn't sure who screamed. She watched as Katie took off toward the restaurant right before she and Hannah turned and ran up the stairs into the house.

"Oh no. Lizzy, what are we going to do? I don't want to stay here alone. What are we going to do? Why did Katie leave us like that? What are we going to do? I'm scared." Hannah was hysterical.

"I don't know. I don't think Katie had a choice. Who screamed? Was it you or Katie?"

"It wasn't me. I think it was Katie because it came from outside. Do you think she's okay?" Hannah was now worried. Remembering the man on the veranda caused her to cry out.

"I think so. I saw her run back to the restaurant. The other's probably heard the storm approaching and woke up to find us gone." Lizzy hoped she was right.

Hannah froze. She whispered, "Lizzy, what if Katie saw that man on the veranda? Maybe that's why she screamed. Oh my God! Do you think he's still there?" The blood drained from Hannah's face. "Do you think he's in the house now? What should we do?"

Lizzy looked around the now familiar parlor area for somewhere safe to hide. She couldn't believe they were back there again. She wanted to run out of the house and back to the restaurant, but she was afraid that Hannah was right, and the man could be in the house.

"Lizzy, I really have to pee now."

"Okay, but let's hurry." Lizzy let Hannah go first. "Don't flush."

After they both finished, they tiptoed back to the sitting area. The door in the back of Hannah's closet had her curious. Where did that lead to? She remembered that someone suggested it might lead to the room behind Hannah's, but no one checked that out. As much as she wanted to investigate, she didn't want to get caught in there with no way out. At least in the parlor, they had a chance to run into another room, or even around the staircase and then down the stairs. Her eyes darted around the room.

From where she was sitting, she could see the entire room and down the stairs. Well, almost all the way down, just not the bottom. Could he be down there staring up at her right then? She squirmed at that thought, and when it got the best of her, she stood up.

"We have to move." She grabbed Hannah's hand and moved just out of the stairway. "I can't see to the bottom of the stairs and that's freaking me out. Do you have any ideas?"

Hannah shook her head no. Her mind was scrambled, trying to keep up.

"We can't just sit here and wait. If the man is in the house, he's gonna come after us, eventually. The others might come for us, but he may still be on the veranda. Not knowing what's going on out there sucks. I think we should move now." Lizzy tried to sound confident in her plan. "We need to see where that closet door leads."

"No! No way! I'm not going in there, Lizzy. That freaky doll is in there. I'm not going. And what if that man's in there? I can't do it!" Tears were rolling down Hannah's cheeks. "Why can't we just wait right here for the others? They're going to come. Cory Ann and Katie will come for us, I'm sure of it. Let's just sit right here, next to the stairs, and wait. It's only been a few minutes. They're gonna come, Lizzy."

Lizzy's heart twisted as Hannah pleaded to stay put. She was scared too, but she didn't think waiting was a good idea. Before she had time to respond to Hannah, they heard the front door open and close. Her heart was pounding in her throat. She prayed it was Katie and Cory Ann coming back for them, but she couldn't know for sure.

"Shh." Lizzy put a finger over her lips and pointed to the stairway with the other hand.

"Oh my God!" Hannah sat wide eyed and shaking.

Lizzy leaned her body to the right, almost completely stretching out on the floor, trying to see down the stairway from where she was sitting. Everything was completely quiet. Even the rain had stopped again. Taking a deep breath, she used her arms to pull her closer for a better view. She had to blink several times, trying to get her eyes to focus in the darkness. She stared into the absence of light for a few more seconds, then pulled herself back up.

"I don't see anything. I don't know what to do. Should I call out? If it were Katie or Cory Ann, I think they would've called out to us, right?"

Hannah agreed. "I don't think it's them." Fright seized her breath.

"Hannah, we have to do something. We can't just sit here and wait any longer. We have to go into the closet." Lizzy hated that it was their best option.

Lizzy stood up first and peered down the stairway. It had been quiet since they heard the door close. She reached for Hannah's hand and nodded that they were going to run toward the room together. They leaped forward and within a few steps were at Hannah's bedroom door. A noise followed them from the stairwell and Hannah stifled a scream as they entered the room and locked the door behind them.

"Someone's coming! Lizzy, hurry, he's coming!" Hannah was pushing her forward. At the moment, the porcelain doll was the least of her worries.

"Did you see him?" Lizzy grabbed on to Hannah just in case.

"No, but I hear him. He's coming, hurry."

Lizzy pulled open the closet door, and they hurried to the back. The door was tiny, and they were in darkness. She glanced back at Hannah one last time, then opened the door and disappeared, closing it behind them.

The room they were now in was even darker and she had no idea which way to go. They felt around for walls or doors. A sudden sensation of claustrophobia came over her and she started to panic. Hannah had crawled up next to her and the room was tight. They inched forward slowly, afraid of what might be ahead of them. Lizzy prayed it was a way out, because if not they were trapped.

"Lizzy, I don't like this. I want to get out of here."

"Me too." Lizzy, filled with anxiety, was having trouble breathing. Dizziness threatened to take over, causing her to act.

She picked up the pace and crawled forward on the floor until there weren't any left. Before she could stop and back up, her body tumbled forward with Hannah in tow, and they fell into the darkness. All she could do was scream and pray. And that's exactly what she did.

CHAPTER 34

Katie

The lightning bolt scared them into scattering, and she took off running toward the restaurant. She looked back, but total darkness covered them. As she approached, the restaurant door swung open, and Cory Ann was standing there waiting for her to run in.

Katie leaned over with her hands on her knees, trying to catch her breath. She paced in a circle before she uttered a word. She hadn't realized how out of shape she was and made a mental note to get back to the gym soon.

"Katie, what happened? Where's Lizzy and Hannah?" Cory Ann nervously asked the question she wasn't sure she wanted to hear the answer to. The look in her eyes was alarming.

Katie held up her hand, asking for another minute to catch her breath. Did she even know what happened? Chaos happened again. She finally calmed down enough to stand upright and answer Cory Ann.

"Lizzy and Hannah are still over at the house. The woman disappeared and so did the man on the veranda. That lightning struck and everything went crazy. I ran, and I thought they were behind me, but when I looked back I couldn't see anything. I thought about turning around, but I didn't know where the man was." She stopped talking to catch her breath.

"Wait. What are you talking about? What man? Katie, why were y'all over there? Why did y'all leave?" Cory Ann was now joined by the others. She was having difficulty following what she was hearing because none of it made any sense.

"I saw a man on the veranda smoking and staring over here. Then the lights were brighter, and I could see movement inside the house. Lizzy found me and saw the same thing. We were going for help, but before we walked out the door, Hannah found us and didn't want to stay here alone."

"She wasn't alone. We were here." Millie sounded irritated.

"That's what I told her, but she wouldn't let Lizzy out of her sight. We agreed to run there and back quickly. And we actually did. We ran past the man, entered the house, and saw a woman behind the desk. But right after she looked up at us, the lights went out again and she disappeared. She was just gone y'all. Vanished. We were gonna run back here, but Lizzy was afraid that the man was still there, so I had checked, and he wasn't. We were about to come back when that horrible lightning struck and sent us scrambling in different directions. I ran and thought they were behind me, but I guess they stayed inside the house. We gotta go after them. We can't just leave them there." Katie was pacing the floor and looking across the lawn at the dark house. "They're still in there and probably waiting for us." Rain pounded the ground quickly creating puddles everywhere.

Katie knew that Cory Ann was willing to go after them. She looked around at the others staring at her in disbelief. There's no question about it; they have to go back to the house and look for them, but should they all go? Safety in numbers. So yes, she knew what had to happen.

"Listen. We have to go back for them. I still believe that there is safety in numbers, so I think we should all go. What do y'all think?" Everyone agreed and that should've made her feel better, but if something happened to anybody else, she'd feel responsible, so she actually became more apprehensive. She hated putting others in danger, but they made their own choices.

Katie and Cory Ann hesitated in the doorway and glared at the house. Katie was looking for the man but found the veranda empty. She wasn't happy to go back into the darkness, but she couldn't leave them there alone.

Cory Ann darted out of the door without notice and Katie ran after her, signaling the others to follow.

"Cory Ann, wait up." Rain drenched her the moment she stepped out onto the lawn.

When she reached the veranda, she sighed in relief that there weren't any new surprises, yet. The house was still dark inside, with only the dimmest of light inside the parlor. How did people function back in the day with such low light? She couldn't imagine how life must've been because she was used to shopping and eating and living a full life after dark. Life back then was very different, and everything had to shut down at nightfall. Her mom often spoke of how the television only had a few channels when she was young. And that at midnight all channels went off air and didn't come back on until the next morning. Again, she couldn't imagine it and was very thankful for modern technology.

Cory Ann snapped her fingers at Katie bringing her back to reality. She was trying to shake off the rain as she leaned against the window, looking inside. The room was empty and no sign of Lizzy or Hannah. She wondered if they were just hiding behind the counter. She wanted to call out for them, but wasn't sure that was the best idea.

Cory Ann whispered she was going in. Katie turned on her phone light and followed her in. They all piled into the front room and since Savannah was the last one in, she shut the door behind her.

They were searching the room when Katie stopped walking. Her ears perked up responding to a noise.

"Did y'all hear that? It sounds like movement coming from upstairs. Should I call out for them? It has to be them."

Cory Ann shook her head no. "We don't know who's up there. We better go up quietly, just in case. If it's them, we'll soon find out because this is the only way out. Come on. If everyone can huddle right here, I can go up and peek at the top."

"I'm going up with you." Katie didn't want anyone off on their own.

"I'll go if y'all want." That wasn't the first time Millie had volunteered.

Katie looked at Cory Ann and then back to Millie. "It's probably better if you stay with the group." Before she got a rebuttal, Katie shoved Cory Ann forward. Her heart was pounding so fast she wondered just how much more it could take before it finally just stopped.

Katie watched as Cory Ann reached the top and crawled on her belly onto the floor, peeking around both sides of the stairway, making sure it was safe. Cory Ann got onto her knees and motioned for her to follow. Once they secured the area, she signaled for the rest of them to come up. Katie checked the bathroom first, then the other four doors. She shrugged, disappointed, then walked back to the group and asked for their thoughts.

A faint thumping sound came from the side of the house where Hannah's room was. A second later, they heard another thumping sound, prompting them to jump into action.

"They're in Hannah's room. That has to be them. Maybe they're inside the closet figuring the door in the back was a way out." She imagined Hannah must be dying by now if she was stuck in the closet with the porcelain doll.

"I don't think we should go in there." Millie voiced her opposition from the back of the group. Katie looked at Millie wondering if she was just scared to go back in or if there was another reason. She didn't sound afraid, but her face looked stoic. Something about the sound of her voice troubled Katie.

"I'm sorry Millie, but we have to go in there. If Lizzy and Hannah are in there, we need to find them. I know it might be difficult for you to go back in, so if you'd rather not, we can split up and meet back at the restaurant." She was not going to let Millie make any decisions or get in the way.

"I'm not afraid. I just think it's stupid to go into that closet when we don't know what could be back there." She glared at Katie and then changed her tune. "But you're right, we have to find them. I'm just worried that it's not safe, that's all."

Katie started to second guess her decision. What if Millie was right, and it wasn't safe to go in there? Maybe she should just call out to them. She knew what Cory Ann wanted to do, but were the others skeptical about going in as well? Was Millie getting in her head and making her indecisive?

"What do y'all think? We have to make a group decision because this choice involves all of us. Of course my vote is to go in and I'm pretty sure Cory Ann agrees with me, but if anyone has reservations like Mille, please say so." Katie looked around at the faces of her friends.

Surprisingly, Sara spoke up and said that she wanted to go forward to look for Lizzy and Hannah. The rest agreed, including Millie. What a surprise? She always seemed to challenge them, then agrees to go along with their ideas.

"So that's it. We're going in." Katie's stomach did a quick somersault right before Cory Ann grabbed the knob and rushed in. So much for giving them a countdown to get ready.

The room was dark and quiet, but more disturbingly, it was empty. She wasn't sure what she had expected to find, but hoped it would've been Lizzy and Hannah. The closet door was open, and she peered into the back. Cory Ann went in and called back that the little door was also open, and she was going in.

Katie's breath bubbled up in her throat. The earlier experience must've left more of an impact than she thought because her mouth was dry, and her hands were shaking. She really didn't want to go into that small closet and definitely didn't want to go through the small door. Thankfully, before she moved, she heard Cory Ann call out to Lizzy. She waited to hear from Cory Ann but instead noticed her backing out of the small doorway and making her way back into Hannah's room.

"They're not there. It's just a dark area, and it had what looked like a shaft that went straight down. I think there might've been stairs, but I couldn't say for sure. I called out to Lizzy, but there was no answer. If they went down that shaft, then who knows where they are? I don't think we should go down there. It looks kinda dangerous Katie. Let's go downstairs and see if we can find out where that shaft goes and maybe we'll find them hiding somewhere. But I don't think they went this way."

"Okay, but at this point, I don't care who hears us. I say we go down and start calling out for them. This entire night has defied all logic and reason, so let's just do whatever is necessary to find them." Katie was dine with all of it. Their tactics hadn't worked for them so far, so it was time to change things up.

Everyone agreed and once again they all headed for the stairway. Katie started calling out before she reached the steps, just in case they were up there hiding in one of the other bedrooms. Disappointed, she made her way down with everyone else and hoped that they would find them soon.

CHAPTER 35

Hannah

The last thing she wanted to do was go back into her room, and she definitely didn't want to open the closet. But Lizzy thought that was their best option, so she buried her fears and went along with the plan. She was chewing the inside of her cheek raw as they moved closer to the back of the dark closet. She thought about Marci and Allie and wondered where they were and prayed that they were safe. Were they together, scared and alone, or with Stephanie? They should've looked harder for them. Were they looking for her and Lizzy now? She wouldn't blame them if they weren't because there was a threat out there. Lizzy and Katie suspected Millie had something to do with everything, but she wasn't so sure. How could Millie get away with kidnapping three people? Unless she had help. A shiver ran down Hannah's body, so she shook her head to push the unwanted thought out of her mind. She had to pay attention.

"Do you see anything?" Hannah waited for Lizzy to answer.

They both had their phone lights on, but it was still dark and creepy. She wanted to cry out for her mother, but knew that wouldn't help. She just wanted to be home in her own bed or at work. Anywhere but there.

"I see the small door and it's closed. I'm gonna open the door and look inside." Lizzy was giving Hannah a play-by-play because she knew she was anxious.

Before they moved into the closet, they stayed close to the bedroom door, hoping that they had just overacted about hearing a noise downstairs. They thought they were safe, but then heard footsteps. Without hesitation, they ran into the closet and were now facing that scary small door. They had to hurry because someone was coming. She wished she would've thought to lock the bedroom door, but she didn't think she did.

"Lizzy, I don't like this." Her nerves were on high alert.

"Me neither. But what choice do we have?"

When Hannah was next to Lizzy, they picked up the pace, crawling forward in the dark space. They were blindly moving forward, and then the floor disappeared from beneath them. They both tumbled down some kind of shaft and eventually landed on something soft at the bottom.

"Where are we? Are you okay?" Hannah jumped up, searching her own body for injuries.

"I'm good. You?" Lizzy fumbled around the ground for her phone that fell from her hand when she landed.

"I'm okay." She angled her phone light to shine on Lizzy. Aside from messy hair and flushed cheeks, she looked fine and in one piece.

"I lost my phone. Shine your light over here. What is this, a mattress? It is a mattress. It looks like the one we saw in the restaurant. Thank God it was here."

Hannah stopped her light a few feet in front of Lizzy.

"It's right there. Why would someone put a mattress down here? And where is down here? Do you think we're still in the house?" Hannah shined the light around the small room.

"Wait. Shine it back that way." Lizzy pointed to her left. "That looks like some kind of opening."

Hannah lit up the area and watched Lizzy walk over. "Please be careful. I don't know about you, but I didn't see that drop off until it was too late."

"It's some kind of tunnel. I wonder where it goes." Lizzy stared into the darkness.

"Look, there's another one to the right. Who does this? Who needs tunnels? This place is getting scarier by the minute." Hannah moved her light around the room.

"Look over there. It looks like a big laundry bin filled with sheets. I wonder if that was a laundry chute we fell down." Lizzy walked back to the base of the shaft. "There are stairs on one side of the shaft and the wall on the other side is slanted like a slide. Maybe the tunnels were here when the house was originally built, and they just converted the space into a laundry chute. Kinda makes sense if they have to change the sheets and linens every day."

"Let's just get out of here. Are we going back up the stairs or are we taking one of these tunnels?" Hannah wasn't happy with either of those options. Sweat pooled above her eyelids and on her forehead. "It's hot down here. Decide, because I don't like this one bit."

"I think we better take one of the tunnels." Lizzy didn't sound too convincing.

"Okay, which one? The one on the right is in line with the shaft we fell down, so let's take the one to the left of that. Maybe at least that one will lead us to the front of the house. What do you think? Because I really don't know?" Hannah didn't want to make the wrong decision.

"I think you're right, so let's go. My light's not working on my phone, so you either need to come in the front of me or hand me your phone."

"How about I get on side of you?" Hannah pulled in close next to Lizzy, looped her arm into hers, and handed over the phone. Her eyes stayed wide open, watching for any signs of danger. They moved slowly, neither one of them brave enough to go any faster.

Hannah hated the silence, so she whispered to Lizzy as they walked. "This is so scary. Where do you think we're headed? Do you think that was the guy from the veranda? Is he trying to hurt us? Maybe he was just another guest looking for help. I really want to go home."

It felt like they were walking forever, and they still hadn't found a way out yet.

"At least the tunnels are big enough to walk through. I wouldn't want to crawl around down here. No telling what else is down here with us. Do you still think that Millie is involved in all of this? I'm not so sure, because how could she do all of that alone? But maybe she has help. Wait, what if that's her guy? The guy on the veranda could be her guy." Hannah felt like she had a light bulb moment.

Aan elbow jabbed into Hannah's side, and she realized that Lizzy probably wanted her to shut up.

"I'm sorry, Lizzy, but I'm terrified, and I hate the silence. It's making me more nervous."

Lizzy immediately felt bad. "I know Hannah. I hate it too, but we need to hear if someone is coming. We have to be careful not to allow a surprise attack. And even though you're whispering, your voice is carrying throughout the tunnel. You're giving our location away. We're gonna be okay. We've been walking for a few minutes now, so we have to be close to getting out of here. Just hold on a few more minutes."

Hannah squeezed Lizzy's arm and shut her mouth.

"And yes, Hannah, I do think Millie is involved in all of this, and I pray she is working alone."

Hannah took a few deep breaths and tried to calm herself down. Lizzy was right that her babbling was putting them in danger. She was going to brave the silence, move onward, and trust Lizzy when she said that they were going to be okay. They had to be.

CHAPTER 36

Katie

She took her time going back down the stairs. She had hoped Lizzy and Hannah were still upstairs, but she'd called out to them and heard no reply. Were they unable to answer?, That thought had been lingering in the back of her mind. What if they were subdued somehow? She shook her shoulders, letting go of that terrifying thought. They were just together a few minutes ago, so she was sure they were find.

The tightness in her chest made it difficult to breathe, but she just couldn't seem to relieve it. That would continue as long as her friends were missing. Her anxiety level was already off the charts. Once they were all back down the stairs, they immediately called out. Searching quietly wasn't working, and she was afraid that time was running out to find them. Millie was the only one that they had saved so far and maybe that was because they got to her so quickly. She wondered why that was, because whoever grabbed her was holding her securely behind the closed door. So why was it so easy to get to her? The others disappeared in a split second during a moment of chaos. She really didn't want to suspect Millie, but there were all these red flags popping up at every turn.

She secretly stole a look as Millie searched like the rest. Maybe she wasn't behind their disappearance, and they were just separated from the group. That thought increased the urgency to find them before she could get her hands on them.

"Lizzy! Hannah!" Katie yelled down the hallway. Their voices echoed through the house. Were they even in the house? She didn't see which way they went when they all ran. For all she knew they could've ran to the highway for help. That idea was comforting.

They searched the tiny front room, unable to find the two that were missing. They really needed to move to the rest of the house and hopefully discover where that chute leads. She doubted they had gone that way, but couldn't be sure.

"Hey. I think we can safely say they are not in this room. Let's go on down the hall and see if we can find the bottom of that Laundry Chute. I know there's a lot of house to search but judging from where the bedroom closet is upstairs, this side looks to be directly under it or at least close." Katie started walking down the hall.

Cory Ann tugged on her arm to slow her down. "We need to check these rooms." She didn't want to pass them up just in case. They needed to be thorough in their search.

Katie stopped in front of two doors, one on each side of her. She wiggled the handle to her right while Cory

Ann checked the one on the left. Both opened but, after a quick search, were empty. They moved forward into a small kitchen area that was connected to another small room with a sofa and television. She realized that was the owners space. Obviously, they didn't always stay here because it was deserted now.

"Lizzy! Hannah!" Katie called out again.

"Hey look. There's coffee in the coffee pot. And look at the table. There's a plate of food and it looks fresh. Do you think someone's here?" Sara asked, hoping that's what it meant.

"It doesn't look like anyone's here." Millie stated the obvious.

"Sara, it's not like it's been days since someone was here. We just checked in about 10 hours ago and the place was filled. That's what I can't understand. Where are all the other guests? Do you think the other people in the restaurant were just dining and not staying in the house? That would account for some of the them." Katie shared her thoughts. "And if that's the case, how did they leave? Remember, that fallen tree had blocked the parking lot. I'm so confused. Everything that's happened since we got here is so strange and I'm having trouble making sense out of it. Like where did that lady go that was behind the counter? She was just gone y'all. And so was the man on the veranda. Although I didn't see him vanish, maybe he's still around. For all we know, they could all be apparitions." Katie sounded upset.

"Listen people. We can't worry about that right now. We have to find Lizzy and Hannah. So stop wasting time and let's go." Cory Ann's voice was commanding. She was starting to really worry that they weren't going to find them, and she couldn't accept that.

"You're right. Let's go." Katie simmered down and listened to Cory Ann.

Before she left the kitchen, Katie touched the coffee cup. It was still warm. She looked over at Sara and nodded that she was right, but none of that really mattered at the moment, so she got in line behind the rest of the group. They were at the end of the house with only two ways left to go. One was out the side door, and the other was through a door in the little television room.

"Which way?" She stood baffled. How did they find themselves all alone in this spooky plantation home, searching for several of her missing friends? She shook her head in disbelief.

"I don't think if that were a laundry chute it would go outside. Then again, maybe back in the day it did since they didn't have inside laundry rooms, or did they? I don't know, but we're gonna search both. Do ya wanna split up or do one at a time?" Cory Ann wasn't making that decision.

"I really think we should all stay together..."

"Katie, I think we should split up. There are seven of us, so at least three to a group. Me, Brittany and Demi will go check out the inside room and the four of y'all will go outside. I still think that would be safe enough.

We need to find them soon." Savannah hoped Katie would agree.

"Okay. If everyone else is okay with that, let's do it. Let's meet back on the veranda in a few minutes. Yell if y'all find anything and we'll do the same."

Katie heard an eerie voice in her head say, 'and now there are four.' She couldn't help wonder if this was some kind of plot to separate them, but it was Savannah who suggested it, not Millie. And Savannah was their friend. She wanted to find Lizzy and Hannah just as much as the rest of them. Katie was becoming more paranoid as time passed and she didn't know who to trust anymore. But she did know, and she trusted Savannah with her life.

They walked out the door and were surprised that it wasn't locked. Outside, there were a few covered walkways that went in a few different directions. She called out, joining the others. They were like ants running in every direction, desperately searching for any signs of life, not just for Lizzy and Hannah. She even found a pipe and was banging on the post to get attention. But it was deserted, just like the house was. There was still a steady rain, but without the lightning, the area was blanketed in darkness, making it difficult to see.

"It's not raining too hard anymore, so maybe we should get to the road and find help." Millie thought that would help.

"We're not leaving them. I know they're here somewhere. Keep looking, we have to find them. Then we can get to the road." Katie didn't even look at Millie when she answered. Did she even realize that she always said the wrong thing at the wrong time?

"I disagree. I think…" Millie's words were interrupted.

"We're not going, and neither are you. We're staying together." Katie stopped and looked at Millie this time. "Sorry Millie. I'm just so worried about Lizzy, Hannah, and the rest of them. I didn't mean to yell. It would be the perfect time to go toward the road, but I can't leave them. Not yet. And besides, I haven't heard a car pass on the road since we've been out here. It is like 4 o'clock in the morning. Please, can we just keep looking for them?" She tried to appeal to her compassionate side, if she even had one.

Millie forced a smile and said, "Sure. You're right, of course."

Katie was upset with herself for snapping at Millie. She definitely didn't trust her, but she didn't have any evidence to support her feelings. And she didn't want Millie to leave the group because then she wouldn't be able to monitor her. She needed to pull it together and try harder to hide her frustrations. That was always difficult for her, but this was too important to mess up. Hannah and Lizzy's lives depended on it, and she would not let them down. Not as long as she was able to keep looking.

CHAPTER 37

Lizzy

L izzy felt bad about telling Hannah to be quiet, but her babbling was making things more tense. And she really thought they needed to keep hidden just in case someone was following them. They'd walked for a few minutes and still hadn't found a way out. She didn't want to admit it, but maybe the tunnels were closed off a long time ago. Maybe they were headed to a dead end. God, she hoped no one was following them. She had to believe that they were going to get out and get back to the rest of the group.

Lizzy could hear a slight whimpering and knew that Hannah was upset. She understood because she wanted to whimper too. None of them were prepared for what they were facing, how could they be?

"I'm sorry Hannah. I didn't mean to jump on you." Lizzy tried to lift her spirits, but she was running low herself.

"I know. It's okay. I was just thinking about Allie, Marci, and Stephanie. Do you think they're okay? I'm terrified for them." Imagining life without her best friends was overwhelming.

"I don't know Hannah. I hope they are. We just need to focus on finding Katie and the group, okay?" Lizzy hated lying to Hannah, but she didn't think they were okay. She was really afraid of that possibility, but she needed to stay positive and push forward.

She kept walking and finally came to a door. She wanted to rush forward and open the door to get out of there, but something didn't feel right. They could be running right into trouble. She'd hoped that the tunnel would lead them to the outside, not another room. She heard Hannah sigh and understood completely. They discussed their options and decided to open the door and find out what was on the other side.

Lizzy hesitated for a second before placing her hand on the doorknob. She was about to turn it when she heard a loud noise. Jumping back, she grabbed onto Hannah and tried to melt into the darkness of the tunnel walls. Panic stricken, she squeezed her eyes shut and held onto her breath.

"What was that?" Lizzy felt the words Hannah spoke because she was so close.

"I don't know." She whispered. "Just wait a few minutes and see if we hear it again."

The noise rang out and this time it sounded like someone hitting a post. The sound was coming from behind them. Lizzy swung around and pointed the light in that direction. They walked back toward the sound and then heard another hit, this time above them. Someone was purposely making noise.

"I think that could be Katie and the others looking for us. Hannah, find something to make noise with. Hurry, feel around for something, anything." Hannah searched around the area she was standing in and there wasn't anything there. "I saw some bricks when we first entered the tunnel, but that's a ways back."

"Lizzy stop. What if it's not them? Maybe it's a trap."

"I don't think so, Hannah. Why would someone make noise and bring attention to where they were if they didn't want to be found? Whoever took the others has to know that there are still nine of us left and wouldn't just reveal themselves. And I mean maybe, but I really think that it's the group searching for us. We need to make some noise."

Lizzy headed in the opposite direction. She remembered that there was another tunnel and maybe that was the way out. Something about going into that room didn't feel right, anyway. The chills that ran up her body was a warning not to be ignored.

"Come on, before they leave." Lizzy was running now.

"Okay, but I'm not so sure it's them." Hannah was reluctant, but followed Lizzy anyway.

They reached the entrance to the tunnel and found the bricks that she'd remembered seeing. She picked up a few and tossed them up to the roof of the tunnel. Thankfully, the ceiling was low, allowing the bricks to make an impact. She ran back into the room they'd fallen into and found a long pipe on the floor. She ran back to the place where she heard the last noise and started hitting the ceiling with the pole. At first she just hit the ceiling a bunch of times in a row, but then she started singing the song, 'You are my sunshine' and tapping the ceiling to that beat. Katie and Cory Ann always teased her because she loved that song, and they would know it was her.

Lizzy repeated that sequence several times before she stopped and listened. Dead silence filled the tunnel again. The tapping had stopped, and they were too late. She continued to tap the sequence all the way back to the room they'd dropped into. Eventually, she let the pipe drop to the ground and covered her face with her hands in defeat. They would never get out of there. She walked back into the room and flopped down onto the mattress. She was so tired and wasn't sure she had the strength to continue on.

When they were walking through the tunnel, it felt like they had walked forever, but running back only took them a couple of minutes at the most. She glanced at the other tunnel, wondering if that one led outside. Exhaustion was setting in, and Lizzy wanted to just lay back and give up. She rocked back and forth, trying to motivate herself to move. She almost screamed when Hannah jumped up and yelled something.

Startled, she looked at Hannah to see what was happening.

"Lizzy. Look! Steps. There are steps going back up. Some sort of ladder." Hannah was shining her light on the chute they'd fallen down. "Look. We can climb back out. Come on let's go back up. Whoever was there before must be going by now."

Lizzy sprung to her feet. How'd she miss that? They can get back up to the room and get out. But what if Hannah was wrong and whoever was there was waiting for them? Maybe they should just try the other tunnel first. They'd been down there for a few minutes now. Lizzy was anxious about making the wrong decision. She should've handled the situation better, but she never claimed to be brave or a leader. Making decisions that involved others' safety made her uncomfortable. She didn't even want to make her own decisions.

"What do you think we should do, Hannah?" Her mouth was dry, zero saliva left in her mouth.

"I think we need to go back up and run out of the house without stopping. Maybe use the element of surprise to give us leverage. I say we slowly, and quietly, go up the ladder, then run as fast as we can without stopping. But we need to hold on to each other. We cannot get separated. We can't let go, okay? I know going down the stairs in the dark will be challenging, but we can do it. We'll just go slower on the way down." Hannah's voice was nothing short of enthusiastic.

"Wow. I should've let you make all the decisions. I agree. We definitely need to be quick and under no circumstances do we let go of each other." Lizzy could see the horror in Hannah's eyes. "We can do this. I won't ever let go of you. I promise."

She was just as afraid, but it was a great idea. Enough time had passed that hopefully the person who chased them down there had given up and went to search for them in a different direction. She prayed that was true. It had to be true.

"Do you want me to go first, or do you want to?" Lizzy stood anxiously.

"I guess I can go first. But you need to be right behind me, like right with me. Once we see that it's clear up there, we have to go. I know I already said that, but I'm kinda scared now that this is not the better choice."

"Hannah, it is the best choice." Lizzy grabbed her hand to reassure her. "We can do this. And in a few minutes, we're gonna be back in the restaurant with the others. Let's go!"

"That's supposed to make me feel better?" Hannah chuckled. "I'm just kidding. The thought of being stuck in the restaurant again is not so comforting, but being back with the others is, so let's do this on three."

Lizzy nodded, waiting for Hannah to count down. She was ready and waited as Hannah grabbed onto the first rung of the ladder. The speed of her heart picked up as if it weren't already maxed out. She patted her chest and silently thanked it for holding on so far. Just a little longer and we're gonna be out of here.

CHAPTER 38

Katie

Relieved that Millie agreed to stay together and not leave, Katie turned her attention back to their search. She'd hoped that hitting on the post would get some attention, but there was still no sign of Lizzy or Hannah. She and the group, well half of the group now, continued to search the grounds. Finally, she suggested they go back inside and see if the second half found anything. She knew she was grasping at straws because they would've yelled if they found anything, but with the lack of a better plan, she headed to the door. Optimism was a rare thing right then.

Maybe they got out when she did, but ran to the road instead. She doubted they would leave like that, but who knows what could've forced them in that direction It might've been their best option. Maybe the only option.

She was the last one, but before she walked in, she thought she heard a noise. A lot of noise, actually. She turned back in the direction she'd just come from. The walkway was dark, but the sounds were radiating up from the ground. Katie stood completely still and listened. She heard three quick taps, then 1 more, and that repeated.

Morse code. It sounded like morse code. She ran back into the darkness and tried to locate the sound. Again, the same sounds.

"Oh my God! Y'all come back. It's them. Listen. They heard me hitting the post. It's them." Katie could hear the tapping right under her feet, and it was moving toward the house. She started humming to the tapping sound and teared up when she put words to it.

"You are my sun-shine! My on -ly sun-shine! It's them! It's Lizzy. She loves that song." Katie's heart was bursting with hope. "They're under this walkway." She ran to grab the pipe she'd used earlier but couldn't locate it. Frustration had caused her to toss it, and the darkness hindered her search.

She looked back at the door and then to the other end of the walkway. The walkway looked like it ended close to that old storm cellar Katie was looking at when she'd arrived.

"Look at the old storm cellar. Could they be in there? It looks like it has storm doors over the opening. Maybe they made their way there, and can't get out. Maybe it has a lock on the doors. We gotta go see." Sara hated the thought of going over there, but they had to.

"Listen. It stopped. The sound stopped over here by the house. I think we should go back inside as originally planned and see what the others have found. That storm cellar looks kind of creepy." Millie was trying to persuade them to go back inside.

Katie had a feeling that Millie didn't want them to go into that storm cellar. What was she hiding? Or was she just overreacting again? It made sense to follow the sounds, and that led them back to the house. She glanced back at the storm cellar, then turned and walked back to the house. Relief washed over her because, truth be told, she did not want to go into that cellar. Ever!

"I think Millie is right. The sounds stop here. Come on, let's go find Savannah and the rest of them. Maybe they found something."

They entered the house and were back in the kitchen area where the others were standing.

"We were just getting ready to head to the veranda to meet y'all. We didn't find anything down here. What about y'all? Savannah saw the look of hope on Katie's face extinguish.

"We didn't see anything, but we heard a tapping sound. It was Lizzy. It sounded like it was underground and headed back in this direction." Katie's face lit up. "A tunnel! I bet there's a tunnel that leads from the house." She continued like a light bulb just went off in her mind. "The closet! That's it! The closet must lead to a tunnel. That's how the person who grabbed Millie must be getting in and out. It has to be there, I know it!"

Katie didn't wait for the others, but instead ran down the hall to the stairway. She couldn't believe she missed that. Although, none of them except Millie had been on the other side of that small closet door. It was too dark to see anything except Millie, who was unconscious, and once they pulled her out, they shut the door. That had to be it. They went into the closet and found a tunnel. The room had to be there for a reason. Overwhelmed with anxiety, she prayed she was right. She was positive that Lizzy was signaling them with that song. Her favorite song.

She stopped at the bottom of the stairs when doubt suddenly slammed into her mind. She had no idea where that came from, but she was now second guessing herself. Her thoughts were foggy, and she felt off balanced, drugged even. She leaned against the wall. When her head settled, she saw Demi coming toward her.

"Are you okay?" Demi went on. "Girl, you scared me. You look like you saw a ghost. What happened? Maybe you need to sit down a minute."

"I'm okay. I guess I'm just exhausted." She glanced up the stairway. "What if I'm wrong? I know I heard Lizzy tapping. I'm positive it was her. But what if they're not up here? We have to go and look, right?" She was desperate for someone, anyone, to tell her what to do next."

"Are you sure? I mean, how did you get a song from tapping sounds? And even if it were them, why would they come back into the house?" Millie was staring at Katie, trying to cast her usual doubt.

Katie glared back and wondered what she was up to. Millie was in the back of the group and apparently didn't agree with her decisions. A few minutes ago, she didn't want her to go into the storm cellar and now she didn't want her to go upstairs into that closet. Another round of fog clouded her brain. Something's not right and whatever was going on had to do with Millie. She was manipulating her thoughts! She had to know!

"What are you doing?" Katie was walking toward Millie. "What are you up to, Millie? Why don't you want me to go upstairs? What are you hiding?" She was getting clearer with each step. "I know you have something to do with all of this. Why? What are you doing?" She was yelling at that point.

"I don't know what you're talking about. Katie, you've been giving me a hard time for a while now. I've been with you the whole time, so how could I have something to do with any of this? I'm not the one that left my friends behind." Millie was returning the fire.

Katie was almost face to face with Millie when she heard movement upstairs. She turned back to face the steps and tried to hear. When she turned back to the group, Millie was gone.

"Where is she?" Katie screamed out for Millie. "Where did she go? Millie? Did y'all see anything?" She swore not to let her out of her sight. She was dangerous and for whatever reason didn't want them to find the others. It was typical though, just when they were about to go upstairs and find them Millie disappears. That's proof enough of her guilt.

Katie started down the hallway, but stopped. She wants me to go after her. Looking at the others scrambling to look for Millie angered her. She'd been playing them the whole time. Why hadn't she listened to her instincts when she was sure Millie was up to something? But she couldn't figure out how she got away with any of it while she was right there with them. The fog in her brain lifted, and she started to think more clearly. The sound. Lizzy and Hannah. Katie ran back to the stairway and started up-ward taking two steps at a time. When she reached the top, she smacked into someone and almost lost her balance, falling backwards, but something grabbed her and pulled her to the top. A hand.

Katie screamed.

CHAPTER 39

Hannah

The idea of getting out of the pitch black room made her feel hopeful. How had they missed the ladder? It was dark, but they'd looked around before leaving the room and taking the tunnel. Going into another tunnel made her stomach crawl, so she was grateful she didn't have to. She was not the claustrophobic type, but was feeling stuck and uncomfortable. She'd noticed that Lizzy was about to go berserk and had been jittery since they'd fallen. Hopefully, the person they heard earlier was long gone and had forgotten all about them.

Fatigue had seized both her and Lizzy, but she prayed they had enough strength left to make it up the ladder and would be able to run out of the house. She smirked at the thought that it had only been a few hours since they'd arrived because it felt like days. It felt like days since she'd eaten. It felt like days since she'd slept. Heck, it felt like days since she'd peed. And it felt like days since she'd been able to sit down and relax. Hannah was so overwhelmed, instead of scared, she was angry. The more she fumed over her circumstances, the more energetic she got.

"Lizzy, are you ready? I want to go now!" Her voice was more commanding than questioning.

Lizzy reached out and grabbed onto Hannah's hand and nodded yes.

"Okay. Here we go. Love ya Lizzy. We're gonna be okay, right?" She didn't wait for a response.

Hannah took hold of the railing and climbed up the first rung, letting go of Lizzy's hand.

She looked down. "I guess we can't hold on and climb at the same time. So when we reach the top, we'll regroup. Just stay close."

"I'm right on you, girl, keep moving." Lizzy was not letting Hannah get too far ahead. They were on their way to freedom and that though exhilarated her.

She ascended the ladder slowly, keeping a close watch on her surroundings and being careful not to fall. She took comfort knowing that Lizzy was right behind her, but was weary of what they'd find at the top. More darkness was expected, but she'd hoped that the room would be empty.

Hannah stopped for a moment when the image of that porcelain doll crossed her mind. She felt paralyzed. Her mind took off on a run and she didn't know how to get control of it, but she had to. She felt Lizzy tug on the back of her shirt.

"Hey. What's wrong? Keep moving."

Hannah's mouth was suddenly dry, making it hard to swallow. Her palms were sweating, causing her grip on the ladder to slip, but she was able to grab on before falling. Leaning onto the ladder for support, she shut her eyes and silently screamed. After a few seconds, she reminded herself that it was just a small porcelain doll and that all she had to do was kick it and it would go flying away from her. It didn't matter if the dolls could talk, walk, or crawl. They were small. A lot smaller than her!

She felt a hand on her leg and looked down at Lizzy. They had to move, and she was holding them up. She reached up with a trembling hand and latched onto the next rung of the ladder. As she moved forward, she focused all her thoughts of getting to the top and then back with her friends. A sadness enveloped her when she thought of Allie, Marci, and Stephanie. Tears welled up in her eyes and she had to fight them back to see. She wiped her face on her sleeve and put those thoughts away for later. Getting out of there had to be top priority, so she willed her mind to get on board with that.

She reached deep inside herself and mustered up the courage to push forward. Suddenly, filled with daring determination and a little angst, she moved quickly, almost racing upward to the top. She was grateful that Lizzy followed suit, and finally they were both safely sitting on the floor behind the closet.

"Are you okay?" Lizzy was staring at her.

"No. But I am getting out of here. I want to go home and no stupid doll or anyone else is going to stop me. Are you okay?"

"No. But I'm with you. Let's get out of here. After I catch my breath." Lizzy was panting. "Where'd you get that burst of energy from? At one point, I thought I was going to have to shove you up the ladder.

Hannah smiled because she had surprised herself. She often wondered what she would do in a scary or dangerous situation and was delighted that she showed bravery in such a strong manner. But her smile quickly flopped because she knew that this was only the beginning, and she would have to endure a lot more before they were away from that place and safely back at home. She allowed herself a brief moment to be afraid, then conjured up that courage again to keep going. They had to keep going. They were almost there. Daylight was coming then they'd be safe.

"All I know is that we are getting out of here and if that means I have to be brave, then I will for as long as it takes. I'm done waiting for someone to come and save us. I miss Allie and I really want to find her. Marci and Stephanie too." Hannah's soft voice was filled with confidence.

"Look at you with all that tenacity. Who knew you had that in you, Hannah? Well, you seem to be ready to take on anything, so let's go find the others. You can lead." Lizzy was finally able to catch her breath and stand up.

With her newfound confidence slipping a little, Hannah's hand shook as she reached for the closet door. She turned the knob slowly and prayed that the dumb doll wouldn't be there. She yanked open the door as if she were ripping off a band aid, swiftly. She stared into the darkness and shuddered. Using the same band aid philosophy, she grabbed Lizzy's hand and almost dove through the closet, exploding into the bedroom.

She shuddered at the sound of movement in the back of the closet. Reaching back, she slammed the closet door shut and immediately ran to the dresser to push it in front of the door to block it from opening. Doll or no doll, this exit was closed!

"Whoa. Hannah, I could've helped you push the dresser had you asked. Are you sure you're okay?"

Hannah shot a look of defiance toward the blocked closet door, then back over to Lizzy. "Did you hear that noise? I think someone is following us again. I told you that, no, I'm not okay, but I'm done being a victim. There's no one coming to help us. I don't understand any of what's going on, but I do know that no one's coming! Except Katie and Cory Ann. I think they are looking for us, but again, they're in the same predicament we're in, so after we find them, we still need to find a way out of here." She glanced over to the closed bedroom door. "Are you ready to go find our friends?"

Hannah walked to the door, and this time opened it slowly, just in case someone was out there. They had made it this far, and she didn't want to put them in danger by being sloppy. She pulled on the knob and its creaking noise sounded throughout the empty house. They waited, looking for any kind of movement that would suggest that they were not alone. She took that minute to regroup and prepare to face their next challenge, the stairs.

The room was dark and just as quiet. She could hear a few rumbles in the distance and figured they were in for yet another round of unexplained storms. The idea that Demi and the others said that it wasn't raining at all until after they'd arrived was outrageous. So if it was only raining where they were, then they could run to the highway for safety. Unless the storms were following them, a thought that at one time would seem bizarre, but not now, they could walk away from the dreadful weekend and get help.

Hannah jumped when she felt Lizzy's hand on her arm again.

"You scared me. You've got to stop sneaking up on me. Give me some kind of warning, please." Hannah clutched her chest. She fumbled for her phone light and, once it was on, flashed it at Lizzy. "It looks like we're alone. Up here at least. Do you need another minute to catch your breath, again?"

Just then, they heard voices from the downstairs area. The sounds were faint, but it was definitely people talking. Hannah felt Lizzy crouch down behind her and yank on her arm to do the same. Somehow it felt safer closer to the floor. She flipped off her light and waited. It sounded like the voices were moving away from the stairway. Her heart skipped a beat when she realized it could be the group looking for them, but she had to be sure before reacting. She crawled across the room to the top of the stairway, staying low, hoping to stay hidden from sight. Looking back to reassure that Lizzy was close behind, she moved forward until she reached the edge of the stairs and then paused.

"Listen, do you hear that? It sounds like several voices. Do you think it's Katie and the others looking for us? What do we do?" Hannah was about to burst with anticipation because the suspense was killing her. But they had to be sure before they exposed their location.

Before she had time to decide, someone had made their way back to the bottom of the stairs, said their names, and was bolting up to the top without hesitation. Realizing that it was Katie, Hannah jumped up and collided with her as she reached the top. The force and shock made Katie off balance and when she was about to tumble backwards, Hannah reached her hand out and pulled her back to the floor. Then another body plopped down on top of them.

"Katie! It's really you! Thank God!" Lizzy was hugging them both from the top of the pile. Her heart swelled with happiness.

"Okay Lizzy, I can't breathe." Hannah was trying to push them off of her. She relaxed for a minute more and endured the crushing of her body because she was overjoyed to have been rescued.

The three of them scrambled to their feet and Hannah turned just in time to see Cory Ann rushing up the stairs, followed by the rest of the group. Her heart was so full.

"Y'all came! Katie, you came looking for us. I knew you would!" Hannah threw her arms around Katie, again and squeezed tightly in appreciation.

"Did you really think we were going to leave y'all? Katie squeezed Hannah back. "Come on Hannah, you had to know that I would never leave you two behind. Never!

"I'm so glad to see all of you!" Hannah walked around, hugging them one at a time.

"Wait! Where's Millie?" Lizzy was frantic as she looked from one face to the next. "Where is she?"

Hannah listened as Katie pushed away from her and, with a grim look on her face, told them that Millie was trying to keep them from coming upstairs. Then, when they questioned her about her motives, she ran away from the group.

Katie sighed. "I don't know where she is. But we're going to find her."

"I'm right here," Hannah gasped as Millie's voice reached the top of the steps.

She turned and stared along with the others, unsure what to do next. She watched as Millie stepped onto the top step where they were all standing, then she leaped forward and hugged her too. Hannah didn't care about the gasps she'd heard spreading across the room. She was just too happy to care about anything. And besides, if Millie was up here, then she couldn't have been the person behind the closet door, She was sure of that.

CHAPTER 40

Katie

Millie was standing at the top of the steps, and Lizzy watched as Hannah went over and hugged her. Surprise took hold of her, and she became completely still for a moment. She knew Hannah was just as suspicious of Millie as she was, so why hug her? Why act glad to see her? As time passed, Katie grew angrier, but she didn't want to make a scene. She wanted them to all move to the restaurant where she felt the safest. And she wanted them to move before something else separated them again. She was positive that was how the person causing all of this worked. They created chaos then struck. She was going to get this message to everyone so they can be prepared for the next attack.

"Can we go now? We gotta hurry back to the restaurant. The thunder is getting louder, so another round of storms must be nearby." Katie stepped between Millie and Hannah to separate them. She turned to talk to the group, but of course Millie spoke up first.

"Maybe we should just stay put. It's already almost 5 am and the sun will be up soon. I thought that was the plan, Katie, to wait until the sun comes up, then run out of here." Millie had a satisfying look on her face.

Katie moved to within inches of Millie's face before saying a word. Her eyes glared into Millie's, and she could swear she was looking into deep dark holes. Emptiness. There was only emptiness.

"Where were you?" Katie's stare intensified. "And why do you always insist on suggestion the opposite of what ever I say? Why?"

"I was right behind you. After you accused me again, I went down the hall to cool off for a second, then came right back." Millie stepped closer to Katie." And I was just reminding you of your own plan."

"No, you didn't! I almost ran after you, but decided that was what you wanted. You were trying to separate us again. What are you up to, Millie? Huh? We are on to you, so you might as well come clean."

Millie's stance softened, and her tone changed. "Katie, how many times do I have to tell you I had nothing to do with the stuff that's happening? You know I've been with you all the time. Listen, I understand you are upset, but please stop taking it out on me. I'm not to blame here. I came to have fun with you guys, not to hurt anyone. Besides, what reason would I have to hurt any of you? Especially Marci. She's been nothing but nice to me."

Katie kept her firm stance but backed up just a smidge. She was lying and Katie knew it, but she couldn't prove anything. And clearly, Millie would not admit to anything. She wasn't sure what to do next, but one thing was for sure, she hadn't changed her mind about Millie being guilty for everything that had happened. Against her better judgment, she backed up and waited until later to bring this up again. The most important thing right now was staying together and getting back to the restaurant.

"What do y'all think we should do?" Katie held up her hand when everyone spoke at once. "One at a time, okay? Savannah, what do you think?"

"I think we need to get out of here as soon as possible. But I have to pee, so should we all take turns while things are calm? The bathroom's right there."

"Okay, let's go to the bathroom before we leave, but again go in twos." Katie waited for Savannah and Brittany to head to the bathroom. "Demi, what do you think we should do?"

Demi threw her hands up in the air. "I don't know. I guess I felt better at the restaurant. I just feel trapped up here."

"How about you Sara?"

"I agree with Demi. I know those creepy dolls were in the restaurant, but at least we have several ways to get out of the restaurant. I feel like it's one way in and one way out up here." She glanced back toward Hannah's room. "Well, maybe there's another way, but I'm not going into that closet. I really need to pee, too, so, Demi, will you go next with me? Whatever y'all decide, I'm good with."

Katie heard the toilet flush and nodded for the two of them to go.

"Cory Ann, any thoughts?"

"You know I have a few. Oh, you mean about what to do next, sorry." She forced a smile at Lizzy, daring her not to laugh.

Lizzy chuckled. "Wow, you sound calm. Maybe it's you who's hiding something after all. Let's hear it. Give us your thoughts on what to do next, please. We're all sitting here in suspense waiting to hear what you have to say." She felt some of her anger start to slip away.

"I say, we all use that bathroom then get out of here. It might look like I'm calm, but my stomach is in knots girl. Getting safely back to the Westbank and out of danger is my goal. Wait, did I just say 'Westbank' and 'safe' in the same sentence? Never dreamed I'd be running there to feel safe. Who knew?" Cory Ann was rattling on.

Demi and Sara returned from the bathroom and Cory Ann declared she was next. Katie met Cory Ann's stare, nodded, and prayed that she had read her correctly.

"Come on Millie, you're with me." Cory Ann pulled Millie toward the bathroom.

"I don't need to go."

"Well, I do, and I need a partner. So, come on." She wasn't taking no for an answer.

As soon as the door shut, Katie huddled the others. She needed to make sure they were all on board with her, and all knew that Millie was a danger.

"Listen, we need to go back to the restaurant. I think we all agree, right? Millie is hiding something, and I have no doubt she took Allie, Marci, and Stephanie. Hannah, why would you hug her?" Katie knew she had little time, but she couldn't help but ask.

"I didn't want to let her know I agree with you. We have to keep her close. If she is dangerous, then I don't want to be the one to upset her." Hannah aggressively defended her actions.

"Did y'all find anything up here? Anything suspicious? And how did y'all end up underground?" Katie wanted to know just in case things got out of hand and they ended up there.

Lizzy answered. "When you ran off, we ran up here and into the closet. We heard a noise, so we went through the small door in the back. It was so dark, and we tumbled down a shaft of some kind. It led to two different tunnels. We made our way to a door at the end of one of them, then we heard banging above us. Was that y'all? Lizzy looked at Katie, who nodded.

"I heard you. You Are My Sunshine, right?" Katie smiled. "I know that's your song!"

"Yes! I prayed you got that. When we first heard the knocking sound, I ran back to the room searching for something to make noise with, but we thought we were too late. Hannah noticed that there was a ladder, so we decided to come back up here and hoped the room was vacant. After we made our way back up and through the closet, we thought we heard someone coming behind us."

"Millie! I'm telling y'all, Millie is behind all of this. She ran down the hall and was gone for several minutes.

Where do you think that doorway at the end of the tunnel led to?"

"I can't be sure, but I guessed it ended around the old storm cellar you were staring at in the yard." Lizzy winced. "I do not want to go back if that's what you are thinking. I just want to get out of here."

Katie wasn't sure what she was thinking. "I bet that was Millie y'all heard coming. She probably ran out the back door to the storm cellar and was coming after y'all. Then when she heard us find y'all, she ran back over here acting like she was close the whole time. I don't want to go there either, but what if …"

"What if what?" Cory Ann was alerting Katie that they were back.

"What if it pours down raining again, and we get stuck over here?" Just as if on cue, thunder boomed, followed by lightning strikes. She felt like she was in some silly sitcom and every time she would say a keyword, like thunder, the crew would unleash thunder sounds.

"Also, I wanted to give everyone a heads up. I believe that whoever is behind all of this is creating a distraction that sends us into a frenzy, then strikes. Please be aware and as hard as it is to do, don't act without thinking first. Your life might just depend on it."

Katie stopped talking, keeping her true thoughts to herself. She was going to say, what if that's where Allie, Marci, and Stephanie were? It made sense because the storm cellar was between the two buildings they had oc-cupied throughout the night. Marci went missing first when they were running across the lawn to the restaurant. It all happened so quickly, meaning Marci had to be in a place close by. But did Millie have time to drag Marci there and get back with no one noticing she was gone? It was so dark and chaotic that the answer was probably. She knew it seemed impossible, but her gut was telling her that it wasn't, not for Millie.

Katie realized the others were watching her, so she pulled her lips up into a small smile and said, "Is it my turn to use the bathroom?"

She, Lizzy, and Hannah darted into the bathroom and shut the door. Katie continued to talk while they all peed, and once she had voiced her additional concerns, they walked out, and she suggested it was time to go back to the restaurant. Once they were safely inside, she would come up with a plan to get into that cellar and see if she was right. And she knew down in her bones she was right.

CHAPTER 41

Lizzy

Lizzy was surprised at how vocal Katie was about her feelings toward Millie. She felt the same way, but didn't want to poke a hornet's nest. If Millie was behind everything, then she was a danger to them all. She was glad that it was finally 5am and prayed for things to remain calm until daybreak. Originally, the plan was that at first light, rain or shine, they were going to run out of there as fast as they could. Now, Katie had thrown them a curve when she said that she thought the missing girls were in that old storm cellar.

Lizzy remembered seeing that storm cellar and was not looking forward to going near it, much less inside. But Katie had a point. It was centrally located and the perfect place to hide a body. Or bodies, in their case. She wanted desperately to find them, but thought maybe it would be best if they went for help instead. She knew Katie wasn't going to wait and would insist that they go check it out themselves. And she also knew that she would stay and assist in the search.

Lizzy tossed ideas around, trying to come up with the best way to approach the new dilemma. They could be walking right into a trap. She squeezed her eyes tight, trying to recall if she saw Millie with them for the last few hours. Katie said that she ran off right before they were found, and they definitely heard someone coming behind them in the closet. Was there enough time to run out of the house, into that storm cellar, through the tunnel, then up the ladder? Then she'd had to run back through, back into the house, then up the stairs. Lizzy was skeptical about the whole thing, but with the recent bizarre happenings, she didn't completely dismiss the idea that Millie could've done it. If the porcelain dolls could walk and talk, then anything was possible.

She shook her head, trying to get some clarity. No one was going to believe any of this and if she was being honest with herself, she wasn't sure what she believed to be true. The others were looking at her, waiting to make a move, but she didn't want to make the wrong decision. Ultimately, she believed they were better off at the restaurant. Once they were safely there, they could discuss their options and make a plan.

"Is everyone ready?" Lizzy looked around at all their faces and wanted to cry. "I'm not gonna lie. I'm really scared, but it's almost daylight. That will give us a whole new perspective on things, so we just have to hold on until then. Does anyone have anything to say before we go?"

Lizzy watched as Millie started to open her mouth, but Katie grabbed her hand and squeezed it tight with a warning. She didn't want any more bickering, and frankly, she didn't care what Millie had to say.

"Okay. Let's go. Once we all get down the stairs, we need to grab onto each other and make a run for the restaurant." She glared at Millie. "Are we clear? Grab on and do not let go!"

Lizzy approached the top of the stairway and immediately prayed that would be the last time she saw that stupid stairway. She felt like she'd run up and down them a hundred times already. She took the steps slowly, one at a time, trying to see ahead in the dark. The house was dead silent, aside from the rain that had started up again, causing a pitter-pattering sound on the roof. She wondered how every time they were to run outside; the rain had suddenly appeared to make things more dramatic. She was so consumed by her thoughts that she hadn't realized she'd reached the bottom and tumbled forward. Shaken back to reality, she watched as the others made it safely down and then, as a group, they headed to the door. They were almost there. All that was left was to run across the water soaked lawn.

She was feeling more optimistic until she opened the front door, and the pitch black darkness of the night slapped her in the face. At least inside the house there were small lights scattered around to cut some of the darkness, but outside was a different story. Fear started to sneak in as she remembered the last time they had all made a run to the restaurant, Marci went missing.

Lizzy took a step back and froze. She considered Katie's warning that the chaos was intentional, and believed she was spot on. Someone was playing with them and forcing their hand.

Surprisingly, no one urged her forward. She knew they were all just as weary of going out the door as she was, but they had to go. Hands wrapped around her arm, and she felt a sudden rush of relief. She wasn't alone and as long as they were all together; they were safe. Without looking back, she stepped forward again and took off running. Just as suspected, the rain had intensified and was coming down hard. When the first raindrop hit her, she realized it was actually hailing. She almost laughed out loud because she wondered how things could get worse and running in hail was definitely worse. It hurt too!

Once she reached the veranda of the restaurant, she turned to wait for the others. Everyone joined her except Katie and Cory Ann. Terror rose up into her throat and almost knocked her off her feet. Why? Why would they do something so foolish?

"No! What are you doing? Stop, Katie!" She watched in horror as the light from a phone radiated toward the storm cellar.

Without thinking, Lizzy ran off the veranda and in that direction. Hannah and the others called out to her, and even though she was only a few steps away from the veranda, she couldn't see them. She fumbled with her phone as she ran and yelled out to Katie and Cory Ann to wait for her. She wondered if Millie had stayed with the group and what she would do next. Was anyone keeping an eye on her?

"Wait for me!" Lizzy kept yelling until she reached the storm cellar.

"Why did you come? Who's gonna watch Millie?" Katie shouted over the sound of hail pounding the ground.

"My thoughts exactly. I don't know, but I wasn't gonna let y'all go in there alone." Her voice quivered as she stared at the doors. "Do you really think they're in there?" The last place on earth she wanted to be was in an old, dark, musty storm cellar. Did people use these things any longer? Her body started to shake, crying out for her to run the other way. Katie and Cory Ann were out of their minds, but she knew it was the right thing to do.

Katie didn't hesitate with her answer. "Yes. I'm positive now." She was staring at something straight ahead of her.

"What does that mean?" Cory Ann looked confused.

"Y'all don't see her?" Katie was staring at the side of the doorway, awestruck.

"See who?" Lizzy followed Katie's gaze. "See who Katie? I don't see anything."

"The lady. She's right there." Katie pointed this time.

Lizzy and Cory Ann looked at each other and were speechless.

Katie let her gaze drop to them. "The ghost I saw earlier. She just appeared and told me to hurry. She said that we didn't have much time. I know it sounds crazy, but I think she's trying to help us." There wasn't an ounce of apprehension in her voice.

Lizzy kept staring, trying to see what Katie had seen, but all she saw was rain, hail and darkness. Her legs trembled when she realized they were about to enter the creepy storm cellar to look for their missing friends. Conflicting emotions consumed her, making her want to scream, but she figured no one was listening. So, she took the deepest breath ever preparing herself for what was about to happen. She took up position behind Cory Ann and said a quick prayer. They were going to need all the help they could get.

CHAPTER 42

Katie

When she ran toward the storm cellar, the last thing she'd expected was to see a ghost. The first time she'd appeared, Katie wasn't even sure the vision was real, but now she had no doubt that this dark complected older woman standing there was not of her world. What she wasn't sure of was what a ghost would want from her?

Initially, she was apprehensive about going inside the storm cellar, but now a strange comfort showered her, and she knew what she had to do. Her friends were in there, hopefully okay, and she needed to get to them. She had mixed emotions about Lizzy showing up because while she felt better having her by her side, that left the others alone with Millie. They were capable of taking care of themselves, but she wasn't sure they were as suspicious as she, Lizzy, and Cory Ann were of Millie. She couldn't worry about that now because, according to her new ghostly friend, they were running out of time. Her choice had been made for her.

She stared down at the padlock once again and was thankful to find it partially open. Someone had been there recently. Removing the padlock proved easier than pulling open the doors. After tugging a few times, the door released, and she let it swing open. Spider webs sporadically covered the entrance, causing her anxiety level to spike because she hated spiders. Cory Ann reached up and swatted the ones hanging in their way and pushed past Katie.

There were stairs leading down into the darkness. She was adding long, dark stairs to her list of things she hated.

"Are we really going down there?" Lizzy already knew the answer was yes, but couldn't help but ask anyway. A small part of her hoped the answer was no.

"I think we have to if we want to save our friends. Maybe we should keep one person here by the door, just in case." Katie was unsure what was best, thought that it might be good to have a look out person. If they knew that Millie was coming, it could make a huge difference. She wasn't positive a warning would change things, but it couldn't hurt.

"I'm not staying here by myself. I go where you go." Lizzy grabbed onto Katie's shirt.

"I agree. We stay together. So let's get this over with." Cory Ann started to make her way down the steps.

All three of them had their phone lights on and after only about ten steps, they reached the ground floor. Katie immediately noticed a light shining from the far side of the room and headed slowly in that direction. Cory Ann reached out and pulled her to a stop.

"Listen, did you hear that?" Cory Ann turned her head toward the sound.

Katie refocused her eyes and tried to look further into the room, but it was too dark to really see anything. She heard a shuffling sound and prayed that it wasn't a mouse. She didn't like them either. Once it was quiet again, they moved forward. Her heart was pounding so loud she would swear it was on the outside of her chest instead of inside. She shined her light around the large, cluttered room as she walked, careful not to trip. She didn't want to have to be carried out of there and needed her legs to co-operate in case she suddenly needed to run. That's not that farfetched because it felt like she'd been running all day.

When she reached the source of the light, she wasn't surprised to find a door.

"This must open to the tunnels." Katie whispered to Lizzy. "This must be the door you found when y'all were down here. Look, it's not closed all the way."

She pulled on the door and, as expected, it opened up to a long tunnel. "You said it was closed when y'all reached the other side, right?" Katie thought that was what they told her.

"It was definitely closed. I grabbed the doorknob to open it, but we decided not to. Do you really think that Millie came down here after us? I guess it's doable, but she would've had to run really fast." Lizzy was feeling claustrophobic again, so she backed away from the tunnel entrance and right into Katie.

Katie stepped back to give Lizzy space and lost her balance, landing on the cold cement floor. She always seemed to end up on the floor.

"Thanks a lot, Lizzy. There's no telling what's crawling around down here. Shine your light so I can see what I'm doing, please." She heard Cory Ann trying to hold back her laugh. "It's really not funny, Cory Ann! And it wasn't my fault, Lizzy bumped into me."

Katie turned sideways, put her legs under her butt, placed her hands on the floor and pushed herself up, but something grabbed her wrist, and she screamed.

"Help! Lizzy, help me! Something has my arm." Katie was struggling to pull free.

She continued to struggle when Cory Ann latched onto her other arm and pulled her free. She scrambled to her feet and all three phone lights lit up the floor, causing all of them to scream.

"Marci! Oh my God! It's Marci! Come on, help her!" Lizzy had dropped to the ground next to her friend, who had been bound and gagged.

Katie kneeled back down and helped remove Marci's restraints. She had duct tape around her wrist and across her mouth. Lizzy started with the tape on Marci's wrist, unwinding as fast as she could, while she ripped off the piece that was over her mouth.

"Marci! Are you okay?" Katie watched a single tear run down her face as she nodded. "Something's wrong! I think she was drugged because she seems sluggish. Marci, can you walk?" Marci opened her eyes and looked at her.

"Where are they? Are they okay?" Marci's voice was weak.

"They? Marci, do you mean Allie and Stephanie?" Cory Ann frantically shone her light around the rest of the room. "Over there!"

Katie left Marci with Lizzy and followed Cory Ann. Allie. They found Allie, who was also bound and gagged. While Cory Ann helped Allie, Katie looked for Stephanie and found her a few feet away from the others. They all seemed to have been drugged, but otherwise, in good condition. Katie hoped they could walk well enough to get out of there soon. She was positive that Millie was responsible, but didn't want to confront her down there. She wanted to get her friends to safety before Millie could stop them. Her heart sank, knowing that Millie had to know by now that they were discovered. Was she plotting her next move? An image of a cornered bear came to mind, and she shuddered.

Katie helped Stephanie walk the few feet over to where Allie was and let her sit down. Stephanie was more alert than the other two and probably could make it out of there with a little help. The other two were still in and out of consciousness, and clearly not able to walk out on their own free will anytime soon.

"What do we do now? If Millie is responsible for this, then she has to know we found them. What do you think she's gonna do?" Lizzy shook her head with concern.

Katie frowned. "I know. I was just thinking the same thing. She has to know."

"Stephanie, do you know what happened? How'd y'all get down here?" Cory Ann sat beside her, waiting for an answer.

"I don't know. I remember falling asleep in the restaurant and the next thing I remember is waking up down here. I couldn't see anything, but I could hear someone moving around. I hoped it was Marci and Allie, but I couldn't be sure. I just woke up a few minutes ago and I'm still groggy. Thank God y'all came! How'd y'all find us?" Stephanie teared up as she continued to speak. "Are they okay?"

"We have to get out of here." Katie's voice was stern. "We need to hurry and take this fight to her before she comes. If we get into a battle with her down her, it won't be good.

She shook Marci again and patted her on the face, but all she did was mumble a few words and move around. Katie scooted over to Allie and was glad to see that she was moving around a little more as well. There was no way either of them were going to make it up the stairs in that condition, even with her help.

She wondered what was happening back at the restaurant. She hoped Millie was still over there and that they were all safe. Time was ticking fast, and she had to decide quickly. Should they get Stephanie out of there and then the others when they can? Her eyes shifted over to the tunnel door that was still open. She took in a deep breath, inhaling the musty smell of the storm cellar, and toyed with the idea of going into the underground tunnel. There were so many things to be considered, and her mind wasn't cooperating.

She made her way back to Lizzy, who had helped Marci move closer to the others. At least now they were all huddled together in one spot. Katie wanted someone else to decide what they should do.

She looked around at the others. "Lizzy?" She stared into her eyes, knowing that she didn't have to say another word.

"I don't know what to do either. I don't think we should go into the tunnel because then they would have to make it up that ladder and that would be harder than these stairs. Stephanie, do you think you can walk on your own now?"

Stephanie shook her head yes.

"Marci is coming around, so maybe if I help her, you and Cory Ann can carry Allie. I think we need to go soon, and I think we need to march right into the restaurant. I hope everyone over there is okay." Lizzy frowned.

"I agree with Lizzy," Cory Ann stood up as she spoke.

"Me too." Stephanie reached out for help to get up.

"Okay. Then let's do this."

Katie told Marci what was happening and got a thumbs up confirming that she understood. She and Lizzy lifted Marci, put her arms around both of their shoulders, and walked her to the edge of the stairs. While Cory Ann helped Stephanie over there as well, Katie went after Allie who was more awake and mumbling. Just as she did for

Marci, she explained the plan and waited for Cory Ann to come and lift her up.

Surprisingly, Allie had become agitated and was almost refusing to move. She kept mumbling repeatedly. Katie got her into an upright position and patted her on the face. The mumbles kept coming and as Allie became more awake, her words were becoming more legible.

"Somebody. Somebody. Somebody. There's somebody. Somebody. Somebody else." Allie was trying to get Katie to understand.

Katie listened to her rant over and over again and became numb when it suddenly became clear what she was trying to say. There was somebody else. Katie spotted what looked like another body several feet away on the other side of Allie.

Overcome with fear and emotion, she yelled out for Lizzy and dropped to the floor. She sat there staring at another body that had been bound and gagged like the others. Had Millie kidnapped someone else? While her mind was scrambling to figure out who it could be, the body shifted and with it came the answer.

Katie was left deflated and without words shocked by the new discovery. Everything that had transpired that night was already unbelievable to her and now the one thing she'd been sure of the whole time just exploded and a whole new set of questions took its place.

CHAPTER 43

Hannah

Her heart dropped as soon as Lizzy leaped off the restaurant veranda to run after Katie and Cory Ann. Hannah's first instinct was to follow, but Lizzy was almost immediately enveloped in the darkness.

"No! Lizzy!" She became frantic. "Katie, come back! Now! Y'all need to come back!"

Disappointed that she couldn't see anything past the veranda, she fell to the floor and cried. Her sobs only increased when her friends tried to comfort her. She felt foolish, but she no longer cared. It was all too much. Everything they'd gone through these past few hours, along with the recent development of Lizzy, Katie and Cory Ann taking off, had collided, and she just lost control of her emotions.

Hannah continued to cry as she revisited all the events. Ironically, recalling everything had begun to make her angrier instead of scared and upset. Her sobs slowed, and she regained her composure. Millie. Where's Millie? She lifted her head to see where the others were. Katie and Lizzy truly believed that she was responsible for everything. And Hannah had started to be suspicious of her, too.

Glad to see that she was still there, she let out a sigh. Millie was seated on the floor a few feet away from her with the rest of her friends. The darkness hindered her sight as she tried to read Millie's expression. Everyone was catching their breath after the run and trying to get settled. The air inside the restaurant felt odd again, but she couldn't determine exactly what was different about it. She glared at Millie through the pitch black room and wanted to scream that she was on to her. But she kept silent and waited.

"Maybe we should go back to our chairs behind the wait station and away from the windows." Millie had stood up to leave the area.

"No!" Hannah responded hastily.

Millie stopped walking and turned toward Hannah.

She lightened her tone. "I think we need to wait here for Lizzy, Katie and Cory Ann. What if they need us?"

Millie walked back to where Hannah was now standing. "Exactly where did they go? Why didn't they follow the plan? It was Lizzy's plan to begin with."

Hannah could now see her eyes and detected the anger in her words. Millie was mad that they had deviated from the plan and wasn't trying to hide it from Hannah or anyone else. She didn't know if she should tell her about Katie's plan to look for their missing friends in the cellar or lie. After taking a moment to study Millie's demeanor,

Hannah decided to tell the truth and see how she would react.

"They went to the storm cellar. Katie thinks that Marci, Allie, and Stephanie are there."

She watched as the look on Millie's face stayed the same. The same angered look was still sprawled across her face. Hannah thought maybe she saw a twitch of her eye, but realized that Millie was really good at hiding her true feeling. Unlike herself, who always wears her emotions for the world to see. She continued her eye contact with her.

"Maybe we should go after them. They might need our help." Millie shot Hannah a smug look.

She was almost impressed with Millie's sneaky disposition, listening to her as she tried to convince everyone that she was concerned and wanted to help. Stalling for time, she decided to play into her game and ask everyone else what they thought should be the next step.

"I don't think we should go after them yet. Katie would've suggested that we all go if that's what she wanted us to do. I say we stay put and wait." Demi looked down at the floor as she spoke.

"I agree. But I also agree with Millie that maybe we should move away from the windows. Just saying." Nervously, Brittany pulled her lips up into a faint smile.

Hannah listened as each of them said their peace. She hated to admit it, but she also agreed with Millie on that one point. They were vulnerable sitting out there in the open, but she really wanted to keep an eye on the storm cellar just in case. If the others voted to move, she would move as well because her eyes were staying on Millie.

"I'm for moving back to the chairs. It felt a little safer back there. But Hannah, if you feel you need to keep watch, I'll wait with you." Sara voiced her conflicted vote.

Hannah noticed that Savannah had been quiet and was staring at Millie with suspicion. Had she caught on to her or had Katie's words of caution earlier grabbed her attention? Whatever the reason, Hannah was glad that she wasn't the only one on guard.

Her eyes wandered back outside and toward the cellar. A glimmer of light sparkled in the darkness and her heart leaped. She smashed her face against the window, hoping to get a better view. Again she saw the light and while yelling to the others, ran to the door and swung it open.

"It's them. I see a light. Lizzy!" Hannah yelled out. "Look over there. I know I saw a light." She wanted to run out to meet them, but stayed put.

"I don't see anything." Millie was next to Hannah in the doorway.

"I saw a light! Look over there!. It was there!" Hannah was pleading for them to believe her.

"I believe you think you saw a light, but maybe it was a firefly. Did you see anyone? Katie or Lizzy? I think they would yell out if it were them, especially after you called Lizzy's name out." Millie was staring into the darkness as she debated with her.

"I don't think a firefly would be out in this weather." Savannah nudged her way next to Hannah and in front of Millie. "Let me look. If you want, I'll go over there with you."

"Y'all are crazy. I don't see anything, and it seems like every time we run out there, something happens. I say we stay put."

Savannah clinched her fist and tried to calm down. "Listen, we know what you think, but if Hannah says she saw a light, then I believe her." She turned her focus back to Hannah. "Again, do you want to go and search for them?"

She didn't know what to do. She really wanted to go find them, but she didn't want to put anyone else in danger.

"I don't know. Let's just wait and watch for a minute. I did see a light, twice, but only for a quick second. Maybe they're waiting for the rain to let up before coming back. I don't know. Millie, you and the rest of y'all can go back to the chair area. I'm gonna hang here a bit longer, then if there's no sign of them, I'll join y'all."

Savannah put her arm around Hannah. "I'll wait with you."

Reluctantly, Hannah watched the others make their way back behind the wait station to the safety of the chairs. As soon as they were out of earshot, she begged Savannah to go watch Millie because she couldn't be in both places at the same time. She didn't share her concern that she was afraid something had happened to make whoever had the light go back into the storm cellar instead of over to the restaurant. She watched vigilantly and prayed while she waited for a sign that they were okay.

CHAPTER 44

Lizzy

Hearing Katie yell out her name made her blood run cold. Her first thought was that something was wrong with Allie because she was having trouble waking up. Her stomach turned at the idea that Allie wouldn't make it after they finally found them. She sat Marci down near the steps and raced back to Katie.

On the other side of the Allie, Katie was crouched down and staring at the ground. Lizzy ran to her side and thought she was going to faint. She blinked several times to clear her vision because she thought she was hallucinating. Katie's face was pale and her whole body was trembling at the sight that was on the ground before her.

"Millie. How can that be?" Katie was in shock and unable to continue to speak.

"Oh Lord! Are you kidding me? What's happening here?" Cory Ann was dumbfounded.

"This is crazy. Is she alive?" Lizzy leaned over Katie's shoulder to get a better look.

"I don't know. You check."

Lizzy didn't really want to get any closer. Thankfully, Cory Ann walked around and put her finger to Millie's neck to feel for a pulse. A nod confirmed she was still breathing. She wasn't sure how she felt about that news. How was Millie down here bound and gagged when she was just with them running to the restaurant?

"Lizzy, was she with y'all when you got to the restaurant? Did she make it there? I mean, how could this be happening? Should we undue her restraints?" She called out to Stephanie. "Did you know she was here? Did you see her?"

Stephanie's weak voice barely made it to the other side of the storm cellar. "No." She leaned down to ask Marci if she knew and after she shook her head no, relayed her reply as well.

While Lizzy was trying to accept what she was seeing, a hand grabbed onto Katie's ankle, causing her to jump back, sending them both to the ground. She bounced back up and covered her mouth. She was waking up, and they had to decide quickly what to do about it. Common sense was telling her if that was Millie, bound and gagged, then she couldn't be the one behind everything. But reason went out the window a long time ago. Katie was seeing ghost and porcelain dolls had come alive, so nothing was as it seemed to her.

"We can't just leave her like that. Can we? Wait. If Millie would've run over here after us, we would've seen or at least heard her. I think we need to wake her up and see what she has to say. Maybe, I don't know, she has an explanation." Cory Ann threw her hands up, confused once again. "Or maybe I should run back to the restaurant and see who's there."

Lizzy didn't comment either way. She and Katie stayed by Millie's side while Cory Ann started for the door.

"Turn on your phone light, Co and yell back when you know something."

After a few seconds, Cory Ann was back inside the storm cellar. "It's still storming, and I really didn't want to go alone."

Lizzy didn't blame her and was actually relieved that she didn't go. Against her better judgement, she leaned forward and ripped the tape from Millie's mouth. She was going to feel terrible if Millie woke up and had a really good explanation, but she had to know.

"Millie. Can you hear me? Millie." Lizzy was rocking her body back and forth.

Millie's eye shot open and startled her.

"Lizzy back up." Katie pulled on her arm.

"Man, I'm tired of all of this. There seems to be a surprise around every corner. I don't think I've ever been this jumpy in my entire life." She stared down into Millie's eyes and saw fear.

This time, Millie started to rant about someone. Could there be someone else down there with them?

"Look, what is she gonna do? We have her outnumbered, and she appears to have been drugged like the others." After she spoke, she leaned in checking Millie's pockets for a weapon. She looked up at Katie. "Just in case."

When she started to pull the duct tape from Millie's wrist, she felt the temperature in the room drop. She looked at Katie first, then Cory Ann to see if they had felt it too. The expression on their faces gave her the answer. The room was getting colder, while Millie's voice became clearer. She latched onto Lizzy's arm while trying to tell her something.

"Where is she? Lizzy, where is she? She's dangerous. You have no idea what she's capable of." She frantically looked around the room. "Where's everyone else? Did she get to them?" She grabbed onto Lizzy's shirt, begging for answers.

"Who Millie? What are you talking about?" Lizzy was almost afraid to hear her answer.

"Billie. My little sister." Millie attempted to stand up, but stumbled.

"What? I don't understand. I thought you didn't talk to your family. And what did you mean she's dangerous? How?" The suspense was killing Katie.

"Listen, there's a lot I have to tell y'all, but we have to find her."

"I think we need an explanation first. And why is it so cold in here?" Cory Ann shivered.

Millie placed her face in her hands. "I'm sorry. I'm really sorry. This is all my fault." As Millie calmed down, so did the temperature.

Lizzy shared a look with Katie before she reached out to help Millie sit up. By that point, Allie was fully awake, and they all waited for her to get Millie upright.

"I know y'all need an explanation, but it's not that easy. Most people have trouble accepting the truth about my family. I have psychokinetic abilities. My whole family does." She let that sink in before going on. "I can move things with my mind. I can manipulate things like the temperature in this room."

Lizzy automatically backed up a step. Overwhelmed by Millie's claims, her first instinct was to call her a liar. But what if it's true? It would explain a lot if she were telling the truth. And the air was getting warmer. She pinched the bridge of her nose and tried to absorb what it all meant.

"So, how did this happen? I mean, how did you end up here?" A light bulb went off before Millie answered. "The closet."

Katie chimed in. "That was your sister that grabbed us in the closet? What, then she pretended to be you? This is crazy."

"Yeah. I had no idea she was here. I have had no contact with her for years. My family abuses their gifts. They use it to steel, cheat and manipulate everyone. I grew up waiting for someone to find out and lock us all up. When I turned seventeen, I left home and only had contact with Billie once since then. I thought she shared my feelings about the family, but she blamed me for leaving her with them and wanted nothing to do with me. I had no idea she would do this."

"I'm confused. How have you been hiding from them? If they have all these abilities, why couldn't they find you?" Cory Ann shrugs.

"It doesn't work that way. They can only manipulate someone or things that are close to them. My mother's abilities were the strongest, but still she had limitations. That's why I moved to New Orleans. Eventually, I was going to move across the country, but that never material-ized. And after a while, I figured I was safe. Then I met Marci and you guys…"

Lizzy's heart broke for her. She felt horrible that she was suspicious of Millie, but technically, she was right. Except it had been Billie all along.

"What are we going to do? She's over there with the others right now. I left Hannah with her! And the weather has the phone service down and there's no one here to help." Lizzy was pacing.

"That's not the weather; that's Billie blocking the ser-vice. And she's probably responsible for the weather too!" Millie looked like she was sorting things out in her mind, and they watched as she started to put it all together. "Her powers have grown. When I left, she could barely move an object and now she was capable of complete manipula-tion. She's manipulated the whole area and apparently capable of holding it for a long time."

Katie was more confused than before. "What does that mean, Millie? The porcelain dolls? That was her?"

"It means that she's created an alternate space and brought y'all into it. The staff never left, y'all did."

"How can that be? Everything looks exactly the same." Lizzy questioned the validity of it all.

"Listen, I know this is a lot to absorb, but it's true and I have to get to her. She tried to drug me so I couldn't stop her."

Cory Ann crossed her arms and stared down at Millie. "What makes you so sure you can stop her?"

"There's another reason none of them came after me." Millie walked through the darkness without a light and stopped at the bottom of the steps. "I'm stronger than all of them, Billie included, and it's time to put a stop to this before she does something I can't undo."

Lizzy's eyes grew wide, but she didn't say a word, not out loud anyway. She prayed Millie was, in fact, capable of doing what she was saying and that she would stop Billie before it was too late.

CHAPTER 45

Katie

The magnitude of what was happening was almost too much for her to fathom. Katie stood there motionless, her mouth hanging open in disbelief. Since Millie's confession, her thoughts had been spinning out of control. Little things that didn't make sense before were now coming together. She looked at the others and knew that they were feeling just as speechless. Alternate worlds, mind control, weather control! And Millie's whole family is out there with the same abilities. Katie couldn't wrap her head around any of it and yet she found herself believing every word that Millie spoke.

She watched Millie walk to the steps and make her way out of the storm cellar. She could feel the energy in the room and even thought she'd noticed a spark or two coming from her fingers. Millie claimed to be more powerful than her entire family, and while that revelation was scary, Katie didn't know what it meant.

She reached out to Lizzy and then gathered by the others, hoping that someone else would take charge and tell her what to do. She wasn't sure if they should be following Millie or waiting down there. A vision of Hannah and her friends came into view, and she answered her own questions.

"We have to follow her. We have to get to the others before Millie confronts Billie. Right? We have to warn them. They have no idea what's about to happen." She looked around at the eager faces staring back at her. "But wait. We can't all go." She pointed to Allie to make her point. "You're too weak to go running around in the rain. It's too dangerous and I have a feeling it's going to get a lot worse real soon."

"I'm coming with you." Lizzy made that clear.

Katie looked over at Cory Ann, who nodded in agreement before walking over to the other three that were just rescued.

"I'll stay here with them, but don't keep us waiting. As soon as you can, get back here, okay? I don't like this at all, but I do agree that it wouldn't be a good idea for all of us to go. Just be careful." Cory Ann sat down at the bottom of the stairs. "Once y'all go, I'll climb up and keep watch. Hopefully, the rain will let up soon and…" She suddenly remembered Millie's words and the true magnitude of the situation registered. What if it's true? "If any of what Millie said is true, then I guess we can expect the storms to get worse before they get better. Just yell if you need me."

When Katie and Lizzy reached the top of the stairs, Millie was standing in the middle of the lawn between the cellar and the restaurant, arms outstretched, and face looking upward to the skies as if calling upon the clouds and the stars for help.

"Should we wait or run past her?" Lizzy stood frozen next to Katie.

"I don't know. My head is telling me to run and save the others, but she looks really scary standing there like that. I hope she doesn't remember that I pulled that tape off of her mouth quickly on purpose." Katie looked nervous.

"Yeah, well, I hope she doesn't remember all the times I questioned her and practically accused her of being untrustworthy." Lizzy let out a nervous chuckle.

Making that many decisions in one night had left Katie exhausted. All the events playing over in her mind were merging, and she was having trouble sorting through them. Billie hadn't actually hurt anybody, so what was she there for? Was she dangerous? Millie seemed adamant that her entire family was dangerous, but it was still nagging her that none of her friends were hurt. Ans she was thankful that that was so.

"What do you think Billie was going to do to them if we hadn't found them?" Katie was fishing for some sort of clarity.

"You know that's been bothering me. Do you think she's just here to get back at her sister for leaving her? Millie sounded like she'd hoped Billie would be like her and not like the rest of the family. Oh, and I bet she's the one responsible for the crazy porcelain dolls coming alive." Lizzy shook her head in frustration. "We can't worry about that now because we have to get to the others before all hell breaks loose out here."

Katie kept her eyes glued to Millie, who was still in the same place, conjuring up something. The rain was relentless, and the wind was howling as it slammed against her body, knocking her around. She grabbed Lizzy's hand and yanked her to the side of the restaurant.

"Maybe we can go through the back."

"No." Lizzy pulled Katie back and stopped. "I think it might be too late for that."

The entrance door to the restaurant shattered, and the glass was swirling around in a vortex. Katie couldn't tell if Millie did that or if it was Billie. She crouched to the ground the minute she saw someone walk out of the chaos and onto the front veranda. The sight of a person walking through a vortex of glass was almost mesmerizing. The lightning was striking at an alarming rate and the rain mixed with the glass, putting on a show like she'd never seen. By the intensity of things, she knew they were running out of time.

She waited until Billie slowly made her way down the steps and out onto the lawn. Then she and Lizzy crawled to the side of the restaurant veranda and slid up, hoping to stay out of sight. They slowly made their way toward the shattered entrance, often stopping to make sure it was safe. The word safe was an exaggeration, but Katie felt that as long as Billie didn't see them, they were as safe as could be expected.

When they were about halfway to the door, Billie's head snapped in their direction, stopping them in their tracks. Katie tried to get as close to the wall as she could and wished she could crawl right through it. She would swear the boards on the porch were shaking under her body.

Katie saw Millie's eyes flash her way for a split second before calling out to her sister. Was she trying to save them?

"I'm over here! Billie! Look at me!" Millie's eyes were back on Billie and her voice sounded almost demonic. "Why are you here? What is it you want?"

Millie's distraction was working to pull Billie's focus away from them, so Katie and Lizzy began to crawl toward the entrance again. She was afraid that there would be glass to crawl through, but it was still flying around in a beautiful vortex and moving forward with Billie as she walked toward her sister.

They reached the doorway and, without looking back, pulled themselves into the restaurant and made it safely to a corner of the main room. The lightning show coming from outside lit up the room, and Katie was disappointed to see that it was empty.

"Where are they?" She looked back at Lizzy and knew she was thinking the same thing. They crawled around the room, careful not to alert Billie, and found themselves in the hallway all alone. The chairs were still lined up behind the wall, but they were all empty. The bathroom.

"They must be in the bathroom. They have to be." Lizzy's voice was shaking with concern.

Katie stood up, no longer afraid of being seen, and pulled Lizzy to her feet. They raced down the hall, forgetting all about the mirrors and the eerie dolls, in search of Hannah and their friends. The sounds from the battle happening outside were so loud and the power coming from them was rocking the building. Katie pushed the door open and stared into the darkness.

"Hello? Hannah? Hello? Anybody in here?" Lizzy held her breath, waiting for a response.

CHAPTER 46

Hannah

The sounds of thunder and lightning had vanished and were replaced by the sweet melody of chirping birds. The dining room was bright, and the light tugged at her eyes. Hannah stretched out her arms and struggled to open her eyes. Her mind was foggy, and she couldn't seem to recall where she was until a vision of Millie raising her hands and blowing out the front door flooded her mind.

The pace of her heart quickened, but she was afraid to move. Slowly, she sat up and noticed that they were all stretched out in the chair area where they had been hiding. She listened for any sign that they were still in danger, but it was quiet, aside from a few birds singing in the distance. What's happening? She stood up and walked into the massive dining room. It was completely empty aside from the tables set and ready for the dinner crowd.

She swirled around to look at the entrance and almost fainted when she saw it was completely intact. That's impossible. She saw the glass blow out with her own eyes. One minute Millie was sitting with them, then the next she was up and marching toward the door like a crazy person. She was mumbling words that none of them understood, and at one point, seemed to be a blaze of fire. She and the others took cover back by the chairs and waited for the worst. But it never came.

Hannah ran to the door and pushed it open. Her body trembled with confusion. What was she supposed to do? Her feet were moving before she had time to think of an answer and she rushed out the door onto the veranda, except it wasn't the veranda, but instead she was back in the hall where the others lay sleeping.

"No Way!" Hannah looked down at her hands, half expecting them to be glowing or something.

She patted her face and arms to make sure she was awake. Surely she was dreaming. Panic was moving in fast, and she was terrified. Sliding off her chair, she knelt down next to where Savannah was sleeping. She nudged her arm, hoping she'd wake up. She needed her to wake up.

"Hey. Savannah. We have a problem." She didn't know why she was whispering, but continued to do so. "Savannah. Please wake up."

When Savannah started to move around, Hannah latched onto her arm. She needed someone else to wake up and confirm that she was not crazy. The other three were slowly moving around, and she wondered if they'd been drugged. Her hand let go of Savannah's arm and clamped over her mouth. "Oh my God, she drugged us."

Savannah reached out and touched Hannah, startling her back into the moment.

"Hannah, What's wrong?"

Hannah grabbed Savannah and led her to the front door.

"Am I going crazy? Didn't Millie destroy this door? Please tell me you remember?"

The shock on Savannah's face suggested she remembered, and Hannah breathed a sigh of relief. Before she could stop her, Savannah ran out the door and disappeared. Hannah was sure of the outcome, but followed her running through the door, anyway. They both found themselves back by the chairs.

"This is insane! What's going on?" Savannah suddenly stopped and was at a loss for words.

"I'm not sure how, but twice I went out the front door and ended up back here." She glanced down the hall, then walked toward the bathroom.

"Where are you going?" Savannah yelled out.

Hannah kept walking and quickened her pace as she approached the bathroom door. She didn't stop and, in one quick turn of the handle, entered the darkness. She fumbled for her phone and turned on the light. As soon as she could see, she ran to the other door and into the storage room. With one quick step, she was up on the chair and pushing open the window. Her heart was racing at full speed with anticipation. She hoisted herself up and out of the window. She closed her eyes and braced herself for the impact of hitting the ground.

She kept her eyes shut, afraid of what she might see if she opened them. She jumped when a hand touched her shoulder, then for a moment thought that maybe she made it out.

"Hannah. Are you okay?" She shuddered when she heard the familiar voice.

"No Savannah! I'm not okay! There's no way out!" Hannah paced. "This can't be happening!" She closed her eyes and screamed in frustration.

The others bolted off their chairs and ran to Hannah.

"Hey, are you okay?" Sara asked, confused.

"No. None of us are okay." Hannah looked defeated and sat down in a chair. "There's no way out. It sounds bizarre, but it's true. There is no way out of here."

Hannah watched as everyone raced around in a frenzy, trying to find a way out. Eventually, one by one, they gave up and joined her. Ideas were flying around, but none of them seemed to be a good option. Hannah chuckled because at least the weather was calm, quite pleasant actually. Under different circumstances, it would be a perfect day to be with friends at a weekend getaway. The hair on her arms raised as she tried to make sense of their situation because her gut told her that something unworldly was happening.

She continued to sit there and personally unravel until she heard a clap of thunder. She stretched her neck to look around the wall into the dining room. The room darkened right before her eyes and the skies let out a roar. The weather changed again.

"Savannah, do you hear that? Y'all listen. Look." Hannah was suddenly hopeful. "Come on, let's try again!" She started toward the door and stopped when she saw Lizzy and Katie walking toward her. The lightning flashed, and she called out to them. "Lizzy! Katie!" They heard her voice and looked her way. Then they were gone.

"No! Lizzy! Katie! Where did they go?" She ran toward the door and once again jumped through it and landed back by the chairs.

CHAPTER 47

Katie

After finding the bathroom empty, Katie's anxiety spiked, and sweat beaded on her forehead. She was terrified that Billie did something to the others. This was all her fault. If she hadn't broken off from the group, they would still all be together. Now Hannah was gone. Her friends were gone. She felt Lizzy's arm on her shoulder, but wasn't ready to face her. It was her fault that Lizzy left the group and followed her, leaving Hannah behind. If she'd discussed the plan with the others maybe things would've turned out differently.

"Katie." Lizzy's voice echoed off the empty walls.

"I don't know what to do. They're gone."

"Listen. I know how you feel because I feel just as bad. Look, we saved Marci, Allie and Stephanie. If you hadn't run off in search of that cellar, who knows what would've happened to them. Your instincts saved them. And remember, they were not hurt, so there's no reason to believe that Billie has harmed the others. There'll be enough time to feel bad about our actions later, but right now we need to figure out what's going on. Let's go back out front and see what's happening outside."

"I don't know how much more I can take. You know I'm not this person. How did we end up with all this pressure on us? I can barely take care of myself and my own problems and now I feel like it's up to me, and you, of course, to save the day. I don't think that's possible. Do you?" Katie was feeling inadequate in the hero role.

She followed Lizzy into the front dining room, and they both fell to the ground in reaction to the fireworks show happening outside. Billie was screaming at her sister but hadn't advanced her position. Katie wondered if Millie was just letting her have her say before she took control of the situation, or if she wasn't as powerful as she claimed to be.

She was in the main dining room again, unsure of what to do next. It was too dangerous to go outside, and too depressing to stay in the empty dining room. She looked next to her at Lizzy and knew she was feeling the same depressed, hopeless emotions. She wanted to scream and shout, but there was no one to hear her, no one that cared anyway. She felt isolated and defeated.

"Lizzy! Katie!" Hannah's voice was loud.

Katie's eyes shot across the room and there she was. Hannah was standing there, safe, and calling out to them. But before she could move a muscle, she was gone.

"No! Hannah!" Lizzy rushed to the place she saw Hannah. "Wait! Hannah, hang on! It's gonna be alright."

"What are you saying? Why do you think it's gonna be alright? She's gone! Vanished!" Katie's voice shook as tears streamed down her face.

"Don't you see? It's Billie. Just like Millie said. They can manipulate everything. She can manipulate time. Billie's doing this. They're not really gone. It's Billie who created this false reality. Oh my God! Hannah's okay. They're all okay." Lizzy exhaled with relief.

Katie stared in disbelief. "But what does that mean?"

"I'm not sure, but if what Millie said was true, I think she uses her energy to create a new reality. I guess when she is weak, the false reality falters. That's why we saw Hannah for a few seconds. Oh! And I bet that's why Hannah said she saw a waitress. I bet Billie has been manipulating us the whole time."

Katie pulled out a chair and sat down. "If what you're saying is true, then how will this all end? What happens if Billie wins?"

"Billie can't win!" Lizzy's voice was strong. "Katie, get up! Come on! We are not giving up."

Katie was exhausted. She felt like they'd been there for days, not hours. She was glad that Lizzy was fired up, but what were they going to do? What could they do? She wasn't about to go confront Billie, and Millie was a little busy. She wished that all of this would just go away. Why couldn't it just be the ghost they had to deal with? She laughed out loud at that last thought. A few days ago, a ghost was the last thing she thought she'd ever see. Now… Katie's eyes lit up.

"What?"

"The ghost. Maybe the ghost could help us." She put her hand out and turned in a circle. "Maybe if we can call to her, she would help. But how do you call a ghost?" She didn't waste time. Katie started yelling, "Hello. Please, I need your help."

"Wait. Stop. What are you doing? What if she doesn't want to help us? I mean, come on, what do you know about ghost?" Lizzy's eyes were wide open, just in case.

Katie ran to the front door to see what was happening. The two sisters were still raging a battle with the wind and rain. She noticed that a beautiful old oak tree had toppled over, and debris was flying all over the place. She could hear small bits of their argument. Millie was surprised at the strength that Billie was displaying, but she still seemed to be toying with her. Billie looked wild and out of control, while Millie appeared to have full control of herself and her surroundings.

"I don't want to hurt you. Why are you doing this? You need to end this now and we can go talk about it. I won't let you hurt my friends." Millie's voice was strong but compassionate. "Let them go Billie."

"You would choose your friends over your sister? You are becoming weak, Millie. That's never been our way." Billie smiled, but it was halfhearted.

"That has always been my way, and I thought you felt the same. I will never agree to hurt or manipulate anyone ever again. And don't mistake my patience for weakness. I will do what I have to in order to protect innocent people."

Billie's rage exploded and fire balls were launched at Millie, who dodged them with ease. She was firing them off more quickly now, and the last few landed on top of the old storm cellar.

"No!" Lizzy screamed and ran out the door. "Stop!"

Before she made it to the steps, she was sucked up into the vortex and tossed down at Billie's feet.

Katie was frantic. She started pleading for help. She was racing to go after Lizzy when she saw her. There she was and this time in full form blocking the entrance. The ghost was suspended in air and just staring at her. She nodded and then vanished.

Katie watched in horror as Billie began to lift Lizzy off the ground without touching her. She was just floating in the air. She glanced over at Millie, who still looked to be in control. Katie thought maybe she saw her flinch, but if she had, she quickly composed herself.

She looked back at Lizzy and that's when she saw her again and everything came to a head. The ghost appeared before Billie, placing herself in front of Lizzy. Everything seemed to happen in slow motion from that point on. Shock tore through Billie, causing her powers to weaken enough for Lizzy to be released. She was able to get up and run toward Millie and the storm cellar. Noise from behind Katie surprised her, and she turned just in time to see Hannah, Sara, Demi, Brittany, and Savannah running toward her.

Outside, Millie made her move and ran toward her sister. The two were tangled in midair with a display of fire, wind, and rain thrashing all around them. Then it all stopped. The rain, the wind, the fire, it all just stopped.

The calmness took over and the light from the rising sun was slowly creeping over the grounds. Katie followed the rays of sunshine, and her eyes landed on a body sprawled out on the ground just below the place where she last saw Millie and Billie tangled up in battle.

"Millie?" She called out but didn't move. She held her breath until she noticed movement and then longer because she was afraid of who the body belonged to.

"We can't just leave her out there. She may need our help." Demi was pushing past the others and heading out the door.

They all followed and stood over the body, praying she was okay. When her eyes opened, they searched out Katie's. A smile gently spread across her face, and she said, "I told you I was stronger than all of them."

The sun was peaking over the main house and the sound of sirens were screaming in the distance. Katie and her friends were standing on the well-manicured lawn, trying to decide what to do next. They were grateful that they were all reunited and safe.

It turned out that Katie's ghost was real and had a hand in helping them survive the night. Grateful, she hoped she would see her again before they left so she could thank her. She would love to know her story, but knew that might not be possible. One thing was sure, she had a connection to the storm cellar and was the source of Katie's obsession with it. Maybe she was trying to tell Katie something about her own demise or warn her of Billie's dangerous intentions. They didn't get to take the ghost tour after all, so she was just as clueless about the history of the plantation as when she'd arrived.

Millie had explained to the others exactly what her and her family's abilities were.

Millie was psychokinetic like she briefly explained earlier. That meant she could move objects and manipulate situations.

"Growing up my family used the same powers to get what they wanted with no remorse at all." Shame blossomed on her cheeks while she continued with her story. "They had come to rely on their powers instead of earning an honest living. When I left, Billie was too young, so she was left behind. That's one of my biggest regrets. But even though she was furious with me, she didn't hurt any of you and I'm grateful for that. We have a lot to discuss, and I hope in the end I can trust her."

She went on to apologize and asked for their forgiveness. She expressed her desire to remain friends with the group but said that she understood if they had reservations.

A few of the front desk staff members had arrived and found that the tree had toppled over across the driveway and called the authorities to report it. Katie asked if there was anyone inside and one lady said, "Of course, there is always someone on the premises." Before they left to go inside the house, the woman commented on the tree and wondered what caused it to topple over, since the weather had been calm for weeks.

The entire group burst into laughter until Katie stopped and raised the same question. "How did the tree topple over if we were in the alternate space?"

Millie looked at her and said, "I don't know. But like I said before, Billie isn't as strong as I am, so maybe she slipped up and let the two worlds collide. It takes a lot of energy to manipulate a situation and an even greater amount to keep it from reverting back."

"Ahh. That's why we caught a glimpse of that waitress and heard movement when there was no one there. Billie's powers must have slipped a few times." Katie was still processing everything.

"Right! She was sleeping when I noticed the lights on in the house, then they went out. Wow this is all so amazing." Hannah's face slacked and a grim look took over. "What was with those creepy dolls? I guess it was cleaver but man that was freaky!"

Katie jumped back into the conversation. "For the record, I knew something was off and I'm glad it turned out that it was your sister and not you. Sorry for mistrusting you."

"Speaking of Billie…"

The first police car arrived, and they watched as two officers got out and walked over to them.

"I'm officer O. Vaughn, and this is my partner, Officer Morgan. Is everything okay here?"

Katie looked over at Millie and then the others and said, "Yes. Everything's great actually."

Acknowledgements

Let me begin by saying, what a journey! These past few years have been amazing, and it couldn't have happened without some special people who supported me along the way.

What If It's True is my fourth book, and like the others, was so much fun to write. I actually stayed in a haunted plantation, and can relate to some of the same fears my characters display, but overall my experience was quite different.

I want to thank my friends and family for allowing me to bounce my crazy ideas off of them and for providing me with valuable feedback.

A big thank you to my beta readers, especially Peggy Morgan and Pam Volek. Your input makes my books that much better. And, aside from reading and editing my books, they listen to me talk about the characters and stories every day. Our friendship is of the precious and unforgettable kind, like the opening paragraph of this book. Thank you for your endless love and support!

There are so many other friends and family who have listened to me rattle on about my writing and have yet to tell me to please stop. So, thank you for that! And without the tech support from those who offer it, none of this would be happening. Kathy Griffin, Charisse Zanca, Danny Bourgeois, Matthew Martin, and Matt Pertuit, thank you!

A special thank you to the people who read my books. The kind and encouraging words that I hear from you all feed my soul. I am still surprised when someone walks up and tells me they enjoy reading my books. Those encounters mean the world to me and make my heart soar high with joy! Thank you!

To my husband, Glenn Griffin. Only because of your love and enthusiastic support, I have written and published four books. When I first suggested that I wanted to write a book, you encouraged me and from that day forward have been nudging me on. Words cannot describe the gratitude and love that I have for you. Thank you!

Most importantly, I thank God for all the Blessings in my life, this writing journey included. Through him all things are possible. My life lacks meaning without him.

OTHER BOOKS BY AUTHOR
D. M. BOURGEOIS:

EDGE OF REALITY

MISGUIDED REVENGE

SLIPPING INTO DARKNESS

ABOUT THE AUTHOR

D. M. Bourgeois, born in New Orleans and currently a resident of Crown Point, Louisiana, writes locally influenced paranormal mystery and suspense. She studied Creative writing at Nicholls State University in Thibodaux, Louisiana. Aside from being a mother, grandmother, and great grandmother, becoming an author is one of her greatest joys. Her first three novels, SLIPPING INTO DARKNESS, MISGUIDED REVENGE, and EDGE OF REALITY were Sliver Falchion Award Finalists in the Best Supernatural category at Killer Nashville Writers Conference.
For more information you can visit D. M. Bourgeois @
Website: dmbourgeois.com
Email: dmbourgeois61@gmail.com
Facebook: dmbourgeois61

www.ingramcontent.com/pod-product-compliance
Lightning Source LLC
Chambersburg PA
CBHW051128190726
48290CB00006B/1732